The MMRPG Apocalypse

The MMRPG Apocalypse

Jeremy Chambless

Published by Level Up in the United Kingdom in 2023

Cover illustration by Sippakorn Upama
Cover by Claire Wood

ISBN: 978-1-83919-497-9

www.levelup.pub

Also by Jeremy Chambless:
The RPG Apocalypse
The RPG Apocalypse 2
The RPG Apocalypse 3

Chapter 1: When Your World Becomes an MMRPG

A bell chimed, signaling the entrance of the first customer in what felt like several hours. I put down the bag of chips I had been stocking onto the shelf and made my way towards the register. I didn't mind slow days at all: in fact, I embraced them.

Cleaning up and restocking the shelves had to be done before I could leave anyway. Getting those jobs done early was the best scenario for me, as I could call it a night sooner. My head turned to eye the customer who just entered—a regular.

"How's it going, Rick?" I asked with a smile. I moved to behind the register, which was located behind bullet proof glass. I worked in a gas station on an off road; usually I took the late shift and I had twice had to deal with attempted robberies.

"Not bad, yourself?" Rick asked in return. "Carton of Marlboro and two scratch-offs." He tossed a wad of cash into the metal tin that was sunk just below the bullet proof glass.

"Ten-dollar ones? With the ladies on 'em?" I asked.

"Those are the ones," he laughed, "you know me pretty well Mike."

"Well, I've been working here five years and you've been coming here even longer than that. I've only ever seen you try those," I said while turning away with a plastic key in my hand.

The cigarettes were locked away and needed to be removed with a key I had tightly wrapped around my wrist. I grabbed a carton and then removed two of Rick's choice of scratch offs. "Maybe this is the day you'll win something," I said with a smile.

My comment got a self-deprecating smile out of him. "It's not about winning anymore. You know it's personal now."

I understood him. He'd developed a habit and while I approved of determination, Rick's bull-headedness here was misplaced. Effectively, Rick was taxing himself at least twenty dollars a week. He looked around the store and then back into the empty parking lot. "Slow day today?" he asked.

I scanned the carton and then the two scratch offs before picking up the wad of cash and unfolding it. "Very slow day, you're the first customer all afternoon." I counted out the cash. "You're a bit over. You want dollar bills or a five?" I asked.

"Give me the dollars, I'll use 'em for tolls. You haven't been watching the news have you then?" He looked at me curiously.

"Boss won't give me a TV to watch even if he knew we wouldn't have customers. He wants me on my feet, working all damn day."

"Well, some weird shit has been happening since this morning, probably why you got no customers."

I finished putting the money into the register and counted out five one-dollar bills. "Like what? Nothing crazy happens here except the occasional robbery or bit of vandalism."

"Well, according to the news, people have been getting attacked like crazy lately." He looked at me intently. "Animals coming out of the woods and mauling people to death. Weird shit."

"Like what? Wolves? Bears?" I asked. This was interesting, but no doubt the news was exaggerating whatever incidents had happened to make a good story.

"Yeah, wolves, bears, dogs, birds. News was showing some shit I'd never seen before, too. Saying they were mutated animals, that it was a virus—trying to keep everyone in doors."

Rick was a sensible man, his beliefs about scratch cards might not be the most rational, but when it came to animals and everyday practicalities, he was no fool. "What do you think about it?" I asked him. "Anything in the stories?"

"I've not seen anything yet, and it's hard for me to believe something like that if I didn't see with my own eyes. But what I can see with my own eyes is that the streets are empty, and no one is around."

I was slipping the money under the glass when the bell chimed again. It rattled every time someone opened the door. My boss had put it on to make sure we never kept a customer waiting. Although the door had opened, I didn't see anyone come in. The shelves created a blind spot, despite a mirror, where I could only see people from the waist up. Parents would sometimes come with their rowdy children, and I could never keep track of the small ones as they ran in search of some sort of sugary candy.

"My advice to you, Mike," Rick leaned in close while grabbing his money, "call it an early night tonight. Not worth the risk, you know?"

"True. In any case, I'll be done early tonight with all this free time. Have a good one."

Rick turned away towards the door, and something pierced his chest.

His body froze in shock as his hand grasped and scraped at a wooden pole piercing his abdomen. His head moved in slow-motion as he tilted it lower to glance at a strange figure before him. A midget-like person with a disgusting green skin covered all over with wrinkles, warts and blisters stood in front of him.

"Wh-wh-what...the fuck...is this?" Rick asked in horror. He tried to turn his head to look at me, but the wooden pole dug deep into his gut was pulled out with a vicious tear. Blood spurted from his chest as his body collapsed with a thump to the floor.

The weapon was a wooden spear about four or five feet long now caked in a thick layer of blood. The creature holding it, however, was nothing of this world. *This...this is a goblin? A small orc?* My mind raced as fear overtook me. This was something out of fantasy.

The figure stared at me through the glass barrier and a menacing cackle come from deep within its throat: a grating sound that brought a chill to the nape of my neck. My hands were shaking at my side as I tried to make sense of the situation.

Was this even reality? Did I actually wake up this morning? That thought held me still, until the blood-caked spear was stabbed through the small gap between the counter and the glass barrier. I dived backwards and off to the side to avoid being impaled.

The spear flailed and shook but could not bend nor reach me. I scurried across the floor to the only doorway into the cubicle and double checked it was locked. The cackling didn't stop and the spear continued to flail around seeking for me.

Eventually the weapon was pulled out and the cackling stopped. The silence gave me a moment to think rationally. I pulled my phone out and dialed 911. It rang and rang, and then eventually it ended with a dial tone. I called again, and then again. Then I tried a few friends and family members. I couldn't get through to anyone. I was on my own.

There was dead silence in the store besides the sound of my heavy breathing. Was the murderous creature waiting for me to think it had left? The front door bell had not rang; it was definitely still in the store with me. I scanned the area around me for a weapon, but there was nothing.

On several occasions my boss had urged me to get a permit for a gun, so that in the worst case I could defend myself. I was kicking myself right now for not following his advice. The thought of having to shoot another person over money had never sat well with me, and so I always brushed off the suggestion.

I stood up carefully and peeked over the glass barrier, rising sufficiently to see Rick's lifeless body. I couldn't see the goblin anywhere. My eyes scanned the store but came up empty. There was no way it had disappeared, I knew it was waiting for me.

My only chance was to make it to the office. There were some items I could use as a weapon there: golf clubs; an umbrella; there was also the mop. The mop was wooden, and I'd be able to snap it and make my own makeshift spear.

I didn't know how fast the monster was, nor how agile. Making a run for the office though was absolute stupidity and I couldn't risk it, not until I knew where it was. Just as I had that thought, a car pulled up outside. My heart was stuck in my throat while I waited for whoever it was to appear outside the door.

A man stepped up and was about to open the door when he saw Rick's lifeless corpse lying in the aisle, in front of the register. His hand reached for the door slowly as he stared directly at me. My hands waved back and forth trying to signal danger, urging him to not open the door.

Nevertheless, it opened with a click, and the bell chimed. He leaned through an opening he'd made just big enough for his head, "What's going on? Does he need help?"

"No! There's a killer in the store. Stay out!" I urged him forcibly.

The man's eyes began to scan the store for any signs of life, and he looked around for over thirty seconds without moving, before the door opened a tad wider and his foot entered. He slipped his entire body inside and then closed the door carefully behind him.

He stayed low to the ground and then looked around carefully again. I was also looking around frantically for any sign of the creature. It was hard to believe, but maybe the creature really had disappeared. None of this was making sense.

"It looks clear," the man whispered while making his way closer to Rick's corpse.

I nodded reluctantly and then moved to the doorway and unlocked it carefully. The handle turned with a click and I stepped out. A weight had been removed from my shoulders. The man stood up as well and seemed to breathe the first breath of air since he entered the store.

It was then that the nightmare began again. That blood-caked spear rocketed through the air and slammed home directly through the side of his neck. Blood spurted from the wound and splattered as high as the glass barrier.

The man didn't even have time to react at all. His body slumped to the floor like a lifeless doll. The cackling started again, and my mind raced a million miles a minute. The opportunity was there for me to make it to the office...

But then what? The creature could toss the spear like an Olympic javelin athlete. Even if I improvised a weapon with a range advantage, it could pin me to the wall with a single throw of his spear.

6

Right now though, the monster's weapon was currently out of its reach—out of its hands.

I had a crazy, barbaric idea, but I wanted to live. I was in shock, high on adrenaline—I needed to survive. My feet moved on their own as I ran past the now collapsed man and confronted the green little monster in the isle.

The look on its face was menacing, and a row of sharp and disgusting yellow teeth appeared as his mouth widened as if to welcome me. A cackle that sent me into pure fear assaulted my ears. "AHHHHH!" I yelled at the top of my lungs and rushed it like a wild animal.

The monster was smaller than me, and so I kicked it as hard as I could. My foot collided with its body and something gave with a crack as it tumbled several feet backward. There was no room for error, no room for hesitation.

I was on top of it within a second. The full weight of my body pinning it down as my hands came down like sledgehammers on its skull. Over and over, I pummeled it with all the rage and anger I could muster.

That hard skull became soft as it cracked under my blows. The struggling I felt below me slowly ceased until the monster was lifeless. I had killed it with my bare hands, hands that were still shaking, and now covered in blood—some of the monsters and some my own.

Congratulations, you have reached level
11

A line of text flashed over my vision and a message spoke directly into my brain. These were phenomena I couldn't explain—

a brief visual alert and a voice in my head that was so neutral that I couldn't tell if it were male or female, young or old.

The monsterf's corpse disappeared, and a bandage floated there above where its corpse once was. I reached out with bloodied hands and picked it up.

You have received Bandage. Heals a small amount of HP as well as removes the bleeding effect.

An item? What was happening? I had leveled up and obtained an item. My mind was telling me this was a dream...but the pain in my hands, the sweat covering my forehead, the chill in my bones...was telling me this wasn't a dream.

The item vanished from my hands like it never existed, even though I had felt its weight, felt the reality of it in my hands. I sat in confusion for a moment longer before embracing the insanity. Leveling and monsters were features of an RPG. If this were one, then the bandages had gone to a character inventory. Finding them would be a good test of my theory. I tried patting the back of my neck and shoulders, hoping that would trigger the opening of an imaginary pack. I tried all sorts of hand motions and gestures and mimes.

Only when I concentrated on the word *Inventory* did I get a result. A menu appeared in front of me, and it was an inventory: a grid with hundreds of boxes and all of them empty except a small version of the bandages in the top left corner. I imagined removing them from their storage place, and instantly they appeared in my hands. It was true then! Whatever was going on obeyed the rules of an RPG.

My shaky hands grasped the bandage tightly and I started to wrap up my sore palms and fingers.

What happened next again told me that the normal laws of science had been altered to allow for RPG-like rules. Instead of having to wait days for my hands to recover under the protection of the bandage, the material quickly vanished into thin air. The wounds and lacerations on my fist flowed away, healing at a rate I could watch.

The cuts healed closed, and their color changed as well. It was as if two weeks of time had passed in just that moment. The wounds were covered in hard scabs, and if I had shown them to anyone, no one would have believed I had received them just moments earlier.

My aching hands no longer ached, and the pain was no longer there—just light scabbed lacerations that were a bit off color. I shifted my attention to the next pressing issue: my level.

I was not unfamiliar with RPG's or video games in general. In fact, I was overly familiar. The reason why I worked at a gas station, why I didn't have a job or promising future, was because I was addicted to video games.

Through high school and college, I put more time and effort into games than my own studies. This lack of discipline came back to bite me in the ass when I flunked out of college. My performance was so terrible that I couldn't even appeal and go on a probation period.

I started to think through the words and phrases that might be used to open your character sheet, and eventually I found it. *Character* prompted a menu that showed me all of my stats.

Name: Mike Reynolds (27) **Class: None**
Level: 1 **EXP:** 7%
HP: 55/55 **MP:** 15/15
STR: 1
AGI: 1
DEX: 1
VIT: 1
WIS: 1
Available: 3
Skills: None

All of my stats were at 1. A pathetically low amount no doubt. What that did mean, however, was that the gains from early levels were incredibly potent for increasing your ability. With three points to assign, I would transform any stat I invested them in. I needed to weigh my options carefully.

These early levels would determine if I lived or died, and judging by my lack of any other options, I would most likely be fighting in melee combat. I glanced over at the spear lodged deep into my last customer's neck and decided it was likely to be my main weapon.

The stats on my character sheet were standard RPG ones and made sense to me when I looked at their abbreviations, Strength, Agility, Dexterity, Vitality, and Wisdom. I was not unfamiliar with their uses, at least if this new world would follow conventional RPG's.

Adding to STR was a no brainer, as I would be using a melee weapon that would require me to overpower my enemy. Increasing my striking power was vitally important to kill enemies and do so quickly.

AGI was also a no brainer, as I needed to be swift to avoid being attacked, and it would also increase the speed at which I would be able to land attacks on my enemies. Being faster would also lend me the ability to flee in case I was in a bad situation.

It was which of the remainder of the stats to boost that was causing me pause. DEX would probably increase the nimbleness of my hands, which would increase my accuracy with thrown weapons and probably my spell casting speed. For now though, I didn't think it would be hard to hit enemies with a spear, nor did I have any spells to cast. I disregarded DEX for now.

VIT would increase my life, which from the looks of it, I only had one of. Rick and the other man hadn't despawned after dying. Had they done so, it might have been possible that the laws of physics were so changed that people simply re-incarnated from a kind of 'saved' point. I told myself it was best to assume I had only one life. The two human bodies suggested that whatever the new rules, they did not include the option for people to re-enter the world after death.

Attractive as it was to put the point into VIT and increase my chances of taking a blow and living, I would have liked to have known about that stat a lot more. Did it affect more than just my HP total? Maybe my recovery speed? Was there going to be some kind of endurance system coming into play?

If VIT did have these extra benefits, then it would be incredibly valuable for healing minor wounds and staying in a healthy shape more generally. The problem was that I had to have a means of defeating whatever monsters and challenges came my way over the early levels. I doubted that even with additional VIT I could survive a spear to the chest. It was therefore off the menu for now.

Finally, there was WIS. Putting a point in wisdom was highly likely to increase my MP and have some positive benefits on spell casting. But currently I had no spells. So WIS was definitely not on my list of required stats for now.

In the end, I decided to put two points into STR and one point into AGI. My stats were now STR 3; AGI 2; DEX 1; VIT 1; WIS 1.

Seeing that I had no skills, the fact they were mentioned in the menu made me question how I could obtain them. There were many possibilities, some systems gave you a start in a skill only after you'd managed to perform a related action successfully, like managing a climb to trigger the climbing skill, other systems showed skills only after you unlocked them by levelling. In others they were dropped from monsters. I didn't have a class either, the choice for which would probably come with more levels as well.

There seemed to be nothing more I could do with my character sheet at this time, so I stood up and rushed to the store entrance and locked the door before flipping the sign to 'CLOSED' out of habit. This was no longer the world I knew, shit had hit the fan. I pulled my phone from my pocket and rang all my family members again, but the call always ended in a dial tone without ever connecting.

Web pages wouldn't load either. It seemed the internet was down, and my ability to gather information was gone completely. For now, I could only depend on myself.

I opted to send a few texts hoping they might become marked with 'Read' instead of 'Sent'. The question now was what should I do? Was sitting still my best option or should I move? I just didn't know enough about what had happened to the world.

Chapter 2: A City Destroyed by the Apocalypse

I was in a building filled with food and water. I had a bathroom and was entirely secure. There were only two doorways into the building. The backdoor was solid metal with a deadbolt, a chain, and even a brace on the door.

The front doorway had a metal framing I could drag across and lock, so even if the glass was broken nothing could get through. The problem was my lack of information. Without a TV or internet, I wouldn't know what was happening anywhere beyond the gas station.

I dragged the metal lock across the door and secured it. No one was getting in, nor was I getting out. The two cars sat in the parking lot: Rick's and that of the unknown man. But I couldn't see anything else. I continuously scanned the streets outside in expectation that more monsters would appear.

Several hours passed and night time rolled around. Not a single car had driven down the street in all that time. Previously, I had let myself believe the lack of traffic was because the gas station was on a back road and slightly out of the way. With a full day having passed without a single vehicle coming past, I couldn't hold on to that belief anymore. No one at all was traveling this road, which meant shit had seriously hit the fan. Still, as far as catastrophic events went, I was in the best spot to be: a low population area inside of a secured building filled with food. This was going to be my home base.

I moved to the main office and grabbed a camo bag and emptied out the contents. The owner wouldn't need it anymore, nor would he need the food or drinks I'd be taking. I packed the bag with several bottles of water and lightweight foods (dozens of protein bars) before strapping it on my back.

The monster's spear was still lodged in the man's neck, and I hadn't had the stomach to remove it. I needed it now, however, for protection beyond the relative safety of the metal doors. I grasped the wooden shaft of the spear in both hands and placed one foot onto the ribs of the body. Asking for forgiveness seemed pointless now: if there was a greater being, he was surely toying with us and didn't care.

The sensation of removing the weapon from the body's neck was awful and something I'd never experienced before. The man's blood had thickened and turned somewhat gelatinous. It made a sloshing noise as it ran onto the floor after the spear tip was fully pulled clean. Blood was caked on the tip of the blade and was even darker than before.

I moved towards the front door and unlocked the cage and then the glass door before stepping outside. I made sure to relock the cage and the glass door on my way out. It was a decision I had struggled with. On one hand, leaving the cage and the door un-locked would give me quick access in case I had to run back into the shop, on the other hand it would give people free reign to loot the store. My supplies there might prove essential. If the whole world were caught up in this disaster, then food might become very precarious. I couldn't risk people or monsters breaking in and taking everything useful, including all the various packets of food. This was a selfish thought, but right now I was solely focused on my own survival.

Across the street from me was a line of thick pine trees and a dense forest began with them. The forest was a great place to go during deer and hog hunting season, but on the other hand was slow to progress through and it provided cover for enemies to hide in and get close to me. My goal was simply to gather some information and be able to sprint back to the gas station if I needed to: it would remain my home base until I learned more about my situation.

Gravel crunched beneath my feet as I walked through the parking lot and past the gas pumps. A chill wind blew past my face and into the distance. I turned my head and looked down the barren street. There was nothing in sight in either direction.

I wanted to see what my home city—Sangeal—looked like. Walking there would take at least an hour. Assuming my truck worked it would only take around ten minutes to get to beyond the forest and onto a road with a good view. I tossed the pack on my passenger side seat and, as a feeling of anxiety rose up in me, turned my key.

Yes! Whatever strange change had taken place, vehicles were still working. My truck started without much trouble. I took one last look at the gas station before pulling out and speeding down the street. No one would pull me over, and no one was even on the road.

I wasn't prepared for what I saw when I cleared the final clusters of trees and the city came into view. Fire had wreaked havoc on all of the northern half, with smoke still billowing from the taller buildings.

The cars I could see down the road ahead of me were totaled and smashed together, others were burned to their frames. Street lights and power lines had fallen to the floor. I pulled up as close as I could to the first residence before stepping out of my vehicle. Glass crunched beneath my feet.

Every step of mine felt heavier than the last. There wasn't just trash, and glass, and burned debris on the streets. There were bodies: people who had been alive just two days ago and were now dead. I didn't dare walk too close to the corpses, but from a distance I could tell that their cause of death varied.

Some looked mangled and mauled; others were burnt and mutilated beyond recognition. Obviously, they had all been murdered. All showed signs of assault except one woman who had no obvious wounds. I walked towards her. When I made it about halfway, I heard a noise behind me: a growling.

My body instinctually froze as every hair on my body stood up. Fear dominated me as the threat of the growl was so visceral. I didn't even want to turn around, but my fear of death overwhelmed everything.

I grasped the spear so hard my hands turned white. My body spun and faced the enemy behind me. It was a wolf with patchy fur that made it looked completely deranged. The hair around its jaws was caked in dried blood. All these bodies seemed to be quite the feast for it.

The wolf crouched lower and seemed ready to pounce at any moment. I knew what I should do in this situation, but acting it out in reality was so much more difficult than when people had talked to me about wolves. It took every ounce of will power to spread my arms wide and make myself look as big as possible.

"AHHH," I screamed at the wolf at the top of my lungs while stepping forward. In normal times, I knew it was possible to scare these animals away by acting intimidating and emphasizing that you were bigger than them. That wasn't the reality of this situation, unfortunately.

As soon as I stepped forward, the wolf lunged directly at me with an obvious intent to rip me to shreds. My reactions weren't fast, but they weren't slow either. I frantically swung out the spear with a single hand and the spear shaft caught the side of the wolf, causing it to skitter to the side.

My response was enough to make the wolf take pause and think carefully. Somehow though, I had the feeling that the wolf would never retreat. If this were a game…then this was an encounter. This was potentially a fight to the death, and to judge by the corpses on the streets and in my gas station, I only had one life to work with.

Both my hands grasped the wooden spear and pointed it directly at the wolf. It began circling me slowly and I kept the spear tip pointed directly at its head. My advantage was my range, and I wouldn't let it get close to me unwounded.

It was fortunate that the wolf only had one avenue of attack and one that was completely predictable. As soon as it leaned low and the muscles of its shoulders tensed, I knew it was coming. Mouth wide, fangs visible, the rush came.

I lunged forward as the Wolf made its charge, spear striking out with pinpoint precision. Either by luck or thanks to my extreme concentration, my spear tip entered directly into the wolf's mouth. There was a moment of resistance and then I felt the spear tip push on through.

It was a one hit kill, and the wolf dropped immediately. The spear was nearly ripped from my hand at the sudden force being exerted on the tip. I had to no choice but to drop it in fear it would snap in half. A few moments later, the wolf despawned.

Wielding the spear had been surprisingly easy and its impact when I struck the wolf unexpectedly light: the muscles of the wolf's jaw and neck had offered no resistance, even though the spear tip wasn't that sharp.

Probably, my having increased my STR to 3 had come into play here. At the time, I wasn't sure how effective it had been to increase my STR, or whether everyone started with 1 of each stat (perhaps I had been weaker than normal). Now, I reckoned 1 must have been the base human start stat and that 3 was therefore a significant improvement.

A beautiful book floated above the wolf's corpse, one whose glow lifted my heart. It was an item of some kind, and I rushed forward to grab it even before picking up my spear. A message was presented to me.

Book of *Summon Skeleton* LV. 2
Cast time: Instant
MP Cost: 5
Distance: 3 Meters
Summons two Skeleton Warriors to fight
for you. Skeletons can only be spawned
from a corpse.
Do you wish to learn *Summon*
***Skeleton* LV. 2?**

The description of the skill was immediately followed by a prompt asking me if I wished to learn the skill. This was life or death, and any increase in power was greatly welcomed. *Yes!*

Warning: You may only learn one Active skill currently. Your next skill slot will be unlocked at level 10. Confirm skill allocation.

This message gave me a second of pause before I confirmed. I checked the EXP I had received from the wolf and it was only a measly 60% of my level. I wouldn't make it to level 10 at this rate.

Name: Mike Reynolds (27) Class: None
Level: 1 EXP: 67%
HP: 55/55 MP: 15/15
STR: 3
AGI: 2
DEX: 1
VIT: 1
WIS: 1
Available: 0
Skills: [A] Summon Skeleton LV. 2

Summon Skeleton was now in my list of skills. It had an [A] next to it, which I assumed meant it was an active skill. That implied there were also passive skills I could learn. Whether I could level up my skills or needed to be lucky enough to find rewards of higher skill level I had yet to determine.

A sudden cackling came from an alleyway as I was contemplating my situation. It was unmistakable in nature. That had to be another of those small but fierce, green monsters coming my way. This was the perfect opportunity to test Summon Skeleton.

I didn't know how to cast the spell specifically, but I figured it wouldn't be complicated. The spell description said a corpse was required so my focus shifted to a body just ten meters away. It was mangled and partially burned already, the face completely unrecognizable. I had to get close enough to cast and that made me a bit queasy. The smell coming from the body was putrid.

I concentrated on the idea of using Summon Skeleton and immediately two Skeleton Warriors spawned from the corpse, which disappeared. Two boney warriors appeared in front of me, one wielding a spear and the other an axe. This...was absolutely fucking sick.

Did they follow my commands? Did they attack wildly at whatever they chose? It could be either and I wouldn't be surprised. There was only one way to find out: test it. My focus shifted back to the alleyway, where the sounds of mocking laughter were coming closer.

Move to the alleyway. Having concentrated on that command, I was very pleased when the two summoned skeletons began walking over to the alley the monster was coming from. They moved neither fast nor particularly slowly. If there was something in the way, they intelligently moved around it. The weapons they held ready looked quite menacing though, even though they weren't particularly fast.

A green, humanoid monster—I labelled it a goblin in my mind—appeared in sight just before the skeletons reached the corner. It held a wooden spear just like the other goblin I'd seen, and the tip of that weapon was also caked with blood. A sudden fear came over me and I wondered if the goblin would ignore the skeletons and throw the spear at me and kill me.

I urged the skeletons to move forward and fight, but far from moving faster they came to a complete stop! Perhaps they could only fight with me in range, or at least had a magical tether to me as their master? Both to protect myself from a possible spear throw and to give them more room if they were on a tether of some sort,

I rushed behind a burnt car and allowed the skeletons to complete the distance to the goblin.

Changing its focus, the goblin rushed at the skeletons, where they efficiently fought it with axe swings and spear stabs. I didn't know if the summoned skeletons had HP or how they worked exactly, but the goblin stabbed and sliced at them, occasionally knocking free a bone from their white frames. Fortunately, they didn't fear damage or death. It took them just ten seconds to overwhelm the goblin.

Congratulations, you have reached level 2!

Chapter 3: Run and Hide or Stay and Level Up?

Level 2! That was a message I had dearly wished to see. If I was going to survive this crisis, I would have to level up fast. Unfortunately, though, the goblin didn't drop any loot this time. Excitement rushed over me as I realized just how powerful my skeleton warriors were. As long as I didn't try to tackle anything too dangerous, my summoned fighters could dispatch foes for me while I kept a safe distance.

Another cackling sound came from a different direction, and then another. Before I could respond to what was happening, there were at least twenty or thirty different enemies coming towards me. They weren't just goblins either.

I saw what looked like zombies and undead, more goblins, and even just regular but dangerous animals of the kind you could have found before this happened. Particularly scary though, were alien creatures I'd never seen before, something like giant lobsters, but thinner and faster moving. My instincts told me these antennae-waving creatures were really bad news. I had to run.

My feet were taking me away before my brain could even give the command. I started to sprint towards my truck, the two summoned warriors following behind me as quickly as they could with their missing bones. These numerous enemies wanted blood, and they chased me with madness.

The army of monsters quickly caught my summoned skeletons and piled into them. A barrage of blows and bites smashed the skeletons to bits and shattered their bones. A connection I hadn't previously realized had been there broke, and I felt a sudden emptiness. Fortunately, this feeling was no more harmful than a loss of the connection. I took no damage when they died.

My left hand holding my spear, my right fumbled for my car keys. Running faster than I had ever managed before, it became clear that my increased STR had probably affected my endurance and speed: both from the pace of my sprint and how long I could keep it up.

A spear flew directly over my shoulder and smashed into the side of my vehicle, leaving a massive dent. My heart was in my throat: a few inches lower and the spear would have pierced through my shoulder and brought me down.

I reached for the car door handle and jerked it open, then leapt inside. For a moment I was looking directly at that charging body of enemies. There wasn't even time to close the door as I started the engine and reversed at speed. Miraculously I managed to avoid crashing into anything and went backwards fast enough to make some distance from the monsters. Only then did I dare to turn the vehicle around, my momentum bringing the door slamming shut.

My thumping heartbeat was all I could hear on the drive back to home base. My heart was beating out of my chest, not with fear, but with excitement. I hadn't felt so alive in…forever. That chase had been the most intense experience of my entire life.

This feeling was scary. It was an adrenaline rush that was absolutely addictive. This must be what daredevils felt, or crazy thrill seekers. My eyes continuously scanned the rear-view mirror for signs that any of the monsters were chasing me. There was nothing. I was long gone.

I'd never have thought that the gas station would be such a welcoming sight. What wasn't welcoming was the person smashing a rock against the metal grating inside the glass doorway. From the back it was hard to say, but their long hair made me think it was a woman.

The sound of my car pulling up spooked her and she immediately ran around the side of the building and out of sight. I parked, then walked over, spear in hand, to take a better look. Sure enough, the front door glass had been smashed by a relatively large rock.

There were marks on the metal gate that suggested she had been slamming into it for a good while. "Come out!" I yelled. "I won't hurt you! I can unlock the front door." There was no response.

I pulled out my keys and unlocked the now broken glass door, and then fiddled with the metal grate. The sliding of metal was a loud screech: surely she heard it? My feet crushed the glass below as I stepped inside.

I grasped the metal gate and began to slide it closed, "Wait! Wait please, let me in!" A woman's voice came from outside as I heard her scurrying towards me.

A moment later I saw her standing in the doorway. She was average height with shoulder-length brunette hair. Attractive too, to say the least. Judging by her youthful appearance, she must have been around my age or slightly younger: in her early-to-mid-twenties.

She paused for a moment.

"Come on. It's dangerous to be outside," I said and made to close the fence again. The hesitation on her face disappeared and she rushed past me and into the shop. I closed the fence and then locked it.

Before I could even finish securing the door, I heard a gasp behind me, "Stay back!" she suddenly said. I turned in curiosity then glanced from her to the two corpses on the floor.

"That wasn't me. It was one of those small monsters. I managed to kill it and now I have the spear to protect myself." My words eased some of her suspicion, but not all of it. I took a step forward and she jerked in fright. "Here, look," I said.

It wasn't a smart use of MP, but I didn't plan to leave the station again today. I cast Summon Skeletons and the corpse of Rick and then the man despawned. My two, armed skeletons took their place.

For a split second I realized I had made a grave mistake, as I couldn't be sure they wouldn't just blindly attack her. Fortunately, they did not. It was probable that I needed to concentrate on a command to attack or perhaps my considering her an enemy would be enough.

"What in the world are those? What did you just do?" The young woman seemed even more shocked at seeing the two skeleton figures appear in front of her than when she had seen the bodies.

"They are my summonings—like in video games. It's now possible to obtain skills and level up...by killing monsters. You must have seen the monsters? Our planet has completely changed, and we need to learn the system that has appeared here and get on top of it."

The woman looked as if she wanted to scoff at my statement, but the animated skeletons in front of her were proof of my words.

"Can't we just hide and try to survive? There must be others. We should try to find them and stay away from the monsters."

"First, why don't we at least introduce ourselves," I said. "I'm Michael, you can call me Mike though."

"Jessica," she responded.

"Hi Jessica. Good to meet you. I intend to use this gas station as my base as long as I'm able, and you're welcome to join me," I said. I couldn't exactly force her to leave, not peacefully at least. Also, I'd never let someone go out there and into danger. Furthermore, I was glad of the company of another person; she could potentially be a strong ally and even just having someone to talk to was a big improvement compared to figuring this all out on my own. "I don't think running will save us. We should work together to survive, level up, and grow more powerful."

Her expression showed unease at the idea. "So, you're saying you level up from killing those things? And that's how you got control of those skeletons?"

"That's what I'm saying."

"I'm not exactly keen on the idea of fighting monsters…" she confessed.

"Eventually we'll run out of food and water, and then we'll be forced to leave. If we aren't strong enough when that time comes then we will die. We have no idea how the world will evolve and change over time. We need to take advantage of the relatively low-level monsters around us and become stronger, now. Think about it."

"I can't think about anything but food right now." Her stomach grumbled, "I'm starving." Jessica went down the aisle grabbing whatever snacks caught her fancy before plopping down on the floor and violently tearing open packets. What I saw was anything but lady-like. A burp topped off the entire scene, "What? I was hungry. Sue me." She must have seen something in my expression.

The day was still young, and I could still use Summon Skeleton one more time if need be. I wanted to go out and hunt monsters, but it was best to minimize the risks I faced until I had a better understanding of what was happening. There was also the issue of my stats, too.

I had gained another level and had three points to allocate. My priorities had changed though, as I was now able to summon minions to fight for me. STR and AGI were still useful, but no longer were my first preference.

I pulled up my stat page and noted that my HP had a potential maximum now of 70 and my MP of 20. From the looks of it, leveling up had granted me 15 HP and 5 MP. I could cast Summon Skeleton twice more today instead of just once, a happy surprise. My best bet now was to focus on surviving while they did the fighting, which meant VIT was a good choice for my new attribute allocation. WIS also looked enticing as well, to boost my MP and allow for my skill to be used more often.

What I had also take into consideration, though, was how long I would be depending on summoning skeletons to survive. Level Ten seemed quite a ways away, but if I started efficiently killing monsters, perhaps it would turn out to be fairly easy to get to. Especially with how many enemies were now available to fight in the city. And a new skill might open up new possibilities that needed high attributes in scores I'd neglected. I just didn't have enough information for a min-max strategy: to go all in on any particular stat.

In the end, I deemed VIT the most useful stat in my current circumstances. I started off by putting one point in to see how it faired. One point in VIT gave me the same HP increase as my recent level up, which was better than I had hoped for. After that encouraging result, I decided to put all three new points in VIT.

I had a long look at my character sheet:

Name: Mike Reynolds (27) **Class: None**
Level: 2 **EXP:** 5%
HP: 115/115 **MP:** 10/20
STR: 3
AGI: 2
DEX: 1
VIT: 4
WIS: 1
Available: 0

Skills: [A] **Summon Skeleton LV.** 2

My HP maximum was now double what it had been at Level 1. As long as I didn't take some kind of critical hit then I should be able to recover from injury...I hoped. There was no way to know exactly how rare an item like Bandage was.

I got myself an early dinner from the fruit and other perishable foods and looked to Jessica, "Tomorrow I'll be heading out to practice my skills and to try to level up, you should come with me and we can progress together."

"I'll think about it," she said. Besides that, she didn't really have much else to say. It seemed neither of us wanted to talk about our family, or our lives. We sat there mostly in the silence of our own thoughts till the night came. I sorted out some jackets and car mats for us to lie on and sleep took us.

The following morning, I woke with a sticky sweat lining every crevice of my body. There was no power, and with that no air

28

conditioning. It was hot, and worse, humid. Every bit of clothing stuck to me as if glued on.

"We should eat the perishable foods now and drink the drinks that will go bad." Breakfast ended up being milk and two sandwiches. Fortunately, they hadn't gone bad yet as the coolers were still maintaining a bit of chill. Today was definitely the last day there would be any refrigeration.

"I'm heading back to the city and I'd like you to come with me. I have an idea that can possibly make leveling easier for you."

Jessica stared at me in silence for a few moments, "I'll come with you, but there's no promise I leave the car..." I appreciated her honesty, and the fact that she would come at all was promising.

"Fair enough. You can see how you feel about fighting monsters when we get there." Once again, I brought a bag with water and food: depending on how well things went we could be there for many hours.

Jessica sat in the passenger side, so I ended up placing the spear and bag in the backseat. The blood on it was now fully dried and the weapon wouldn't stain the truck's interior, not that it mattered. "I'm gonna lock up, if you need anything say so now." Pulling the gate open and closed and padlocking it was not light work.

"I'm good," she said while getting in the passenger seat and looking at me impatiently. Well, at least the hesitation from last night seemed to be gone. That alone was good progress. We took off towards the city after I finished locking up.

The smoke from smoldering buildings had completely disappeared, but a new stench had taken its place completely. A smell of death and decay wafted over the entire city. I would have rolled up my window, but I knew that in a few moments I would be outside with the stench anyway.

I parked a ways out this time, just in case the noise of the truck would attract attention. "We go on foot from here. Will you be joining me?" I asked.

Jessica thought on this question for a moment, "I doubt I'd be much safer in the car if something came around." She wasn't wrong. At least I had the spear and my skeleton warriors to fight for us. Although I was going looking for battle, she probably would be safer with me.

I felt melancholy looking at the city and wondering how my family was doing. They didn't live here, but I doubted that any other town nearby had fared much better than this. The possibility my family had died where they lived was very real. I put one foot in front of the other and tried to get rid of that thought.

We surveyed the city entrance for several minutes and saw nothing, not a single enemy to fight. This was our cue to move in and start making progress. This was a chance to gain EXP and also potentially find more allies. I refused to believe the entire city had been wiped out. Other humans must have adapted and be leveling up.

We moved steadily but cautiously, carefully clearing every corner and alley we passed. Stores that were unlocked were worth checking for goods and in case there were any survivors. Eventually, we came across our first enemy.

Half way down the road was a monster that was clearly a zombie by the looks of it. Presumably, it was slow, but it had powerful muscles that had caused its clothing to rip. "Would you like to give it a shot? I asked, "Try to kill that zombie and get your first level." Up until now I hadn't tried to form a party with her: I had no intention of carrying someone if they were going to be dead weight.

If she showed initiative, she deserved a fair share of experience and loot but otherwise I would help her survive as much as I could, while focusing on my own progress.

"I just have to stab that thing, right?" she asked with an expression of determination. I nodded and passed her the bloodied spear.

She took the weapon in both her hands and then stabbed the air a few times, then looked at me for approval, as if asking 'like this?' I silently nodded and we moved forward. The zombie noticed us when we were about ten feet away. Possibly by hearing us but since we had been pretty quiet, more likely by our scent.

The entire bottom jaw of the zombie was missing and splotches of hanging dead skin covered the decaying body. A hoarse gurgling sound escaped its throat as it moved at us. I was expecting something slow moving, but instead it was quite quick.

Although not as fast as a living person, the zombie had some speed in those dead legs, and after just a second it was already close enough for Jessica to stab. "Mike…Mike, Mike, Mike!" Jessica said frantically as it closed.

"It's okay, just stab at its face," I said from beside her. I wanted to stay out of the battle, so she got the experience. This was probably one of the safest foes to fight solo. It had no ranged abilities, could be outrun on foot, and probably could be knocked over with any object quite easily.

Jessica steadied herself and to my surprise stopped backing away. She turned her body sideways slightly and then stabbed out with all the strength she could muster. I was pleasantly surprised when the spear tip went through the lower jaw and up into the head of the zombie. It fell to the ground and nearly dragged the spear tip with it. The monster collapsed, quite dead.

"Did you level up?" I asked.

"Yes!" She said while exhaling, it seemed her heart was beating quite fast despite the calmer appearance she was maintaining. "I reached level One!" she said proudly.

"How did the spear feel?" I asked.

"I don't like it. When I stabbed that zombie, I could feel the impact of my actions clearly. I don't like it at all." There was some truth to what she said. It was much easier to hit a button and watch something die than use the tool yourself to kill it.

"We don't have any other weapons at the moment, and you don't have a skill. The spear will have to do for now. Should we continue or do you want to head back to the truck?" I wouldn't try and stop her if she decided to go to the truck. Forcing her against her will was not an option, but I definitely would continue to hunt for experience gain and drops.

"I'll continue," Jessica said with firm determination.

Chapter 4: Forming My First Group of the Apocalypse System

"Until you get a skill, you'd better hold onto the spear."

Jessica didn't look too pleased, but I admired that she didn't complain and simply tied up her hair and hefted her weapon, soon finding it was most comfortable to rest it over her shoulder. We kept walking in the hopes of encountering more easy prey. My plan was to let her slay any zombies we found, while I killed other, more dangerous enemies with Summon Skeleton. Hopefully, Jessica would hit level 2 before long, at which point I would try to form a group with her. Once the idea of doing so had crossed my mind, I had tested for a group formation menu by concentrating on Jessica with that thought in mind and the option had appeared. For now though, I thought she would level faster if I wasn't taking a share of her zombies.

The outskirts of the city had few encounters—one zombie for Jessica and three of the goblin type for me—but as we moved in deeper the amount of enemies became increasingly numerous. Looking down some of the longer streets I found the numbers gathered in the distance alarming. It was as if the entire city had become some sort of massive spawn point for creatures.

If this were a game, it was no dungeon crawl. Maybe it was more of a sandbox type of game, where there was no obvious goal and plenty of different hunting grounds for us to explore? Or what if there was some final quest or goal I was supposed to be working on? The city, with a center full of monsters, felt like a hunting ground for us, and we were new 'players' to the game. That was how I'd be approaching the situation if I had a game controller in hand. Only now we were playing a real-life game and our lives were on the line.

Carefully making our way through the quieter streets, eventually Jessica and I met our next encounter, and this time it wasn't a zombie, or a goblin, or anything I'd seen before. This was a four-legged creature about the size of a large dog that had no eyes. The joints of its legs and arms bent at an odd angle and it looked completely alien. A tongue constantly escaped its mouth and licked two antennae located atop its head.

Creatures I'd never seen before required my full focus, and no holding back. I found a nearby body and cast Summon Skeleton immediately. I beckoned for Jessica to hand me the spear and stand back.

After I urged the skeletons to attack, they ran forward like two reliable guards. They rushed the small creature and started to chop at it with their axe and spear. At first the alien seemed alarmed, but then nimbly dodged their attacks with complete ease. It 'looked' at me, and then I felt my heart drop.

Instinctively, I knew what would happen next: it jumped at me with those odd legs and rocketed through the air. Fortunately, I had started to raise the spear in preparation for such an attack and I got the point into line just in time to impale it. The battle wasn't over though, as the creature hadn't died immediately.

Those long legs extended downward, and I could see razor sharp talons extending and scraping towards me, which threatened to grasp my arms. My only option was to drop the spear on the floor. A second later both my skeleton warriors arrived and chopped the creature to a pulp, nearly destroying our only weapon in the process.

Congratulations, you have reached level
3!

It seemed this type of enemy gave considerable EXP. Probably because of its good mobility. Fast monsters were dangerous monsters, regardless of their size. I wiped the sweat from my brow I checked my stats. Curiously there was a new entry listed in my skills tab.

Name: Mike Reynolds (27) Class: None
Level: 3 EXP: 1%
HP: 130/130 MP: 20/25
STR: 3
AGI: 2
DEX: 1
VIT: 4
WIS: 1
Available: 3

Skills: [A] Summon Skeleton LV. 2,
[P] Sixth Sense

There was a skill there called Sixth Sense, with a [P] in front. The P must mean passive, but what did it do? By concentrating on it, I opened a sub-menu that provided an explanation.

Sixth Sense: Your sense of danger is
superb. Trust your instinct.

So, if I had a feeling that something was wrong…that feeling was probably right? This was some form of premonition, and in a game setting with danger lurking at every corner, would be considered a godly advantage. Perhaps I had hit the jackpot, but I'd need to understand more how the skill worked. If it was just a vague alert, well, that would still be a huge help, whatever the game system, but might it be directional? Or give me some intuition as to the nature of the danger? If so, my chances of surviving this apocalypse had just doubled or tripled.

Given encounters with such dangerous monsters were likely to happen again, I decided against waiting to form a party with Jessica. I concentrated on the idea of grouping with her and mentally said *yes* to the menu box that asked me did I want to do so. She looked at me curiously and then I saw her name and HP bar appear. It floated there in green above her head, and there was even a place for her hit points– 55—at the side of my vision. At first, I thought this was going to be a distraction and bother me, but as soon as I stopped thinking about Jessica as a group member, her stat completely slipped from my view.

"I can't baby you," I said to her, "If we work together we can survive, and maybe even find people to help us." I didn't want to die, and a part of me now wanted to see how far I could go in this new game world.

My fears of having to baby Jessica disappeared when we fought the next mob. It was a goblin and my skeleton warriors rushed it and began attacking. Something I never expected also happened: Jessica charged it as well, and in the end it was her who stabbed her spear through the monster's neck.

She looked back and a touch sharply said, "I can pull my weight."

I could only give a wry shrug in response. "Let's keep going." The EXP gain had been cut cleanly in half, which was a welcome result. If it had been participation based, that would have made sharing it more complex.

Seeing that Jessica had fighting spirit was a blessing, but now I felt it necessary to guard against over-eagerness, "So far so good, but we must cherish our lives more than anything. Be prepared to run if we have to." We continued to hunt the peripheral streets and I felt increasingly confident we could level up again like this. Zombies and goblins were extremely common in the outskirts and we made those our targets.

We ran into a zombie and goblin combo and I didn't feel the need to run. My skeletal warriors dogpiled the goblin in order to keep it from chucking its spear, while Jessica went face-to-face with the zombie and dispatched it cleanly.

That battle brought Jessica to Level Two and I was getting close to Level Four. This was as smooth a way to get a start in the game world as I could have hoped for.

We rounded another corner and engaged a single goblin. As ever, my skeletal warriors showed no fear as they rushed it like two berserkers. Jessica went to engage as well, and in her haste failed to see another foe whom I only spotted coming out of the corner of my eye.

From an alley on her right-hand side, a spear flew like a missile. The tip burrowed itself several inches into her thigh and she immediately let out a scream and fell to the ground. I rushed to her and put my hand over her mouth to smother her screaming.

Noise would have enemies crawling all over us in moments, and she couldn't exactly run very fast. I didn't dare remove the spear and instead grabbed the one from her hand. "Try to bear the pain for a minute!" I said in a low voice and turned to the alley.

My skeletal warriors were just finishing up their goblin when I reached the one who had caught Jessica with his spear and pierced him through his chest, killing him in one blow. I rushed back immediately after to inspect my partner's wound.

It was deep, and with blood pooling around her, potentially life threatening. "Do I remove it? What do I do?" I asked. I didn't know. If the spear remained in her thigh she would die but removing it might kill her even faster. Some sort of torniquet first maybe? Then pull it out? My time to respond to this crisis was up, as new monsters came around the corner.

Two zombies, a wolf, and one of those odd alien creatures started closing in on us and fast. They were eying Jessica hungrily as she did her best to crawl away on the floor. I didn't want to lose my first and only friend in this apocalypse.

I separated my skeleton warriors and sent one on the wolf and one at the weird alien crab. The two zombies weren't anywhere near as agile as their companions, so I opted to ignore them. They seemed the least threatening for the moment.

I rushed to join my undead warrior at the wolf and stabbed out frantically. The snarling wolf, however dodged my spear thrusts and the warrior's axe by constantly edging back. Fear was starting to over-take me as I realized this battle was way over my pay grade.

I gave the order to my warrior to try to subdue the wolf as best as possible. The axe dropped from the skeleton's hand and instead it did its best to grab the wolf. That didn't seem to be working either though in evading the warrior, the wolf turned away from me: I thought I saw a chance and leapt forward.

There was a searing pain in my leg as a claw came across my calf. It shredded my jeans and rent flesh, but I had distracted the wolf. My skeleton warrior managed to bear hug the beast. Ignoring the pain in my leg, I stabbed the spear repeatedly into its gut. I didn't stop until the yelping ended.

Almost immediately after that, the two zombies reached me and attacked. One caught a spear to the head and quickly collapsed, while the other managed to bite into my extended hand. My skeleton warrior tackled the zombie to the ground and held it down, a bit of my flesh torn off by the pull of its rotten teeth.

There were multiple status messages happening all at once, which I could only ignore. My spearhead came down again and stabbed directly through the Zombies skull. Now there was only that weird alien creature left.

My adrenaline was pumping and despite searing pain from my leg and arm, a newfound bravery came over me. I once again directed my warriors to try to grapple the creature. Their attacks weren't fast enough to damage the alien, but working together one of the skeletons was able to grasp a limb in its boney hand, even at the cost of the other skeleton's rib cage being destroyed.

Once the alien crab was unable to use its full speed, killing it was as easy as slipping the spear through its hard exterior and collecting the EXP. With the battle over I surveyed the area for a belt or cord for a torniquet and spotted something that was desperately needed.

There was a skill book, and then also a single bandage floating there. I grabbed both without hesitating and rushed to Jessica. "This is going to hurt, try to bear it and don't scream." Her forehead was drenched with sweat and her face was red. She managed a nod and put a large portion of her t-shirt into her mouth.

Grasping the spear in her leg firmly, I ripped it out in one fell swoop. What I had feared became a reality as blood started to gush from the wound with every pulse. Using the bandage that had dropped, I 'wrapped' it around her wound.

The bleeding stopped immediately, and the healing power of the bandage meant that even the wound closed over slowly. There was still a raw, pink indentation in Jessica's thigh, but the life-threatening nature of the wound was now gone. I wiped my brow and forced a smile, only to realize my vision was starting to blur.

Jessica said something appreciative, but I found it hard to focus. I was feeling incredibly nauseous and dizzy. Something was terribly wrong, and I decided to read the status messages from earlier.

Congratulations, you have reached level 4!

You have received an infection. You will lose HP overtime.

I checked my hit points in a panic. I was down to 65 from 145.

The zombie had bitten me, and I had failed to appreciate the fact that maybe I could become infected? Was I going to become a zombie? Having used our only bandage to save Jessica, I didn't know the solution. It was possible I was going to die, and I couldn't help but selfishly wish I still had the bandage.

I nearly collapsed while trying to stand after removing the spear. "Are you okay? What's wrong?" Jessica asked in a panicked tone.

"One of the zombies bit me." I said, "we need to get back to the car." My vision was growing darker and my head even more fuzzy. An encounter with a monster now would be disastrous. With Jessica leading me by the hand, our rush back to the car was a fog that went in and out.

All I knew was that I didn't want to die. I almost didn't realize it when we reached the car, and Jessica forced me into the backseat. "It'll be okay," she said. I used my 6 available attribute points and put them all into VIT in a last-ditch effort to survive: then I blacked out.

Chapter 5: Am I Going to Mutate into a Zombie?

The next time I opened my eyes the gas station ceiling came into view. My head was pounding, and I was covered in a thick and disgusting layer of sweat. I tried to sit up but could only let out a low groan before falling back down.

"You're awake! How do you feel?" Jessica must have heard me as she came to my side.

"Like complete shit," I said plaintively. "How long have I been out?"

"You've been lying there for two days…when I first got you back, you were burning up and murmuring while unconscious the entire time. It got so bad I was sure you were going to die. You were like that for a full day, and then the fever broke, and your temperature started to come down."

"Water…please," I said. I felt incredibly dehydrated, and my stomach was begging for liquid to fill it. Despite that, I couldn't help but smile. I was alive. I was alive! I opened my stats and took a look at myself from the view of the game system I was now a part of.

Name: Mike Reynolds (27) Class: None
Level: 4 EXP: 35%
HP: 30/235 MP: 30/30

STR: 3
AGI: 2
DEX: 1
VIT: 10
WIS: 1
Available: 0

Skills: [A] Summon Skeleton LV. 2, [P] Sixth Sense [P] Bravery [P] Mutated

To judge by my low HP, I was just outside death's door. Putting the 6 points I had available into VIT had most likely been essential in my survival. I turned my thoughts from my narrow escape to the two new passive skills I could see.

Bravery I had seen when checking my status before my collapse, but the situation was so dire I hadn't had time to check it. *Mutated*, however, was completely new. Naturally, I read each of them.

Bravery: Helps you find the strength to overcome adversity.
Mutated: You have been changed in an unknown way.

Bravery was definitely useful, and perhaps it had been a factor when I had overcome my instinct to run when Jessica was down, and two zombies and a wolf came into view? But I also had felt a strong desire to help the only person I knew for sure was still alive. I couldn't say for sure, obviously, life or death situations were something completely new to me. It was possible that Bravery had stopped me from fleeing in fear. I was never particularly brave.

Mutated, however, worried me. Getting the skill must have been a consequence of being bitten by a zombie, but in what way was I mutated? The 'passive' tag didn't help in any way to

43

understanding it. A horrible thought occurred to me. Perhaps I was going to turn into a zombie? I guessed I would need to wait and see.

Jessica returned with a bottle of water and some chips. She opened the top and the bag for me before sitting down beside me. "Thanks for saving me. Those monsters would have torn me apart. If you hadn't put yourself in between them and me, I'd be gone."

"Teammates help each other out. You paid me back already by getting me back here, safe and alive." It was then that I remembered I had picked up a skill book from one of the monsters. There had been no time to look at it before.

I pulled it out and the thick, glowing tome hovered above my hand. Jessica looked on in awe, "Is that what you meant by a skill book?"

"It is. Mine gave me the power to summon skeletons. This will be yours and it could make all the difference to us. Let's see what it is." I turned the cover for both of us to read the front page.

Book of Sharpshooting LV. 1: Fires a projectile with pinpoint accuracy. Requires: Projectile Weapon.

I drew a blank…"Isn't this kind of useless right now?" We didn't have a bow or a gun or any kind of projectile weapon.

I didn't bother reading the other skill stats because it wasn't even usable at the moment.

Jessica looked up from the book and had an uncertain tone in her voice. "Should I learn this? It seems a waste. Perhaps you should hold on to it and maybe we will find a projectile weapon, or a different skill book."

I nodded and when I put the book away, felt that Jessica didn't seem too bothered about it. Did she appreciate how important a skill was for our survival and progress? I was disappointed this hadn't been more useful.

It suddenly occurred to me to ask, "Did anyone else come by the garage while I was out?"

My question wasn't just based on hope for more human allies, I was also concerned about our food supply. As time went on resources would slowly become scarcer. People would continue to search for food and water, and that would eventually lead them here not as friends but rivals.

"No one," Jessica responded.

I found that I was more relieved than disappointed. I finished my chips and took another big gulp of water before laying my head back down. Right now, I felt too weak to move. Fortunately though, I could see my HP was steadily recovering. Even in these few minutes I was 2 HP better. It seemed to me my HP was ticking upwards a little faster than before I was knocked out. Probably, VIT made a contribution to the rate of restoration as well as the absolute HP score.

In another day I would be back in fighting shape, and we could return to the city to explore more. I was determined to continue leveling up; whatever the meaning of this game, it was clear that levelling was central to it. My main fear was that things may have changed in these past two days.

Despite having been asleep for nearly two days already, drifting off again wasn't difficult. My body felt like absolute trash, and after eating and drinking my fill I went back under without any delay.

The following morning I felt renewed, and seeing that my HP had recovered back to full, was good to go.

"Are you ready to try to get more E.X.P?" I asked Jessica. She must have felt trauma from her injury and near death. Once you experience that fear, it stays with you and is hard to get rid of. I was almost expecting her to say 'no'.

"Let me eat my breakfast. We should spend a bit more time being careful, though. A spear in the leg is not something I ever want to experience again." She half laughed.

Her mood was surprisingly cheerful and I admired her for it. I also noticed that she wasn't walking with a limp at all. "Does your leg hurt?"

"Just a dull aching since it was bandaged. It's been slowly getting better since then though." She looked at me, "what about you? Are you sure you're ready?"

"Good as new. My ten VIT has ensured that." To Jessica I wanted to project that I was calm and composed, but in truth I was worried. Out of necessity, I had put a ton of points into VIT, even though my combat tactics were to rely on my summoned skeletons. If the monsters in town had become tougher in the last two days and if there was no scaling for my current skill, we might become stuck, unable to progress. Level 10 seemed to be far away.

Trying to be more positive, I reminded myself that if the zombies and goblins remained easy kills, then we could slaughter them without care, in which case level 10 would be reachable in just a few days grinding by our two-person party. The risk of a ranged attack against us was my biggest concern and probably Jessica's too from what she'd just said. It was fine to say we'd go slowly but those attacks were the bane of our existence. There were so many places for enemies to hide and attack from.

We had crowd control problems too. Only zombies could be dealt with efficiently en masse. The rest of the monsters—the goblins, wolves, and especially the aliens—were big threats and fighting more than one at a time increased the risk of injury several fold. We hadn't even cracked the outer zones of the city either. What lay further towards the center? Would monsters be getting stronger? Would they change and evolve as time went on?

I shifted my thinking to the present and stopped worrying about the what-if's. "I'm gonna fill up the tank and then we head out. Would you lock up?" I said to Jessica before tossing her the keys. She had already gained my loyalty and trust.

The city's appearance hadn't changed much over the previous two days. The biggest difference was the smell. It had grown milder, as the corpses had already dried out in the sun, having reached their peak stench around the time of our last journey here.

As we moved carefully down a wide street, I realized that my outlook had grown bleaker. Several days without seeing another person didn't bode well for the survival of humanity. Was everyone holing up as long as possible? If that was the case, they would be forced to find food and water and new shelter in the coming days.

Were monsters going to be what I needed to worry about most? People could be terrible, and even more so when it was 'us or them'. What if we met people of higher level, was there anything in the system to stop PVP? Or was it going to be that the strongest set the rules?

As we moved, I realized that while the buildings looked the same, the pattern of the spawns was different. When we started to see monsters, they were always in large groups. There were no more singles, only packs of them. Although they moved around, it always seemed to be within a limited area.

Being careful was no longer a suggestion but an absolute requirement. "Let's avoid the goblins at all costs." I suggested. For now, their ranged attacks posed a serious problem. The alternatives were packs of zombies, our little alien friends, and a new monster type that I hadn't seen before.

The streets were now crawling with enemies to fight, which potentially meant more EXP, but also way more danger. Fortunately, both Jessica and I were wielding spears from goblin enemies. With my two skeleton warriors we had four bodies to fight with.

"What about those over there?" Jessica pointed to six zombies. Her choice was good, they were a risk, but it was lower than for any other group of mobs we'd seen.

"All right. Let's see how they react to being attacked," I suggested. "Maybe it's possible to pull them separately." Even if we somehow pulled five or all six of them at once, I felt we could handle the fight.

I took a moment to find a corpse and then I summoned my skeleton warriors. Jessica had picked up some rubble from the ground and looked at me. Her intention was clear; she was going to try to beam one of the zombies with a rock.

It was a good idea so I gave a nod. "Worst case, everything starts coming, we run like hell and don't look back." She gave a nod and then tossed out the piece of rubble. My expectations weren't high, but to my surprise she managed to clock the zombie directly in the head.

The zombie that was hit turned in our direction immediately, even though it didn't know exactly where we were. There was a moment when I thought it might come alone, but then four more turned and began rushing in our direction as well.

"This is fine." I assured her. "Let's move back a bit." We moved off the debris we had perched on and into one with a lot of wreckage around us. We positioned ourselves between several to-taled cars. We could easily funnel the incoming mobs one at a time here.

I sent the skeleton warriors out first, with instructions for them to deal with two zombies on their own. They would do well: the scratching and biting attacks of the zombies would have a lot less effect on bone than skin. That left four rushing zombies for Jessica and I to deal with.

The remaining zombies came at us while awkwardly tripping and hobbling over the corpses and downed infrastructure. They battered into the burned car frames with almost no sign of intelligent pathing. With no windows to block us, we stayed on the far side of cars and pierced their heads from one side of the car to the other when the opportunity arose.

My skeleton warriors easily cleaned up the original two, and I received a very welcome system message that filled me with relief.

Summon Skeletons has leveled up.

I opened the skill description for Summon Skeleton and took a look at what had changed.

Summon Skeleton LV. 3
Cast time: Instant
MP Cost: 7
Distance: 3 Meters
**Summons three Skeleton Warriors to fight
for you. Skeletons can only be spawned
from a corpse.**

I had gained one more warrior at the cost of 2 extra MP per cast. I cast it again on a zombie before it despawned and three fresh warriors appeared in front of me. My hope had been that a new level would increase their strength, and that this was true was as clear as day looking at them.

Their boney frames now supported a few pieces of metal armor. The axes they wielded were slightly larger now. Looking at them was enough for me to see they were definitely more dangerous.

"Got another bandage," Jessica said while walking over to me. So far, neither of us had found a single equipable item yet. I was starting to wonder if they even existed. Up to now, I had been convinced I was in an RPG system. Yet an RPG without drops and gear wasn't really an RPG.

Perhaps though, the issue was that we hadn't killed much more than twenty enemies, if that. Maybe this was a system where gear was rare, and that wouldn't necessarily be a bad thing. It meant whatever we found would be that much better and more valuable when it did drop.

For now though, we had to find a way to level given the change in monster behavior. There was no point continuing along these roads that no longer had easy pulls, and instead we went in the other direction, but still along the outskirts of the city. Our search for an encounter we could handle ended up being a walk of over thirty minutes of movement away from our vehicle, which was not a great idea in itself.

"Wait…" I said. There was a commotion ahead of us, some shuffling inside a former grocery store. "Do you hear that?" I whispered.

Jessica looked at me and nodded her head, and then we both started to scoot forward stealthily, eventually we reached the corner, and she peeked her head around to take a good look. "There's people!" she said in an excited but low whisper.

Chapter 6: After the Apocalypse Humans Can be Scarier than Monsters

"People?"

"Two men, just inside," reported Jessica, and I couldn't help but lean over her back and take a look. Sure enough there were two men. They hadn't noticed us, and as soon as I saw them I had a bad feeling.

"Don't tell them about leveling or anything." I whispered to her, "don't reveal anything." I tasked my skeleton warriors to disappear behind the wall.

Jessica must have seen something in my expression, "What's wrong?" she asked. "Do you know them?"

"No, but there's something…something that might be my Sixth Sense skill. Let's just be smart about it. They could be as dangerous as monsters."

"We can always avoid them…" Jessica suddenly said. It was true, we could avoid them, but I wasn't certain how Sixth Sense worked, and we could really use more people in our group. Maybe I had a negative feeling looking at them because something bad was going to happen to them? I couldn't be sure.

"Just be on guard," I warned before stepping out. It took the two men a moment to notice me, and then they noticed Jessica who also came around the corner. Surprise raced across their faces as they eyed the bloodied spears in our hands.

They were clearly looking for food and water, and from the looks of it had no weapons. Keeping my spear lowered and making myself look as non-threatening as possible I slowly entered the store. Only after entering inside could I get a better look at them.

They were both similar height—a little under six feet I judged—and had short, unkempt black hair. There was a similarity in their long faces: they were related, probably brothers. Age wise, they were both a good bit older than Jessica and I, mid 30s probably. As I looked at them, it was the younger one that gave me a terrible feeling.

"People? Real live people? We haven't seen anyone in days." The older one spoke up first, and he sounded genuinely relieved.

"We neither. You're the first people we've seen. Are you hungry? Thirsty?" I asked. It was better to be amicable to start and see what happened. Not only that, we had months of water back at home base, I could spare some now in good faith.

"Both," the younger one said while moving forward. I tossed him a bottle of water and two candy bars, which he caught without a thank you. My eyes couldn't help but follow his, and his eyes couldn't help but stare at Jessica.

The look he gave her wasn't pleasant, or curious. It was a hungry look, and not for the food he was currently about to eat.

"Excuse my brother…he's lacking in manners," the older one suddenly said while letting off a small laugh. "We appreciate the food, right?" He moved behind his brother and gave him a playful smack on the head.

"Right. We appreciate it."

The more I looked at the younger one, the more I had a bad feeling. Even the older one, whom seemed nice and friendly, felt fake. It felt as if I was talking to someone with a mask on, hiding all of their emotions. He was even harder to read than the younger one, which worried me.

"How have you guys been surviving? Out there, I mean," the older brother asked, "we have been scraping by like rats…but you two seem well off enough. You even have spare food and water to share."

I appreciated the fact that Jessica said nothing, letting me come up with our response. "Just like you two, scraping by like rats. We managed to come by these spears, which gives us some protection. We can dispatch the zombies, but have to avoid everything else," I continued, "finding food and water isn't that bad if you can move around."

"Do you have somewhere safe you're staying?" he asked. I almost felt bad lying, but my Sixth Sense was telling me these two were bad news. Trying to team up with them would only lead to harm, especially to Jessica.

"No, we're just constantly on the move. We were passing through trying to find any survivors, see if there's even a small semblance of normalcy in this hellscape," I responded.

"Right, right," the younger one forced a smile.

I didn't want to continue talking anymore, and honestly wanted to get away. My feeling of danger only grew worse the longer we were near these brothers. "We're going to take our leave now. Stay safe." I grabbed Jessica by the wrist.

"Wait, please wait," the older one suddenly said. "Is it possible you can take us with you?"

I turned and said as firmly as possible, "I think its best we part ways here. We can barely protect ourselves. Small numbers seem to be the best bet to go unnoticed." I hoped that sounded convincing, even though it was not at all my belief. In fact, I believed the way to cope with this system was to create a large group, a raiding party even.

Having more numbers, capable leveled individuals with skills and items, was definitely the best bet. The people though, they needed to be the right fit. These two were definitely not that, and my decision was solidified even more when I saw the younger brother's expression in response to my words. It was a look of pure malice.

I didn't wait for his response before turning and hurrying out with Jessica. "The young one is bad news and the older one is crafty as a snake. We can't trust them: the old one tries to hide it, but the young one can barely manage to contain his lust."

"The younger one was seriously creeping me out," she acknowledged. "They took your decision surprisingly well, though."

"I'm not so sure. For a moment there I think the older one dropped his façade. He wasn't happy about my refusal, but I didn't want to stay around and argue the issue." We started to retrace our steps and hurried back towards the truck. "And they're following us."

Even though whenever I looked back, I couldn't see anyone, the reason why I knew they were following was this bad prickling on the back of my neck. It kept coming up and eventually I turned fast enough to spot the older brother jump back behind a corner. Judging by their actions, it didn't seem like they believed my story. Clearly, they had hostile intentions. My biggest worry was that they might have got levels and skills I didn't know about.

The brothers had been sneakily keeping pace with us and doing a good job of staying hidden. No doubt they were watching how we handled the encounters on our way. The number of monsters on the outskirts we were moving through was low, and we avoided dispatching anything that wasn't a zombie. I really wanted to avoid showing my hand, and even if they didn't know already, to alerting them to the fact leveling was possible. I didn't use Summon Skeletons the entire way back.

Our EXP gain therefore was pitiful, but not every day could be super fruitful. When we arrived at the truck, I was relieved that we could drive off and lose the brothers. But at the same time, I had bad taste in my mouth. Two humans who meant us harm turned out to be scarier than most monsters. We could go back to EXP grinding once the looming threat of the brothers had disappeared.

Slamming the truck door closed, Jessica gave me a smile as we raced out of town. She didn't seem unhappy to be leaving without having gained another level. Her temperament had grown on me. A steady presence throughout our expedition, she was quick on the uptake.

"We'll take Route Eleven and try again tomorrow from the north. Hopefully, we'll never see those guys again. They are serious trouble." Despite getting away from the brothers and putting miles between us and them, the ominous Sixth Sense feeling loomed over me. Falling asleep wasn't easy that night.

"Mike, Mike, wake up!" It was pitch black when I opened my eyes, it must have been some time in the middle of the night and an acrid smell made my eyes water. I looked at Jessica and could barely make out her figure in the darkness. "Fire! There's a fire!" She kept shaking me.

The grogginess of waking disappeared in an instant. Adrenaline kicked in when I realized there was a growing light coming from the back of the building. As I stood, smoke assaulted my face and entered my lungs.

"Grab whatever you need," shouted Jessica, "we have to get out!"

My head was already resting on my bag, and I scooped it up and packed it with whatever I could grab in a hurry. My hand scraped the pitch-black floor and eventually I grasped the spear in my hand.

"Good to go." I rushed to the door behind Jessica. With no light it wasn't at all easy to get the gate unlocked. My hands fumbled for the padlock and eventually I managed to scrape it open. "We can store as much as possible in the car, let's try and make a few trips."

The gate opened with its normal grating sound, and I stepped outside. That bad feeling that was following me must have been this fire. At least that's what I thought, mistakenly.

Something smacked into my skull with tremendous force and sent me to the ground. "Ahhhh!" I groaned. My vision was swimming and dizziness assaulted me. I turned on my side along the floor in time to see a figure illuminated by the firelight. It was the older brother coming towards me with a rock.

Having seen that I wasn't unconscious, he came at me again with full force. He was going to bash my head in if I didn't do something. I didn't want to kill anyone, but I didn't want to die. The spear was still half-gripped in my hand.

It was possible he didn't see the weapon in the darkness, with me being on the ground, but I lifted it. I didn't hesitate to orient the point towards him as he came towards me, and the tip pierced directly into his midriff. It stopped him in his tracks immediately.

"Ahhhh....?" He said a low moan that was almost a question. I shoved hard and the shock caused him to drop the rock at his feet. His hand reached down to feel what had pierced him, and I felt his firm grasp on the spear tip.

I was terrified, but I used the little remaining strength I had to push the spear and twist it in his gut. The weight of his body falling ripped the spear from my grip. He was dead...I had killed someone.

Everything was happening so fast that Jessica didn't even realize what was happening. "Careful!" I yelled at her. The younger one was somewhere lurking in the shadows. No doubt she would be his target. As soon as I had warned her though, I heard her scream out.

"Let go of me!" Jessica screamed. Two figures wrestled in the darkness, the younger brother had grasped her from behind, his hands around her neck.

"Shut up you bitch!" I could make out that he was pulling her backwards. "You're both going to die." There was fury in his voice.

I managed to stand despite waves of dizziness and nausea. "Don't do this," I said, "this is a mistake...we can work it out."

"You're going to stand right there." He said to me, "and watch while I take care of business." It was then that he started fumbling with Jessica's pants with one hand while the other was at her neck. With the moonlight strengthening as a cloud moved, I realized that hand wasn't empty, but was holding a knife.

There was nothing more to say. This man was deranged, and it was clearly us or him at this point. He was more concerned with vengeance and lust than survival. I needed to edge away from his brother's corpse, at least a little.

I started to circle while speaking only to distract him, "This can go a different way," I said, "if you rape her, I'm going to kill you right after. Stop now and we can all leave here alive." I was lying.

Regardless of his actions, I had steeled my resolve. He was dying tonight.

The younger brother didn't instantly respond, which meant he was pondering my threat. His eyes remained locked firmly on me, knife to her throat. It was then that I cast Summon Skeletons on his brothers' corpse, hoping I'd moved around far enough he wouldn't see the skeletons in the darkness.

Good. His glittering eyes were still on me. I sent my summoned allies all the way around the back of the building and tried to add the thought they should be quiet to my mental instruction. Whether this helped or not, the skeletons moved carefully and soon came around the building to be behind our enemy. I wasn't sure how to go about attacking him though. If I tasked them to restrain the younger brother, he might slit her throat in the struggle.

In the end, I decided that zero risk was the best option. I tasked one of the skeletons to bash his skull in from behind. An axe to the back of the head would leave no room for error. I made sure the target was specific as possible. I didn't want any possibility the skeleton might also attack Jessica.

My heart was in my chest as I looked at the younger brother, "Just let her go!" I screamed as if distraught to cover the skeleton's advance. Moonlight shone on a raised axe that struck violently downwards. A cracking, mushy sound came from where he stood.

Jessica must have felt the knife drop because she staggered forward, gasping, "it's over."

Behind her, the man's body collapsed backwards into a heap on the floor. Jessica rushed over to me and buried her face into my chest clasping me tight. "I thought you were going to die."

"You did good," I said. It must have been hard for her, being held captive. And if she had tried something instead of waiting for

58

me to set up the skeletons, she might have provoked him into killing her.

We had survived this ordeal, but we'd lost our base. The fire had spread beyond control. Our home was being burnt to the ground and there was nothing we could do about it. There wasn't even time left to grab any more supplies. All we could do was check the aftermath in the morning.

My stomach was curdling in disgust. I had just killed two people. The thought continued in my head over and over: *It was us or them*...I looked at the new corpse and used Summon Skeleton simply to get rid of it. I couldn't bear to look at it.

Chapter 7: New Mobs, New Skills: Another Day in the Post-Apocalypse World

We ended up sleeping in the car that night, which actually didn't turn out to be that uncomfortable. There was more bad news though: the two brothers had slashed every tire on all the vehicles.

The gas station was basically destroyed. The following morning, we searched the still warm ruins and managed to find some drinks that had escaped destruction in the coolers along with a small amount of untouched food. Maybe a week's worth.

I managed to find another bag in Rick's truck that Jessica could use, and we took whatever our backs could carry. From here on out, we would truly be like rats scraping by. This incident had changed my outlook, hardened my resolve.

I never again wanted to look at someone and feel scared or the need to avoid them. No, I was determined to become so strong that no one could threaten us. Whoever met me with harmful intention would learn to avoid me or fear me enough to never try to take me down.

Killing the two brothers hadn't resulted in any EXP gain, which told me something. Whatever or whoever deigned this apocalypse didn't want the playthings having any incentive to hunt each other.

Unfortunately, human nature was going to work against that design. This wouldn't be the last time I would need to deal with enemies in the form of humans. I was sure of it.

There was nothing left tying me to this place anymore, so we set off on foot towards the city. After a brief discussion Jessica and I had agreed we could level there, and also scavenge for food and water. It was the best place to be but it was more than an hour walk on foot, which further showed the determination those brothers must have had to find us.

"A mistake now will cost us our lives, but not giving our all will do the same," I said. "Leveling is the number one priority." It had occurred to me that leveling would eventually bring me to a state where I could not be easily killed by normal weapons. That rock smashing into my head should have made me unconscious, but it only stunned me momentarily. A single night of rest had healed the damage completely. More hit points, more abilities, and more strength in general—then no one could take advantage or look down upon us.

Once at the outskirts of the city, I found the first corpse available and summoned skeletons. From then on, we worked together to grind up EXP. It was necessary to take risks for some of the pulls because our encounters were double or triple packs of mobs. We took them all on, even goblins. For goblins specifically though, we always took cover and I pulled with my skeleton warriors. After they aggroed the goblins, I would pull them back into an enclosed space. Once there, we destroyed them without fear of spears being thrown unexpectedly from side streets.

By mid-afternoon, I had reached Level 5 and Jessica had got to Level 4. The required EXP per level was steadily increasing, and I expected she would be Level 5 before I even reached Level 6. Still, our increased power meant that our killing speed against the monsters of these streets had increased tremendously.

Up until now Jessica hadn't decided on a specialization, and we still hadn't found a skill for her to use. In the end, like I did, she put a few points in VIT and ended up saving the rest. I kept my three stat points in reserve as well. For now, I was pleased with how smoothly I was progressing.

Name: Mike Reynolds (27) Class: None
Level: 5 EXP: 1%
HP: 250/250 MP: 28/35
STR: 3
AGI: 2
DEX: 1
VIT: 10
WIS: 1
Available: 3

Skills: [A] Summon Skeleton LV. 3,
[P] Sixth Sense [P] Bravery [P] Mutated

I hadn't gained any new passive abilities, which was disappointing. My intuition was that defining moments would possibly grant one. In which case I might gain another passive skill should I kill more people. The thought was disgusting, but it crossed my mind all the same: this new world had attuned my mind to efficiency.

There was no place for normal human decency in the world anymore; not that I wouldn't act in a proper manner, but my attitude would never be the same. People would be treated with decency until they didn't return that decency. Then I would be merciless.

The hierarchy of the world had changed a week ago, and I didn't want to be on the bottom rung of that ladder. "Let's pick up the pace," I said, confident we could tackle larger groups. "The sooner we hit Level Ten, the sooner we can stop worrying about others and focus on surviving."

Having said that, I had the thought that there would always be a concern that we would run into someone else actively leveling up, someone with hostile intentions. In a dog-eat-dog world, the threat of assault was even greater for Jessica. She was a woman, and the chances something untoward happening to her was much greater than for me.

Jessica didn't seem at all displeased with my suggestion; in fact, she openly welcomed it. "I want to find a skill today. I can't keep holding you back." While I didn't think she was actually holding me back, I understood her sentiment: there was a limit to what she could accomplish with just a spear when I already had three beefy warriors with large axes.

We pushed deeper and harder into the city and reached places we hadn't seen for over three days. "Let's not get tangled up and lose our direction," Jessica warned me. We were pushing quite fast, and in the case of needing to escape, there was only one path—the one we entered through.

Further towards the city center the monsters were becoming more powerful, which gave us both pause. It was clear from just a glance that they were stronger and would be more difficult to battle. There were still goblins, and zombies and those weird crab-like creatures roaming about, but now too there were ghastly looking female humanoid figures that floated above the ground. "Banshees" Jessica labelled them and I went with that. Without risking pulling one, it was hard to decide if they were like ghosts; they were translucent and perhaps that meant weapons would simply go through them. Another new monster type were big brutish monsters—like ogres—with bulging muscles and huge meat hooks as weapon walking around.

To top it all off, there was a mega-sized ogreish, meat-hook wielding foe who was obviously different than the rest. Despite a similar hair-covered body and set of ragged clothes and weapons, he was just huge. A boss, an elite enemy perhaps?

The good news though, was that none of the new mob types were organized in a pack. If we wanted to, it was possible to get them separately and at worst we might have a goblin or zombie as an addition. "Let's pull one of the meat hook guys," I suggested.

Looking at our potential targets from the corner of the building we were hiding behind, it seemed like an ogre would be melee-based monster, and would use the meat hook to attack, while the banshee might be a spell caster or have some unexpected skill, which could prove difficult to fight, and more dangerous.

We waited until an ogre came close enough and then I sent out a skeleton warrior to meet it. Once it came back, we brought it through an alley and waited on either side of the exit. Three skeletons surrounded its burly body while Jessica and I stabbed at it with spears. The monster had a lot of hit points, but I could tell right away we were going to win, despite the ferocious blows of its weapon. In the end, the ogre managed to smash apart one of my skeleton warriors before dying, which was troublesome. Regardless of whether I needed to resummon one skeleton or three, the MP cost was still 7. My WIS being so low meant my MP regen wasn't that high. The 7 MP would take several hours to recover.

The monster however, was worth more EXP than six goblins. Just four more of these and I would hit Level 6, and Jessica would be right behind me. I bit the bullet on the skeleton warrior, and we waited for another ogre to cross our path and pulled it the same way.

This time, I made sure to micromanage my warriors, making sure never let the same one get hit twice in a row. There was no guarantee this was effective because I couldn't see any HP bar over my summoned skeletons, but we killed three ogres without losing a warrior.

Another benefit to stepping up the challenge was the increased drop rate. We obtained two skill books in only four kills, which seemed absolutely insane. I wondered if that would change over time, that skills came more often at low levels, to get us going. Another thought I had was that stronger monsters were gradually pushing outward from the city center and that if humans were to have any chance, we'd need these skills: eventually there would be no place completely safe from their spawning. These lower-level monsters would cease to provide a path to those starting out, and harder monsters would continue to appear. If that was the case…people who weren't actively leveling now would lose their chance forever and try just to go into hiding.

The first skill to drop was a defensive one.

Book of Bone Armor LV.1
Cast Time: 1 Second
Duration: 10 Minutes
MP Cost: 10
Covers the body in a shield of bone,
greatly reducing damage taken from
Physical and Magical attacks.

Bone Armor was active skill that didn't have any damage dealing potential, which nevertheless was quite enticing to me. One of the biggest fears I had was of encountering people with guns. Did it really matter how much HP you had if someone shot you in the head with a gun? Maybe this would save me. Unfortunately, I couldn't get a new skill slot until level 10.

Book of Quagmire LV. 2
Cast Time: 1.5 Seconds
Duration: 15 Seconds
MP Cost: 5
Summons a quagmire in the targeted location. Enemies caught within have reduced action speed and movement speed.

The second skill was interesting too. Frustratingly for Jessica, neither allowed her to deal more damage. Of the two skills, Jessica definitely preferred Quagmire, but she was hesitant to learn it. "Let's kill a few more and maybe we'll find something."

The Quagmire skill honestly wasn't bad, and if she used it in conjunction with my skeleton warriors, it was unlikely there was a foe nearby we couldn't deal with. Regardless, we pulled three more of the fat brutes and actually found not a skill book, but an item: a weapon, to be precise.

Crude Composite Bow: A bow of decent craftsmanship.

There was no damage range on the item, but it looked promising, assuming we could get a regular supply of arrows. This drop acted as a reminded that we still had the unused skill book Sharp Shooting, and maybe going down the route of becoming an archer was the right one for Jessica.

"Try it." I handed the bow to her and she took it in her hands. I watched as it disappeared and reappeared: Jessica must have been putting it in and out of her inventory several times. Eventually, she grasped the bow and pulled back the string to get a feel for it. To both of our surprise, once the bow was fully knocked, an arrow materialized on the string.

"I guess it's not a game world for nothing," I said. So the bow didn't require arrows: honestly that was a huge benefit and meant the archery strategy was viable. Carrying arrows around and worrying about how many you had would have been terrible. "Maybe you should take Sharp Shooting as your first skill: it is the right choice to go with the bow," I suggested.

Jessica was silent for a moment, and then looked thoughtful, "Wouldn't Quagmire be just as good? Enemies can't dodge my arrows if they can't move…It would make hitting them easier. Quagmire would also make escaping much safer, too."

It seemed that she had been thinking about the way forward much more carefully than I had. Both of her points drew attention to the benefits of Quagmire. Damage didn't seem to be an issue at the moment, while anything that increased our chance of surviving a bad pull was definitely welcome.

"In the end, it's your decision. I think Quagmire is also a good choice when you put it that way." I passed her both books and allowed her to choose. She put the bow away and held one in each hand.

It took her around a minute of careful contemplation before she passed me a book back, the other she kept and learned. "Level Ten won't be that far off," Jessica said, possibly to reassure herself of her decision. The book I had in my hands was Sharp Shooting, and it seemed she valued the overall benefits Quagmire brought to our party more than her damage rate.

"Let's keep pulling," she proposed, "just because I have a bow doesn't mean I can shoot it well. I'll need some practice, for sure."

"If you have unspent attribute points, STR and DEX may help," I said. I couldn't be certain, but STR would definitely make drawing the bow easier. The question was how useful DEX would be to her overall accuracy. Only time could tell.

Jessica nodded thoughtfully, "I'll try without making any changes, and then add a single point at a time and go from there." With that, I began pulling more enemies into our EXP blender.

"Whoops, sorry," Jessica said, as on the second pull she shattered the skull of one of my skeletons. When an ogre was crowded by my skeletons, she sometimes had trouble hitting the monster, even though it wasn't moving. It was disappointing that the game system allowed party members to harm one another, or at least their summoned allies, because that skeleton was destroyed.

Soon afterwards though, she announced, "It seems DEX helps my accuracy more. I've been putting in points one at a time and can tell the difference.

After the third ogre was dispatched efficiently, Jessica called out with delight. "I'm Level Six now! Those extra points in DEX should help a lot."

"Congratulations!" I felt admiration for my lithe friend who each time she drew the bow looked more and more the part of an archer: a beautiful one. She had closed the gap to me. A quick check on my character sheet showed that the difference was only around 20% EXP.

"I should be able to pull a single Banshee from a distance now, let's do that and find out what they are," Jessica suggested. After putting in her new points into DEX, it seemed she didn't have any problems hitting a non-moving target accurately in the face. I also didn't need to worry about using Summon Skeleton to pull anymore.

"If you can hit that one from here in one attempt, I'll agree," I said. The banshee I pointed to was a fair distance away, so it wouldn't be easy to hit the slender floating frame. It was also moving at a slow pace as well, which was encouraging if we discovered it was necessary to run from it.

It also occurred to me that if Jessica could hit the banshee while it floated along at long range, then she could probably get at least one more shot off as it came towards us. She nocked the bow and took stance. Even the way she held the bow looked more refined than before—more elegant.

I watched with extreme concentration as she released it, the slightly glowing arrow making a perfect arc in the air and piercing directly into the side of the banshee. The monster let out a low wail on hit and then turned in her direction. She drew again and released a second arrow: another direct hit!

The banshee picked up pace and then suddenly stopped, a blue glow forming between her ethereal hands. "Careful, get in cover!" I shouted. The banshee had started to cast some ranged attack. Jessica immediately canceled her current pull back and dropped low behind an abandoned truck.

Less than a second after she hit the floor, a projectile thumped into the side of the vehicle. Whatever it was shattered on impact and caused shards to fall all over the concrete. I couldn't help but crouch down to get a better look: it was ice. The banshee had shot some kind of frozen projectile at her.

As soon as Jessica was out of line of sight, the banshee came floating at us with incredible speed, and into melee range. My fearless skeleton warriors rushed at it, completely surrounding it and raining axe blows down upon it. The banshees couldn't manage to cast another spell before it faded into ghastly shards and then fully disappeared.

"Seems banshees are also on the menu now," I said happily. They gave even more EXP than one of the ogre-types did. About six of them would bring up to my next level. As long as we could pull individual banshees then it was clear we should continue to do so. There was the danger from their spell though, and we didn't yet know how much damage it did.

If the pull was bad and Jessica was hit by the freezing projectile, would she die? I doubted it would take one shot, but couldn't know that for sure. And there might be secondary effects, like being slowed or frozen to the ground.

"Another?" Jessica asked.

"Yeah, go again. This time just take it safe though and hide after the first arrow. We can't afford to make mistakes; we only have your one bandage," I replied. Until we had built up a store of remedies we needed to be as efficient and smart as possible.

Jessica waited nearly five minutes before a new banshee moved into a location that was safe to pull from. Flawlessly, her arrow once more smashed into the monster and this time the banshee never had line of sight on Jessica and it didn't pause to try to cast. It ran at us and was met by my skeleton warriors. Once held in place, Jessica shot arrow after arrow at it.

We had now developed a strategy for every enemy nearby and were employing it flawlessly. All that was left was to continuously pull and kill them. The EXP started to flow in, and so did the items.

Ration: Satisfies a certain amount of hunger and thirst. Three uses remaining.

An item that looked like a biscuit dropped, and that was definitely super useful. An item that we could eat and could be stored, with no expiration date, was invaluable.

Minor Healing Potion: Instantly restores 75 HP.

I had been expecting potions to exist and was glad to finally get one. Bandage was super useful, but it took time to 'wrap' the wound. Using this heal, however, was as simple as pouring the liquid into your mouth.

Morning Star: A large metal ball covered in spikes on the end of a chain. When it hits, it deals massive physical damage.

We had found several weapons before, which wasn't exactly bad. From the point of view of starting out, you needed a decent weapon to kill enemies. You could make it through the first two or three levels without armor or spells.

I hadn't been fighting in melee though. My spear was 'melee' and I considered swapping for the morning star, but the range the spear had was almost twice as much. I would be putting myself in considerable risk getting close enough to use the new weapon, especially to the meat hooking brutes.

It was when I was about to put the spare weapon into my inventory when I looked at my skeleton warriors and had a bright idea. I beckoned one over and had it drop the axe it currently wielded to the floor. After that, I instructed it to take the morning star from me.

To my delight, it was able to take the morning star and even wield it. I made it swing the spiked ball around and then checked that I could take the weapon back. Jessica was smiling.

"What?"

"You are like a mad scientist, experimenting on your Frankenstein monster."

"I feel like one. And I've another test I want to make." I returned the weapon to the skeleton and then re-summoned them all.

Two of the summoned skeletons came up with axes, but I was thrilled to see the third was wielding the morning star. When I tried to request the item back this time though, it couldn't give it to me.

It seemed that I had permanently equipped one of my skeletons with this new weapon, but the original copy had been lost in the process of despawning and respawning. Neither Jessica and I were going to use the morning star anyway, so the loss wasn't that great.

I still had a concern though, which was that the weapons wielded by my warriors might be purely cosmetic. It was possible that I had wasted a good melee weapon for a skin transfer. We decided to pull a brute to test this and see if the functionality had at least changed.

As the brute closed in, Jessica casted a Quagmire and I restrained my two axe-wielding skeletons in place. The skeleton with the morning star went to town on the monster.

I counted the amount of attacks required for the creature to die, and then did the same with an axe wielding skeleton. The result wasn't really a surprise but was very welcome all the same: the morning star-wielding skeleton had killed the ogre-type monster almost fifty percent faster than the skeleton with the axe.

Not only had I learned that I could continue to level my Summon Skeleton skill, I could equip the summoned warriors with weapons and perhaps with gear too. My original attitude to the skill had been too unappreciative. The scaling potential of Summon Skeleton was large, and it meant that I should move in this direction as my full focus.

A strong summoner was definitely a force to be reckoned with. It was one of the few classes that could fight many enemies at once. Your minions were tanks and damage dealers at the same time. Not only that, you were much safer during combat than if you were in the front line. If I continued to scale my warriors, defensively and offensively, I would be well off. Potentially, I could be a one-man army. That thought continued to cycle through my head until I convinced myself it was a fantastic idea.

Chapter 8: Enter the Necromancer

Our killing speed increased significantly with the addition of my Morning Star warrior and we both reached level 7 within the hour.

Name: Mike Reynolds [27] Class: None
Level: 7 EXP: 3%
HP: 280/280 MP: 12/45
STR: 3
AGI: 2
DEX: 1
VIT: 10
WIS: 1
Available: 9

Skills: [A] Summon Skeleton LV. 3, [P]Sixth Sense [P] Bravery [P] Mutated

I had been stockpiling my stats, waiting for a clear build path to show itself. A part of me expected the low-level skills to be simply that: low level. As you progressed you would get stronger skills, and I hoped to hold out until then before allocating more stat points.

Fortunately or unfortunately, my thinking had been too naïve. There were multiple paths to scale Summon Skeletons with, and it was worthy of early investment. There was also no indication of how classes were acquired.

Was every class available to everyone? Were certain classes locked behind attribute requirements, skill requirements, passives?

I could miss my chance at gaining a sick class if I gimped myself early.

In the end, I put 5 of the 9 available stat points I had into Wisdom, so I had a bit more MP and MP regeneration to work with, my testing was putting me at a dangerously low level. The result was that my mana pool went up to 70. Each point of WIS had given me 5 MP, the same MP increase as a level. It was also good to note that allocating a point gave an immediate 5 MP on allocation. If I ever was in a situation where I had no MP and had free points to spare, putting them in WIS would give me MP immediately.

"Just three more levels to ten," I said to Jessica while wiping my brow. We had been hard leveling for the majority of the day. The sun was coming down over the horizon and night would be rolling around soon.

I was of the mind to try the rations for dinner but decided against it. It was smarter to eat the perishable foods now and try a ration later. We made camp in a half-destroyed home and called it a night. The next day would mark exactly one week since this all began.

A voice woke me the following morning, and it wasn't Jessica. It was another message transmitted directly into my brain, presumably transmitted to everyone: *Class change has now become available! Acquire a class change stone and you will be able to obtain a class. The stone can be acquired through defeating particularly difficult monsters. The harder they are, the more likely the drop. Do your utmost!*

The phrasing made it feel like an actual person had spoken to us, and it wasn't just a system message. Someone or something was actively watching over this 'event'. I felt sick to my stomach at the thought that someone or some beings were enjoying this amount of suffering.

"Did you just hear that?" asked Jessica and I nodded. "Doesn't 'particularly difficult monster' sound exactly like that giant ogre thing we saw yesterday?" Jessica asked me. There had been a meat-hook wielding foe that was twice the size of normal ones walking around a particular section of the outskirts of the city. Just looking at him would tell you he was special.

"It could be, yeah." I responded, "He looked kind of dangerous though. I doubt my skeletons can take more than a single swing of his meat hook."

"Quagmire and a particularly good location would help. I think it's possible to take him if we're smart about it," Jessica said. I didn't disagree with her, but such a pull came with substantial risk. New classes sounded amazing though and gaining one would boost our leveling speed and power no doubt.

There was another issue too: "If it only drops a single stone, who gets it?" I asked.

Jessica didn't even take a moment to think about it, "You, obviously. You're definitely more battle capable than me at the moment. I can ride off your coattails afterwards. I'll just get the next one."

"Thanks. Let's try for another level each before we fight him. Use Quagmire whenever you can, maybe it will level up also and we'll be a bit stronger for the fight." She nodded in response and we had a quick meal before heading out.

If luck and a bit of hard work would have it. Getting level 10 today was definitely possible. Our current system of dispatching enemies removed a lot of risk, and adding Quagmire made it almost non-existent for zombie and goblin pulls.

We moved to our hunting ground from the day before and began pulling every banshee and brute we could find. The EXP to level had gone up considerably. A banshee and brute before would give somewhere around 20% of level six to seven, and now they were giving just around 6%.

This didn't seem like an issue before, but as we got better at killing enemies, we realized they weren't infinite. In fact, after killing ten of them at a quick pace they became scarce in the streets we were working.

There was a respawn time we hadn't encountered before, and it was giving us some trouble. "We'll have to move around," Jessica said.

Our current position was amazing because we could get to a high vantage point by my giving Jessica a lift to the top of a bus shelter, and she could see enemies from there. Once Jessica pulled them and dropped to ground level, we funneled them through several cars—some burnt to a crisp—to pick them off one at a time.

The ruins of vehicles had provided a miniature fortress for us, and with my skeleton warriors, our enemies just couldn't get to us at all. But when I was around 70% EXP there was nothing left for us to kill and we were forced to start moving northward.

The thought hadn't crossed my mind before, but as we moved I realized we were surrounded on all sides. The path of retreat we cleared yesterday had refilled with new enemies, and to leave the city we would need to fight our way out.

We scouted out a new location that had a plaza in front of a library. From the steps of the library entrance Jessica could pull with her bow and there were a few abandoned cars that would break up the attacking groups. Although not as perfect as our last spot, it wasn't a bad set up and we set about our grind once more.

Congratulations, you have reached level 8!

It had taken us just two hours to level, which to me was amazing pace. Jessica and I were killing enemies nearly as fast as we could pull them safely. The large brute, too, had also made an appearance at the end of a long street.

When we took a break and went to the top of the library to take a look around; from there we could see the giant ogre from time to time north of us. Even more interesting was that he now had a pale, yellow glow around him. My speculation was that he was holding something valuable, probably the stone mentioned in the announcement, one that gave new class options.

Not far away was a six-story office and that gave us another way of grinding, we could pull to the stairwells where the monsters were confined as they came at us through the doorways. In this way we cleared our way to the very top. My jaw nearly dropped at the reality of the situation. It was possible to see the city center, and located there was a peculiar phenomenon.

It seemed to me there was a beam of light, or an aura, in the very center, and from there monsters were appearing. They were dispersing in a way that suggested rings of difficulty existed based on the distance from the center. Having fought our way in past the outside ring, that of goblins and zombies, Jessica and I were on the second, banshees and ogres, and there were probably three more rings before you came adjacent to the aura.

The area we were fighting in had packs of banshees and brutes, and beyond them was a new monster type that roamed alone. It was a demi-human type of enemy, with the head of a snake but the torso and limbs of a human. It held a long weapon in its hand, maybe a spear? A trident? I couldn't exactly be sure.

This pattern continued as I looked further towards the center: next there were packs of that snake monster and new formidable, enemies roaming about. Even worse was that these enemies were pushing away from the center slowly, which meant overtime even the outermost ring of the city would be over-run by mobs that were probably far too tough for us to tackle. Just like if anyone hadn't yet got started on leveling, they wouldn't have a chance against packs of goblins or zombies, we too could fall behind so far that we'd have no other option than to run and hide.

"Can you see any more of those elite ogres?" I asked. It was important to me that after we obtained my stone, we made effort to locate one for Jessica. Both of us moved away from the wall facing the distracting center of the spawns and started to scan the ring that we were within, Jessica moving to the opposite side to me.

"There's a few more I see that could be special fights," she said. "Over there, doesn't that banshee look a bit too big?" I came beside her, traced her finger, and could see the enemy she was pointing at, maybe a quarter mile west of us.

That was encouraging. It suggested the elite mobs were numerous, and there would be no shortage of them. "You know…if these skill changing stones aren't soul-bound, one-time drops…" I said, "we can collect them. They will be valuable."

"Trade them? For food? Water? What do we even trade them for?" Jessica asked, turning her vivid eyes to mine.

"We could trade them for assistance. Not everyone will be like those brothers and building a guild—a raiding party—might be the way to go. Those stones could get a lot of loyalty, maybe." I suddenly felt like I could be a raid leader, but wouldn't it be possible? Couldn't I find people, promise them a leveling stone, and assist them in getting started—they might be appreciative enough to follow me—a real life guild.

"You might be getting ahead of yourself," Jessica said as if reading my thoughts; she did give me a smile though.

"Maybe, but first let's get a stone and find out if it's possible to trade it." I smiled back. "Let's head towards fatso and see what we can do with the terrain there."

She nodded and we set off north, towards the center, on its trail. We took out mobs on the way and were halfway to Level 9 when we reached its location. Even better, Summon Skeleton had leveled up once more.

Summon Skeleton LV. 4
Cast time: Instant
MP Cost: 10
Distance: 4 Meters
Summons three skeleton warriors and a skeleton general to fight for you.
Skeletons can now be summoned without a corpse. If the skill is cast without a corpse, only one skeleton is summoned. The skeleton summoned is chosen at random.

The upgrade to the skill had solved a serious issue I hadn't even considered. If there were no corpses, I essentially had no minions. How could I kill the first enemy once these corpses were no longer abundantly available? Especially if we were facing into nothing but tough ones. At least now I could summon a single warrior to get the corpses flowing.

Best of all, Jessica had also leveled Quagmire to level 3. She read out the new stats: cast time 1 second, duration 20 seconds and MP cost 7.

The cast time had gone down significantly, and the duration was up by 25 percent, all at the cost of 2 extra MP per cast. I wasn't sure if the effectiveness of the reduced speed had gone up also, but I hoped it would.

We also managed to find two more Rations, a Bandage, and a Greater Elixir of Dexterity. The Dexterity elixir increased the stat by 7 for one hour. That went to Jessica, obviously. It more than doubled her current Dexterity stat if she drank it and she decided to save it for an emergency.

There was also an item drop: our first non-weapon item.

Banshee's Wail: Accessory
HP + 20, Fear Resistance +5

This was a ring that had the face of a banshee engraved atop it. Her mouth was open as if screaming. I insisted Jessica take it over me, as I didn't feel in danger at all with my current HP, which was at 300 and felt like a lot in comparison to my 50 at Level 1. I could take six times the damage of a person who hadn't enhanced themselves at all through levels.

I wasn't sure if Fear Resistance meant you didn't get scared, or there was a skill called Fear that would make you become terrified and or run. Only time could tell.

Our battles had not, unfortunately, resulted in a new passive ability in my ability list. Nor had any of the existing ones changed or gained any levels either. I didn't know if passives could level yet, but it would make sense if they could.

81

After clearing the area fully and scouting for a pull location, we found one that was promising. It was an alleyway between two businesses that was about the right size for the big guy to enter but too narrow for him to make full sweeps of his meat hook. The plan was simple: pull him into the alleyway and lock him in with skeletons on both sides.

I cast Summon Skeleton on a nearby corpse and observed my new minion: the skeleton general. He was over a head taller than my warriors and instead of wielding two-handed weapons, wielded a sword and shield.

His body was more covered in pieces of armor and even his bleached skull was hidden beneath metal headgear. It looked to me as if he was meant to be the tank for the weaker skeletons, which was perfect given the circumstances.

Rather than risk Jessica getting the aggro, I decided it was best for my new skeleton general to pull the elite ogre, and so I positioned myself on top of a bin, I where I could fully see the action happening. When the elite pathed back towards us and was clearly a single pull, I sent my new summoned skeleton out. He approached the target slowly, banging his sword into his shield over and over.

Fortunately, the sound wasn't loud enough to pull monsters from far away, but it did immediately attract the attention of the ogre boss. As soon as I saw it charging towards us, I hurried the general back into the alleyway: all the while he turned and taunted the huge monster even more.

Our enemy didn't seem to have any intelligence at all, and rushed into the tight alleyway without fear. Once its burly body had fit between the high walls, I sent two warriors behind and a single warrior in front to join the general, just in case.

Jessica casted Quagmire as soon as the ogre was in a proper position and began unloading arrows into its thick and leathery skin. Metal hooks rained down over and over into my skeleton general, who was so busy trying to block with his shield and deflect them with his sword, he couldn't even take the time to retaliate.

Clang after clang rang out with every strike, and my heart was in my throat. The shield arm of our tank never fell, but the bones of my general were brittle and were no doubt taking an incredible beating right now.

Jessica's decision to select the skill Quagmire was absolutely the right one, as even with it, the brute was hammering blow after blow at incredible speeds. My warriors continuously hacked and slashed at the back legs while Jessica put arrow after arrow towards its face.

Blood started to seep from the numerous wounds on its face and legs. My skeletons were chopping like loggers taking down a great tree. A particularly powerful blow rained down on my general and sent him to his knees.

There was another, and then another, and I heard the bones of his frame crack. He was being smashed into the concrete. A sickening feeling washed over me as things were going bad. This enemy had such a ridiculous amount of health, and no amount of damage seemed to slow it down or phase it at all.

Another blow came, and the arm with which my general held his shield broke off and the shield crashed to the floor. The next blow completely destroyed his upper frame, and he disappeared just like that. As soon as I saw him fall, I issued the command to the warriors to stop attacking and concentrate on slowing it down as much as possible.

"We're losing this…" Jessica called out.

"We need to get back immediately." There was no way my regular skeletons could stop its approach, and the ogre was now looking at me with incredible fury. Two of my warriors grappled the back legs and one was in the front trying to block its path.

A single hook came down on the front warrior and smashed it into pieces. The pile of bones clattered in front of its feet. They couldn't even survive one attack. My only solace now was the brute's legs had been absolutely mutilated, and with my skeletons holding it down, it was finding it hard move forward.

My worry didn't disappear despite the brute being locked down. It suddenly managed to grab one of my warriors and smash it into the concrete wall, followed by the other. All of my skeletons were gone, and there wasn't a corpse to spawn new ones from.

I cast my summons anyway, and by sheer luck my skeleton general came out. He was ordered to stand firm and keep the ogre boss from us while Jessica and I fell back. A sour enemy closed the gap, however, a terrible feeling washed over me, worse than any I'd felt before.

The meat hook in the brute's hand launched out like a rocket in my direction. A chain rattled behind it that continued to extend from his hand. I could see the blur of metal approaching, but it was so fast that I couldn't even react.

With a rush of air, the weapon went just past my body, and then I felt the most indescribable pain ever. My eyes looked at an arm that now had a hook pierced through it, and then my world started to spin. The brute had pulled me with the hook, and I was rocketing through the air.

My back collided with the concrete wall and I flopped to the floor. Every bit of air in my lungs was expunged in an instant. I

84

panicked as I realized I couldn't breathe; my lungs weren't working at all.

The taste of iron filled my mouth an instant later and I felt another powerful tug on my arm. The brute was preparing to slam me into the concrete once again, and this time it wouldn't be just a short slam. I was going to be sent like slingshot into a complete pulp.

My skeleton general managed to reach the enemy as soon as the chain went taut. His sword stabbed upward and into the armpit of the brute and sliced down, severing muscle and tendon. The chain suddenly went limp and the brute's arm dropped to his side lifelessly.

Jessica hadn't panicked either, and was still shooting arrow after arrow into the face of the creature. One eye had already been completely punctured and ruined, and blood was dripping all over its face.

Every time the monster breathed out of its nose blood bubbles would pop and then move down its horrendous lips. It was on death's door, but so was I. Gasping and forcing air to enter my lungs was painful, but I needed to breathe.

Fortunately, my general clearly wasn't just a tank as it assaulted with great swordsmanship. With the attacking arm of the brute mostly disabled, it was free to use the sword as it pleased. I watched as the blade entered into the monster's ribs and sliced clean across. There was an explosion of blood and guts that caked the general's white frame deep red.

The giant brute fell backwards and collapsed with a quake. It had finally died.

Congratulations, you have reached level 9!

Pain was radiating from my arm and traveling throughout my back and neck. It was so unbearable that I could hardly think. Jessica raced over to me and was already pulling out a Bandage and trying to wrap me.

"Wait, wait please." I managed to get out. Wrapping me with the hook in my arm might heal the wound around it. I was terrified, not that I was going to die, but that I was about to be in the most excruciating pain I'd ever experienced in my life.

I pulled out the Minor Healing Potion from my inventory and removed the cork with my one hand before gulping it down. A cooling feeling raced through my entire body that alleviated some of the pain.

"I need something to put in my mouth," I said. "My shirt; help me with my shirt," I pleaded. Jessica grabbed the bottom hem of my shirt and started to roll it upward until it was near my mouth in wad. I bit down on it and used my good hand to grasp the hook.

The pain scared me so bad I almost wasn't brave enough to remove the hook. I praised the bravery passive more than anything else right now. My hand started to shake and then I ripped the metal out with as much force as I could muster.

The wad of fabric couldn't hide the sound of my muffled scream. Blood and a bit of flesh exploded outward as the hook came free. Blackness swam over my vision.

"Hang on! Hang on." Jessica's fingers were on my arm and then came a huge relief from the pain. The darkness started to fade slowly as I looked at the wound. The damage was so bad that one Bandage wasn't enough. I didn't even need to ask, as Jessica grabbed a second and wrapped me up again.

Only after the second Bandage did the gaping hole close and the bleeding stop. The aching remained there though, and moving my arm made it feel even worse. I looked at Jessica whom comforted me, "The Bandages are meant to be used, and it's why we have them. We use as many as we need."

I nodded while falling back onto my back. For a moment there the pain was so bad I would have actually preferred to just pass out. It was my desire to see the benefits of having leveled that kept me going. I opened my stats and took a look.

Name: Mike Reynolds (27) Class: None
Level: 9 EXP: 20%
HP: 65/310 MP: 29/80
STR: 3
AGI: 2
DEX: 1
VIT: 10
WIS: 6
Available: 10

Skills: [A]Summon Skeleton LV. 4, [P]Sixth Sense [P] Bravery LV. 2 [P] Mutated [P] Pain Resistance

So passive abilities could level! Bravery had reached level two and I had a new passive ability called Pain Resistance. It seemed clear that using the passives would make them level up, which meant I could increase my resistance to pain by taking more of it. I looked at Jessica curiously, "Do you have any passive skills?"

She paused for a moment, "I have something called Extreme Concentration." It made sense to me now why she hadn't ceased releasing arrows when I was hurt. I was thankful though, because if she had panicked, I might be dead instead. There were times to remain calm, and that was one of them.

Only after it was clear I wasn't going to die did we take a look at the area where the ogre had died. There was a triangular blue object floating there that illuminated the air around it. Just looking at it would tell you it was special.

We both approached, and Jessica beckoned me to reach out and grab the blue pyramid. I took it in my hand.

Class Changing Stone: A miraculous stone that allows one to pick a class. A User can only use this item once.

The decision had been made beforehand that I would use the stone, but I was still curious. I kept it in my hand and then passed it to Jessica. There was nothing stopping me from doing so, and it seemed she could accept it from me even though I had looted it.

"It seems my plan to trade these might be plausible," I observed.

"I guess, but take it back." Jessica passed me the stone. I couldn't hesitate any longer and triggered it. A menu appeared before me a moment later with class choices. I started to read through them one at a time.

As I looked through the classes I realized almost all of them were generic: with choices like mage, knight, and cleric and variations of these. They didn't seem like anything out of the ordinary; it was only when I got to the bottom of the list that something caught my eye.

There was a class listed there called Necromancer and it was out of alphabetical order. It was like the menu had added it on, perhaps because of the skill I'd been using. I made a note to myself to see if an archery related class was offered to Jessica when she used one of these stones. A part of me refused to believe there were simply these generic choices and then a very specific class of Necromancer, that seemed fine-tailored to the player themselves.

I had learned the skill Summon Skeleton and had brought it up to level 4. That must surely have resulted in this choice appearing? If so, that meant picking a particular skill and building a specific way could allow you to manipulate the system to obtain certain class options: hypothetically, of course.

Once inside the menu I realized that I couldn't get out of it. There was no way to go back without picking my class. It was impossible to know what you had before you used it, and no way to back out and alter your build to get a new class.

As soon as I confirmed there was no backing out and my options would not change, the decision became easy. In the end, Necromancer was the right choice for me. I selected it and the menu disappeared. There was no drastic change to my appearance, but a few status messages had appeared.

Congratulations, you have become a Necromancer!
Proficiency in summoning undead has increased. You can now spawn one additional skeleton per seven base levels and one additional reanimated corpse per fifteen base levels.
You have learned the skill Reanimate Dead LV. 1
You have learned the skill Decay LV. 1
You have learned the skill Skeletal Mastery

Full of excitement, I immediately checked what each skill did.

Reanimate Dead: Allows the user to reanimate the corpse of a recently defeated enemy. User can only have one reanimated corpse. User cannot reanimate an enemy killed by another User. Cannot reanimate Elite and boss type enemies.
Cast Time: 2 seconds
MP Cost: 25 MP
Distance: 1 Meters

Decay: Afflict your opponent with undead magic causing them to rapidly decay.
Cast Time: 1.5 Seconds
MP Cost: 10 MP
Distance: 2 Meters
Skeletal Mastery: Minions deal 15% increased damage and have 10% increased maximum HP per level.

Both new active skills sounded incredibly sick. The passive skill also boasted extreme scaling potential. I was excited to open my stats and see what had changed.

Name: Mike Reynolds (27) Class: Necromancer Level: 9 EXP: 20%
HP: 65/310 MP: 29/160
STR: 3
AGI: 2
DEX: 1
VIT: 10
WIS: 6
Available: 10

Skills: [A]Summon Skeleton LV. 4 |[A] Decay LV. 1| [A] Reanimate Dead LV. 1 | [P]Sixth Sense | [P] Bravery LV. 2 | [P] Mutated | [P] Pain Resistance | [P] Skeletal Mastery

It seemed my HP hadn't changed at all, but my base MP had doubled. Now that I had a clear path ahead of me, I decided it was time to use my available points. There was no going back from Necromancer at the moment.

In the end, I put two points into STR, six points into WIS, and the remaining two points into VIT. While I wouldn't be using STR in melee combat, it was still useful for carrying things and physical endurance. My stats were therefore now STR 5, AGI 2, DEX 1, VIT 12, WIS 12.

At 95 out of 340, my current HP total was still pitifully low, but the thrill of wanting to try out my new abilities trumped that. I had enough MP to cast everything I needed to cast as well. It was time to head for the Banshee elite and Jessica's stone.

Chapter 9: More Survivors of the MMRPG Apocalypse

There were plenty of corpses along the way to the area where I hoped to pull the banshee elite, and I used Summon Skeleton on the first we encountered. Being Level 9 granted me +1 to my skeleton count. Four warriors and one general appeared. It was a beautiful sight to behold.

"Can we stop on the way and kill a brute?" I asked Jessica like a giddy child. I didn't want to waste time, but I couldn't wait to try out my new abilities.

"Fine, just one; you can use your new reanimate spell on it," she caved into my eager tone and we veered off course just a bit. Jessica pulled a brutish ogre with an arrow, and I instructed my skeletons to trap it. Once they had it surrounded and unable to reach me, I cast Decay and watched the magic happen.

The flesh of the creature started to visibly wither and rot. Patches of leathery skin fell off and then after about five seconds there were no more changes. The ogre was still alive, which meant that my new spell had an upper limit in terms of damage that was less than an ogre's hit point, but it had to be doing something at least.

Once my test was done my miniature army of undead was instructed to dispatch the brute. I was on top of the corpse as soon as it fell. Reanimate Dead was cast, and its body shook in place before crawling back up to a standing position. I felt that with my recent advances, my overall power had easily doubled.

The skin of the ogre was darker now and more decayed, and just by looking at it you could tell it was an undead monster. It joined my skeletons and moved with them in a pack. I truly felt like a Necromancer now.

I didn't have any other reason to delay and the two of us moved with one goal in mind: dispatch the elite Banshee and obtain our second Class Changing Stone. We didn't have an exact location for the boss mob, only a general idea of the area it roamed.

Jessica spotted it several blocks west of us, and I knew that as long as we were careful as we travelled, we wouldn't miss it. There were mobs in the way, but Jessica no longer needed to be careful about pulling ogres. I simply sent my horde of undead to hack each monster to pieces. It only took them a few seconds to overpower an ogre and cut it down.

Banshees warranted a bit more respect, and we still dragged them out of line of sight of any possible adds. Once isolated, they died just as fast. After the first banshee we killed I swapped my undead ogre for a reanimated banshee. I figured that I had enough melee minions already, and several times I'd seen them blocking each other anyway. With the raised banshee I wouldn't be missing out on damage.

There was also an added benefit to resurrecting the banshee, and something I hadn't been sure would even happen. The reanimated banshee actually used its original skills. Its ability was a frost bolt attack, and it froze the target and applied a deep chilling effect.

When that frost-based effect was paired with Jessica's Quagmire, the opponent literally couldn't move. It became frozen in place for many seconds, even without the assistance of my skeletons holding it down.

Somehow, the feeling of power we currently displayed gave me a euphoria I almost couldn't explain. I felt like I was on top of the world—what was left of it at least. I started to look forward to those dangerous boss fights.

We located the banshee elite after moving three blocks over, and by then had accumulated nearly 80% EXP towards level 10. Jessica was merely 10% behind me as the difference in early levels clearly didn't amount to much.

Killing the elite banshee would put us both at Level 10, and also give Jessica access to her class. I was already getting excited for her to progress, maybe even more so than she was. Regardless, I didn't let that excitement get the best of me.

We meticulously scouted the area that the boss was pathing through and discussed a possible plan of attack. We were going to pull her back and block line of sight from possible adds, but weren't sure on the best spot for this yet. We didn't want something too claustrophobic either, where her spells might be hard to avoid, and yet not too open so we could restrict her movements.

Planning the pull wasn't easy: not without knowing the banshee's capabilities. It was clear to me it would cast a frost attack, but just like the elite ogre, probably had additional skills as well, not to mention the increase in HP and damage.

In the end, we decided on an intersection filled with totaled vehicles. We would pull her around a building and then position ourselves in the middle of the street behind the cover of wrecked cars. That way I could stay close enough to the fight to remain completely concealed behind cover and have my summoned undead creatures fight.

Jessica also felt the position was relatively safe and reckoned she could even shoot arrows through the burnt car frames. The building directly behind us had been cleared out from mobs and was our designated path of retreat. "Are we ready to go?" I asked.

We had spent a reasonable amount of time figuring out our plan, and by now I had recovered back up to half HP. It wasn't exactly the smartest decision to go ahead without me being maxed, but I felt my HP was high enough to avoid being one-shotted. So I gave the green light for Jessica to go ahead and pull the elite.

The boss was too far away for me to send skeletons, and my lack of full HP made me wary about leaving the enclosure we'd found.

"Pulling." Jessica said as she nocked an arrow. She was sounding like a seasoned veteran.

The arrow flew along a beautiful arc and landed directly in the banshee's neck. A ghastly wail escaped the elite's mouth that caused my skin to crawl. There was something so supernatural about the sound. I felt that it wasn't a sound that should exist in this world.

Jessica didn't need to be told to hide, as she had immediately crouched behind our barricade and removed herself from the banshee's vision. It rushed through the air towards us at extreme speed and passed by the building we planned to fight it at.

My skeletons were positioned there already, and the general intercepted her cleanly. My reanimated banshee was in the middle of the street and had already started casting Frost Bolts. As soon as the general had the aggro of the elite, Jessica cast Quagmire and then began nocking arrows as fast as her STR would allow.

The first thing I noticed was the increased speed at which the elite was able to cast Frost Bolt. I couldn't exactly time it accurately, but by feel it seemed to be somewhere around two or three times faster than the standard version of the banshee.

Fortunately, the banshee elite chain-cast Frost Bolt as her main attack, and solely focused on my summoned undead. Bolt after bolt continuously pelted the skeleton general, who could only hold his shield in place and block as best as possible. Even if I wanted him to retaliate, he couldn't. His shield hand had been completely frozen, and that frost had also encased his upper body in ice.

The slowing effect from my own banshee's bolts and Quagmire was clearly reduced on elites, and only managed to slow her action speed. Much better news was that the extra damage I had gained from skeletal mastery and my two additional summoned undead added up to a lot of damage.

We were absolutely demolishing the banshee with almost no issues. As she got lower in HP, her body began to glow a darker color and she finally began to cast a different skill. Jessica and I both ducked behind our vehicle barricade in anticipation of it landing.

Fear overwhelms you. You are terrified in place and cannot move.

That was the status message I received, and it seemed LOS had no bearing on her ability. My thoughts hadn't stopped, but my body literally could not move. Unfortunately for the banshee, and very fortunately for me, it seemed that my minions were immune to Fear. Although Jessica and I couldn't move my minions continued to demolish her.

Jessica got out of the Fear several seconds before me, probably thanks to the effect of her Banshee's Wail ring, which gave Fear resistance. Still, the elite's freeze attack was over five seconds long, and judging by how fast it was able to cast Frost Bolts, that was enough time for it to hit you with four or five casts.

As I stood back up, it was just in time to witness my skeleton general explode into shards of ice. He had tanked his final Frost Bolt: a job well done. The banshee elite started to spin and cast Frost bolts on every Skeleton Warrior around it.

After ten seconds had passed, she killed three more, but that was the last of her attacks. She let out a final mournful wail and exploded into a ghastly mist that floated away with the wind.

Congratulations, you have reached level
10!

I immediately summoned my skeletons again and we approached the corpse together.

What we wanted most was there: a Class Changing Stone floated above where the Banshee had been. Floating next to the stone was a black piece of clothing, our second item drop that wasn't a weapon.

Jessica didn't hesitate to pick up the stone, while I grabbed the item.

Demonic Garb: A cloak imbued with dark powers. It provides decent protection from physical attacks.
WIS +3, HP + 30

I couldn't resist putting on the cloak immediately and then turned to Jessica, "I kinda look like Van Hellsing, don't you think?" I did a small little twirl.

"A little bit, maybe," she laughed. "Should I use the Class Stone now?"

I thought about this for a moment and reckoned that in a perfect world she shouldn't. If possible, we should find out what skills and stat combinations gave her what class choices. Unfortunately, that wasn't possible.

No amount of delaying would allow us to find and target a specific class choice for her and in the meantime her added power would allow us to snowball in our levelling. Then too, I desperately wanted to find and recruit people under our wing. Influence would give us safety and security.

"I think it's best you use it now," I said, "read out the special classes at the bottom."

I could see her eyes go blank for a moment as she used the stone. About thirty seconds later she read out two options: "Trapper and Control Mage."

"Control Mage probably focuses on CC, which means it won't be dealing damage. When I think of the word 'trapper' I think of people catching raccoons and foxes in traps."

"I do kind of like the bow," she said.

"Well, a trapper might also be something like a hunter? Hunters use bow and arrows often too," I said. "I really want you to make the call though, because as far as we know there's no going back."

I could see that my words weighed on her heavily. On balance I reckoned she should pick trapper; her stats had already favored in the direction of an attacking class. She was pumping STR and DEX currently and was wielding a bow, which is probably why the trapper class even appeared. But I didn't want to make this life-changing decision for her.

Quagmire was definitely a spell caster's ability, and was the most likely reason she had even received the option for Control Mage. It seemed more and more likely that both your skill and stat distribution affected your class choice.

"I want to keep using the bow," Jessica finally said. "I'll gamble with trapper."

"I think that's the right call."

A moment later I could see that she had come out of the menu.

"Skills?" I asked her.

"Well, I think I use traps," she said. "I have Ankle Snare, which allows me to snare an enemy in place for twenty seconds and something called Anomalous Trap. It says that I can turn any spell I know into a trap."

"So you can make Quagmire into a trap?"

"At least I think so." She read the description word for word to me: "Allows the user to place a trap that inherits a selected skill. The trap will use the selected skill when triggered with twenty percent increased effectiveness."

The only skill she currently had right now was Quagmire, so that meant she could use Quagmire traps. Presumably it would auto trigger when dragging a monster over it, and would even have an increased effect.

"What about your passive skill?"

"Expert Tracker: Your senses are heightened. Allows you to detect entities within a certain distance from you."

"That is actually super useful" I said. "Can we test it?" I asked. I wanted to see how well her tracking skill performed. Jessica nodded and we walked to an area we hadn't explored. There was a full building in front of us, and there was no way she could see the enemies on the other side.

"There are...goblins inside the building, close to us; a banshee just past the building; and two ogres beyond her. I can't feel anything beyond them." I felt very encouraged by this report. The distances seemed significant enough that we should be able to sense enemies well before they could see us.

"Also…there's something on the third floor of this building…" she added, "I don't know what it is, but I think it's people? It doesn't feel like an enemy."

"Are you sure? Can you track other people? How do I feel?"

"I don't know. The description says 'entities' not enemies. Also, it's hard to tell because I can see you and you've been near me for so long. There's no particular feeling I could describe it with besides natural."

"We should approach them," I said, "if it's people who have been hiding for a week they may be on death's door."

Jessica agreed with a nod and we forced our way into the building. It became clear moments later why they were trapped.

Goblins were roaming the hallways with their maniacal cackling. My fear of them had disappeared completely, and Jessica only needed to nock a single arrow and put it in a goblin's throat for it to hit the floor.

Jessica led me up to the third floor and down the hall to a room labeled three-zero-seven. Our journey here had been completely uneventful besides the goblins. Still, for someone who wasn't even Level 1 they were a considerable threat.

"Shouldn't you hide your skeletons before we approach them?" Jessica asked.

"No. I want them to see. Only when they see can they understand our strength. My undead will act as a deterrent if they are hostile, like those brothers, and incentive for them to join us if they are friendly." I wanted whoever we met to be slightly afraid us. That would eliminate any thoughts of betrayal or backstabbing. If we had shown the same strength to the brothers back at that time, they may have decided against following us.

I tasked my skeleton general to come forward and cut down the door. He approached and was about to strike out when Jessica interrupted, "Can't we just knock? We don't need to destroy everything."

Destroying the door sounded more fun and would definitely provide a shocking entrance, but I let out a sigh of agreement, "Fine, knock and see if you can get them to come out."

Jessica pounded on the door, and possibly didn't know her own physical strength now. I had to give her credit though, it was impossible for them to not have heard the banging and the door still stood. I heard shuffling inside but it seemed they didn't want to come out.

"Come out, we are friendly," Jessica said, "I know you're in there, it's okay." The fact the voice talking to them was female might have appeased their fears a little bit. As the shuffling grew louder I realized someone was approaching the door.

A voice came from the other side, "Who are you? Why are you here?" It was also a female voice.

"We're here to help. We can help you get out of here," Jessica replied and glanced at me. I nodded. Surely the idea of escape would appeal to whoever was beyond the door like a fresh glass of water when you were dying of thirst?

Hushed whispers came from the other side for several moments, "How can we be sure you don't have bad intentions? How can we trust you?"

Jessica seemed almost annoyed, but didn't lose her temper, "Because if we wanted to, we could bust down the door and skip the chit chat," she retorted.

We both heard more heated discussions and even raised voices, "How can we be sure they aren't monsters that can talk?" someone said in an angry voice. I didn't disagree with the idea, it was always wise to be cautious.

"Listen, ask us something. Ask us anything about life before this catastrophe happened and we can tell you. Like, I don't know, my favorite band was Radiohead," I finally spoke up. "We aren't here to hurt you. This is a chance for you."

There was complete silence on the other side, Jessica shook her head and whispered, "Radiohead?"

But then the lock of the door clicked. It opened a tad bit as a woman's face came into view and looked at us. The chain lock on the door was still there just in case.

Feeling awkward, I waved at her and Jessica did the same. It seemed seeing us was enough to be convincing, as the door shut again, and the chain was undone, and the door fully opened to allow us entry.

Following my earlier idea about displaying our strength, I ordered my summoned skeletons to fully enter the room. Beyond, the eyes of the two people there went wide as saucers and I could see the look of despair on the man's face as he turned to the women. "I told you they were monsters." He couldn't hold his own tongue.

The women's face went white as a sheet of paper and she fell backwards onto the couch. "We aren't monsters," I said plainly. "I'd like to explain this to you once, so listen carefully, even if it sounds unbelievable." I looked at the both of them and received a nod of understanding. "You two have probably seen the little green men running around, which is why you're locked up in here. Long story short, the world has an RPG system and you can level up. Did you hear the message about class changing?"

"We heard it," said the man.

"Good, then that saves me a bit of explanation." I pointed to my group of skeletons, "These are my minions, summoned by a skill. Skills can be obtained by killing monsters. Levels and items are obtained in the same way. Are you starting to get the picture?" I asked.

There was still some disbelief on their faces, but the large skeleton general—who reached nearly to their ceiling—as well as the floating banshee couldn't be questioned.

"Are you two brother and sister? What is your relationship?" Jessica asked.

"We're boyfriend and girlfriend," the man spoke up first.

"Names?" I asked.

"I'm Lucas, she is Rebekah." It seemed she was still almost too stunned to respond. The man however was taking the situation quite well.

"I'm Jessica and this is Mike. We are…comrades."

"What do you want from us? Why would you go out of your way to save us?"

I actually enjoyed his frankness and lack of naivety. "Well, with the world going to shit now, there is power in numbers." I said. "It isn't just monsters as you can imagine, but also other people." I paused. "We have already been attacked by two men and almost killed by them; so right now, I'm interested in finding people to join us to make our group stronger."

Lucas looked to be in his mid-twenties and, promisingly, he had a short, military haircut. He held a strong stare and never faltered while I spoke to him, there was no interruption on his end either. He was waiting for me to finish.

103

So I continued, "Basically, I want your loyalty—both of you. We can shelter you; feed you; help you gain skills; levels; and gain your new class. In return for that, you will be our allies."

"When you say allies, you don't mean slaves, do you?" Lucas asked bluntly.

It was a good question, "Are you familiar with a guild system? One person leads the guild and makes the executive decisions?"

"I'm familiar."

"Good, then it would be like that. Major decisions will be made by me and Jessica, while you are free to make minor decisions on your own. You will be free to go off and do as you please as long as it doesn't interfere with our goals. When you're needed for something bigger, though, I'd expect you to come and assist us the best of your ability. That sort of alliance."

"So like a king and his subjects?" His tone rebuked me.

"No, because a king has guards and prisons to enforce his rule. I'm proposing voluntary co-operation and that you repay our help with loyalty. It's just that I'm reserving the right to make the final call on strategic goals."

Lucas looked at his girlfriend who was still looking from me to the skeletons and back. "What exactly are your goals?"

At this Jessica raised one eyebrow as if to say: *Yeah, what are your goals?*

I should have talked over my guild idea earlier with her. "For now…I don't have a major goal besides surviving by levelling up. The world is still in the process of changing, but I'm sure major boss fights and raid encounters will come along." I spoke more confidently than I felt. In truth, I couldn't be sure anything was coming besides stronger enemies.

"This is a good deal for you," I added, "If we were to leave you here now, you would die as soon as your food and water supplies run out. You are already too far behind to make a start on the game ladder without help."

Jessica got his attention. "I'm no gamer. But that's the world we have now and it's level up or die. I think if you could see the situation from a better vantage point it would help your decision. There are monsters everywhere and more coming by the day."

Lucas and Rebekah shared a glance. I understood they wanted time to decide what they should do. For some people, hiding and risking death would be their preferred choice. Living a life of battle and danger was absolutely not going to be for everybody.

"Come with us and see what the city is like now. We can guarantee your safety, and you will be able to see the situation for yourself," I said. Lucas nodded and looked at his girlfriend, it seems she was finally coming to a decision too as she nodded her head as well.

"Good," Jessica offered them her hand, which they shook. "Let's leave immediately."

Chapter 10: To Survive the MMRPG Apocalypse Humans Need to Group

Our destination was the tallest building of the city, just four blocks back in the northern direction. This was a landmark which allowed me to recognize the inner part of the city and because of it, I had recognized the increasing rings of difficulty resonating from the center.

The monsters we had dispatched earlier hadn't respawned yet and I could see the eyes of Lucas and Rebekah looking around in confusion: there was no danger around us. They seemed skeptical as we approached the tall building and made our way to the roof.

Once on top they looked out and their eyes nearly fell from their sockets. The challenge we faced was clear as day from above, with the myriad of enemies below and in the distance. A clear division of difficulty and monster variety as one approached the center.

Their eyes traced the distance and then eventually the immediate few blocks we had already cleared, "Don't tell me...you two cleared these blocks yourself? That's why there are no monsters roaming about?"

"Right, we cleared them," I said. "And don't let that make you think they are easy. Can you see the stratification of enemies? Right now we are in the second-most outer ring. Those goblins you fear so badly are in the most outer ring. They are cannon fodder to us at this point.

"Do you see those brutish monsters? One of those hitting you would kill you two times over as you are now. You are trapped within this ring and would never escape alone," I continued.

"You should join us, we have to work together," Jessica said. "We just want allies to help us survive. Everything seems to be getting harder and only groups of trustworthy, like-minded people are going to be able to cope. Helping you get started is our way of building a relationship and showing our sincerity."

Her words were like the cherry on top of the conclusion the view was leading them towards. I didn't know she had such a way with words, and the two immediately were more convinced hearing the argument for solidarity among survivors from someone as charming as Jessica.

Lucas leaned in close and started whispering in Rebekah's ear. The hesitation they were both feeling seemed to disappear, "What do we need to do?"

"Does that mean you will join us?" I asked.

"We will join, and follow your direction as long as you are not irresponsibly putting our lives in danger." His response told me he truly had thought about it. He wasn't just blustering with his answer, and I immediately had high expectations for Lucas.

"Good, we can power level you to start. Getting your class change immediately isn't wise as the selections are determined by stat and skill choice. It would be a good idea to start thinking about what you would like to be, when I say that I mean in the sense of class-type: spell caster; melee fighter; tank; or something else.

"We only have one skill book currently available, but it isn't useful without a ranged weapon." I added. With that, we walked back down to ground level and returned to the building we had slept the night prior.

Our spears were located there, even though we weren't using them anymore. Jessica and I each passed one across, and they took them with evident fear on their face. "Don't worry, you just have to stab. We'll pin them down. It'll be fine," I promised.

We headed a bit more inward towards an area that had monsters available. "How about setting a trap?" I suggested to Jessica.

"Quagmire?" she asked.

"Yeah, and then pull an ogre."

She nodded and then set a Quagmire trap before pulling her bow from her inventory. The visual of the bow appearing in her hands out of thin air both shocked and excited Lucas and Rebekah.

She pulled back the string and the two couldn't look away as an arrow materialized out of light on the bow string. She put an arrow directly into the thigh of an ogre and ensured it would run right through her trap.

As soon as the trap was triggered I sent all my skeletons to swarm it, and instructed them to hold the monster in place. They didn't attack, and merely constrained its limbs. With Quagmire and my skeletons holding the brute in place, it couldn't move even in the slightest.

"Now it's your turn. Just go up and stab it. The skin is quite thick and leathery, so you'll need to put some force into it." I caught myself, "Oh wait, you two should make a party. One of you just needs to think it and it will invite the other."

Lucas halted his advance and then turned back to Rebekah. It seemed to me he was picking everything up quite quickly. Once the two were in a party together they approached the brute with spears drawn.

Rebekah stabbed half-assed and couldn't even break the skin while Lucas did his best to drill the tip into the ogre's neck. He pierced it once, he continued to stab it over and over in the same place like a madman.

Blood gushed out of the wound and covered the bulging belly of the monster before dripping to the floor. Some was spurting onto my skeletons, who were holding strong. After dozens of seconds and at least twenty stabs, the ogre went limp and collapsed to the ground.

"I gained two levels," Lucas said with a smile.

"Me as well," Rebekah chimed in.

"Good, so this tactic for power levelling does work." I sighed in relief. Just doing this a few more times would get them close to Level 5. From there they would be able to battle in the outer ring with goblins and zombies and the alien creatures relatively safely with a proper battle strategy.

I instructed them on how to open their stats and gave a brief description of what I believed each stat would do. I didn't have any opinion on what Lucas should do stat wise, as he seemed comfortable going into melee range. His options for classes were completely open.

Rebekah, however, seemed uncomfortable with being anywhere near a foe. I suggested she consider a ranged class, and decide if she wanted to cast spells, or use ranged attacks, or even play a support role.

Just as I had done, Lucas added some points to STR for an immediate boost in his power. It was a useful stat even outside of fighting, and wouldn't hurt to have a few points in it to start with. It would make damaging the ogres even easier.

Rebekah didn't use any points at all, and it seemed Lucas was completely fine with her not contributing to the kills. Five more brutes were all it took for both of them to each hit Level 5, and I wasn't sure if it was pure luck or the relative difficulty, but three skill books and two items dropped.

It was possible there was some sort of dynamic scaling. Defeating monsters of much higher level or stronger than you provided better loot: which made sense from a fairness standpoint. Did that mean lower level monsters dropped you nothing? I'd assume they still would, just that drop values reverted to default, which in my experience had been very low.

I collected the items and the skill books and took a look over them.

Book of Wind Slash LV. 3: Allows the user to strike out with great speed creating a blade of wind that travels through the air to cut enemies.
Cast Time: Instant
MP Cost: 6
Distance: 3 Meters
Requires a sword to be equipped.
Book of Healing LV. 2: Allows the user to use the spell Healing Touch. Healing Touch restores 25% of the target's maximum HP.
Cast Time: 2 Seconds
MP Cost: 15
Distance: 5 Meters

Book of Energy Bolt LV. 1: Shoots a concentrated bolt of energy at the target.

Cast Time: 1 Second
MP Cost: 5
Distance: 4 Meters

None of the skill books held any appeal for me except Heal. The fact that full support skills must exist was a given but it was the first I'd seen drop. There was no guarantee all skills were weighted equally, though. Perhaps healing abilities were incredibly rare, because they could save a life.

As for the items that dropped:

Carbon Steel Nodachi: A beautiful
Samurai sword that measures over 6ft in
length.
AGI +2, DEX +1, Attack Speed +10%
Geloas' Eyes: A pair of goggles that
greatly increases vision.
DEX +4, True Strike + 10.
Grants the user Clear Vision.

I pocketed Heal and then presented Energy Bolt and Wind Slash to show them to Lucas. He seemed interested in Wind Slash as a skill, and then when I presented the Nodachi to him, he was completely sold.

He took the book from me and learned it on the spot, which prompted me to hand over the Carbon Steel Nodachi. As for Rebekah, her only option was Energy Bolt. I was hesitant to allow her to learn Heal. She had yet to prove herself under stress and a healer had to be able to make smart decisions in an instant.

Heal was just too useful of an ability to hand it out irresponsibly. If I gave it to her and she decided she didn't want to live this type of life, and I discovered Heal was incredibly rare, it would be a disaster.

"You can wait to learn a skill as well, if you'd like," I said to her.

"No, it's okay. I'm happy with the idea of using magical spells," she confessed before learning Energy Bolt. As for the Geloas' Eyes, I passed them to Jessica happily. The goggles looked like they would work wonders for her tracking ability, and I was curious what the special effects were.

"This is incredible!" Jessica cried.

"What does Clear Vision do?" I wondered aloud.

"Clear Vision grants the user perfect vision," she seemed to be narrating from the menu that only she could see. "True Strike gives me a ten percent chance to land a critical hit."

This was really welcome news, and I felt a surge of elation. Soon too, the newcomers would be adding a great deal to our combat strength. The Nodachi Lucas wielded looked so menacing I doubted he would replace it anytime soon.

"It's getting dark, we should head back," Jessica said. I agreed and didn't feel like sleeping on hard concrete anymore.

"Why not come back to our apartment?" offered Rebekah, who seemed to be coming out of herself. "We have a spare bedroom."

Only after I was safely in bed did I take the time to look at my own stats. Killing the Elite Banshee had pushed both me and Jessica to Level 10. It was possible for me to learn a new active skill now. I opened my stats.

Name: Mike Reynolds (27) Class: Necromancer Level: 10 EXP: 13%
HP: 230/385 MP: 133/210
STR: 5
AGI: 2
DEX: 1
VIT: 12
WIS: 12 +3

Available: 3

Skills: [A]Summon Skeleton LV. 4 |[A] Decay LV. 1| [A] Reanimate Dead LV. 1 | [P]Sixth Sense | [P] Bravery LV. 2 | [P] Mutated | [P] Pain Resistance | [P] Skeletal Mastery

In the several hours since we downed the Banshee, I had recovered a decent amount of HP and a decent chunk of MP. The question I was asking myself was if Bone Armor should be my next active skill.

My biggest fear was dying to something unexpected. Right now, it didn't feel like we could afford to make any mistakes, even though my HP already felt incredibly high given my level. Honestly, that feeling was just pure stress, and it was accumulating slowly.

At the same time though, leveling for the next few days was going to be purely grinding mobs we could deal with easily. I didn't want to abandon Lucas and Rebekah just because they had gotten their skills and could nearly fend for themselves. There was potential in this group for the longer term.

Tomorrow would be another day of assisting them, and then Jessica and I would make preparations to move towards the next ring. There was still time to see a few more skill books drop, and by the day we made a move inwards, I could make a decision.

There was also Jessica to consider as well. Her spells could be used as traps, which meant even non-normal skill choices could work. The only limiting factor was the drops we received and our own creativity.

I never thought sleeping on a bed could feel so good, and it was the first time in a long time that I didn't feel anxious about closing my eyes. Nothing was going to wander upon us and attack us in the night. But before I fell asleep, I heard Jessica from the bed at the other wall.

"You did well today Mike. And with Rebekah and Lucas, I feel hopeful for the first time since this disaster."

"You too, I don't think they'd have given this a try without you," I said.

I waited for a response but could hear her breathing was deep and steady. Like me she must have been exhausted and had fallen asleep. I let myself do the same.

Chapter 11: Power Leveling in a Post-Apocalypse City

Waking up after the sun had already risen was an oddity, but damn did it feel good. A sleep that refreshing could only happen because Jessica and I had reached our first goal. A huge weight had been lifted from my anxieties after hitting Level 10 and especially after getting the Necromancer class specialization. With Jessica as a Trapper and potential support from the newcomers too, as far as I was concerned, our current position was solid and safe. With this set up and the level of the monsters we'd faced, we could survive on the outskirts of this city for as long as need be: my main fear was that the challenge could grow too fast for us. Although we were leveling well, the world was evolving and changing alongside us.

We all rose bright and early, and ended up eating the remaining rations Lucas and Rebekah had in their apartment. I showed them the consumables you could find from drops, including HP potions and even actual Rations.

During the night, the monsters nearby had all respawned and the streets just outside the apartment were crawling with them. Jessica and I had to play cleanup to start the day off, because pulling and restraining a single ogre for our companions to kill wasn't possible: there were just too many monsters, and we didn't want to risk Lucas or Rebekah's safety.

What was apparent though, was that this ring had grown too weak for Jessica and I now, and slaying multiple ogres and banshees at the same time was no longer a risk. My skeletons were able to take multiple hits from these monsters, and the damage they dealt was outstanding.

Only after we had cleared a safe space to work with did we start pulling for them. The goal for the day was to get them to Level 8. By then they should be able to level alone, and we could discuss the best way forward. I wanted to resume levelling up as soon as possible and I was sure Jessica felt the same. Once Lucas and Rebekah were safe in this area, I reckoned it might be best to split up and they agreed on that point. I did my best as we pulled each mob type to explain their abilities and what was dangerous about them.

Jessica's pulls included the zombies, goblins, and the four-legged, alien-type creature. The grind was effective but dull and it wasn't teaching them a lot. Lucas was simply chopping mobs to bits in full safety while Rebekah shot Energy Bolts. When they expressed that to me, I agreed it was safe enough for them to be more ambitious. As soon as they reached Level 6, we decided to let them start clearing for themselves, moving towards the edge of the city.

On my advice, both Lucas and Rebekah put points into VIT and started to pull for themselves, making sure to be careful of thrown spear attacks from hidden goblins. Jessica and I were down to only a single bandage between the two of us, and I didn't want to use it due to their carelessness.

I turned to Jessica, "What do you think? Should we leave them to it and try pushing further in?"

She pondered the idea, "Hmm, I'm sure those two will be fine, but we would be going into the unknown. I think we could handle it, but don't we need to farm two Class Changing Stones first?" Of course, this was something I had forgotten. We had promised Rebekah and Lucas that we would provide them with a stone so they could choose their classes on reaching Level 10.

There were more elites in the next ring of enemies than the one we were in, but I reckoned that we wouldn't be able to handle them at our current strength, not with the risk of adds that were themselves a challenge. Here, the non-elite ogres and banshees were no longer a threat to us, and while they gave very little exp—each kill was around three or four percent of our level—it honestly wasn't bad for battles that were almost risk free.

To get to the elites of our current ring was probably an hour walk on foot, but we had reached a strength that we could travel this layer without much fear. Jessica could immediately discover any hidden enemies, and my skeletons were the perfect shield.

After a discussion, we parted from Lucas and Rebekah. They were going to continue their own grind, while Jessica and I went to get their class stones, with a plan to meet up again at their apartment.

Jessica and I started our journey north again, towards where we had defeated the elite banshee. Between us, we had decided she was the weaker of the two elites. My skeletons countered her Fear, and her Frost Bolt took way more hits to down my Skeleton General than the constant pounding from the elite brute.

The boss was merely a four block walk over, which took around thirty minutes given we were meticulously downing monsters. The idea that there was some form of dynamic scaling for loot seemed plausible, as we weren't finding many drops. From about twenty kills, we did, however, manage to find another two rations and a hit point potion. Truthfully, this was easy and safe leveling for us, and after making the thirty-minute walk decided we would get all the EXP we could from this area.

As we moved and fought, Jessica and I discussed what we would do after the elites. So long as the EXP gain was 3 or 4 percent of a level, we would continue in this ring, but once the EXP per kill was down to below 2 percent, it would be time to travel inwards. This was probably only two levels away or so. As we finished clearing the remaining monsters in the block of space we had previously chosen for the boss fight, the elite banshee was nowhere to be found.

"I guess maybe it takes longer to respawn than regular mobs?" I questioned.

"Maybe." Jessica said. "It doesn't matter how soon we find them anyway; we'll be grinding here for a bit regardless." She wasn't wrong, and when I looked at it that way I wasn't in a rush at all.

We eventually did come upon an elite, but it wasn't a banshee.

It was another ogre, and although I felt sick to my stomach looking at him, we managed to find a good place to pull him and defeat him. There were no untoward hooks thrown this time and the fight ended with just a few of my skeletons being destroyed.

Having an increased effect on Quagmire and the reanimated Banshee made so much of a difference. When the boss died, I was anxious in case a class changing stone might not drop since Jessica and I had already class changed, but that wasn't the case.

A stone did drop, which I pocketed away. There was also another item that dropped.

Leather Gloves: Tight fitting gloves made out of a leathery but dirty-looking material.
AGI +1, DEX +2
Grants the user Nimble Fingers.

Again, this was another item made for Jessica, and honestly I wasn't unhappy about it. The gloves were definitely made from the disgusting skin of the brute, and just that color made me feel sick. Wearing it on my hands all the time was a no go for me.

Jessica told me that Nimble Fingers increased attack speed by 5%, which wasn't a small amount at all. The way she nocked arrows and sent them flying was growing more and more incredible. She'd really taken to this new world and I felt lucky to have her at my side.

Her archery had gone beyond what had previously been possible for a human, mostly a result of the assistance of increased stats. The time it took for her to pull the string back and aim was already less than a second, and her accuracy was on point.

I knew it was on point because I tested her. As we moved forward, looking for more enemies, I would occasionally pick up a baseball-sized rock and toss it in the air and call on Jessica to hit it. So far, in five attempts, she hadn't missed a single one. An arrow went directly through each rock and split them into pebbles.

This had become somewhat of a game for me, but evidently more of an annoyance as time passed for her as at last she pleaded, "No more please." The constant nocking and shooting might have been tiring on her, and I happily obliged.

With the EXP from the elite brute and then that from another ten kills, we both managed to hit level 11. I had also gained another skill up in Summon Skeletons, which granted me an extra skeleton.

Almost as if my complaining about the rarity of loot had been heard, we managed to get three items as well, two of them equipment and one was another HP potion.

**Long Hunting Bow: A bow of
considerable size. It takes great strength
to fully draw it.
DEX +1, STR+ 3**

There was no added passive skill, but the bow itself was clearly an upgrade to her crude short bow. Just the effort required to pull it back showed how much more force it would shoot with.

**Skull Mask: A face mask made out of the
skull of a dead animal. You look Demonic.
WIS +2, VIT +2
Grants the user Intimidate Living.**

Putting the mask on, I pulled up my stats immediately to take a closer look at this item.

I noticed that unlike the black on white colors of the game menu, which were the usual ones, Intimidate Living showed in purple, probably indicating that it was item granted. I read the description:

**Intimidate Living: Living enemies feel fear
when looking at you, making them less
likely to attack. The wearer has a small
chance to cast Fear when attacked.**

From what I understood, the mask acted like threat reduction, reducing my chance of getting aggro? This could be important if my minions were going down: I might not be the next target once they did. I had experienced what Fear did firsthand, and if it proc'd, that would be amazing.

Besides that, the stats were good enough to warrant my wearing it. "Do you feel intimidated when you look at me?" I asked Jessica.

She looked me up and down and then smiled, "No, you just look kind of silly to me." I guessed that in her eyes I wasn't a threat, or simply that the mask didn't affect allies. New people we meet might not feel the same. Having a skull mask gave me a bit of allure and mystery, which I liked.

We continued to head north, beyond the point Jessica and I had previously ventured. It was just more of the same, an endless waste of destruction and debris. I started to wonder if we would ever find more people. If they had survived, it was probably well away from the city and not towards the dangerous core.

The likelihood that we would find people that hadn't started their leveling journey shrank each day, while those that had grown in power could be potential enemies. This wasn't a pleasant thought at all: having to kill another person or be killed by them.

Sometimes in my sleep, I saw the image of the older brother dying, and I was thankful that I had immediately cast Summon Skeletons on the younger one's body in the darkness. I don't think that sight would have ever left my brain if not.

It was this line of thinking that prompted me to turn to Jessica, "Hey, I never asked you, but what do you want?"

"What do you mean?"

"Like, what do you want to happen? Where do you want this all to go? Save the world somehow? Find a nice quiet place and live? What goal do you have?"

Her face lit up with an 'oh' and then she went silent, "For now, I think I just want to survive. If possible…it would be nice to find a spot less affected by this mess and continue to grow as a Trapper. Then I could choose my adventures better instead of being thrust into them. Maybe even help a community thrive." She paused, "I guess what I'm trying to say is that I want some control back."

My current goal was also to survive, and it was that simple in my head. I hadn't thought beyond this to the level that Jessica had. Since I no longer felt death was looming at every corner, I had more time to contemplate on my future. "Some control doesn't sound so bad," I agreed.

"Probably, its cities and population hubs that are most affected by this catastrophe. If we moved to the country, maybe there would be monsters, but nowhere near as bad as this. Especially those enemies in the inner rings."

"Right," Jessica nodded. "But I don't think we should just leave. Not now, anyway. This is where we can get levels and new gear. And I worry that if we drop our pace, we'll fall behind and never have a chance when in the future some monster finds us."

I liked the way she spoke about 'we' and not just 'I'.

Chapter 12: The Challenge of the Apocalypse MMRPG Deepens

The next hour or so was spent walking in silence, I wasn't concerned about the need for stealth, it was more that I was caught up in my thoughts about the world we faced and presumably Jessica was too.

The enemies roaming these streets and less built-up areas, were mostly zombies and goblins. My skeletons had no difficulty with these.

Eventually though, through the mindless slaughter, we did encounter another elite enemy, and this one was a Banshee. Between Jessica's new hunting bow and my extra skeleton warrior, the Banshee went down incredibly fast.

The only thing the elite dropped was another stone, which was fine.

"Can I have your old bow?" I asked Jessica. I had decided upon another small goal of mine, and that was to gear out all my skeleton warriors.

I hadn't attempted to put any equipment other than weapons on them yet, because it was too costly and neither Jessica nor I had full gear yet. But losing left over or unusable weapons shouldn't be an issue. She handed it over without hesitation and I allowed my warrior to take it.

My army of minions was actually looking incredibly fierce. My skeleton general led the front, 4 skeleton warriors by his side—one with a menacing mace—and a single warrior wielding a bow stayed at the back beside by my reanimated banshee.

At level fourteen I would gain another minion from Skeleton Mastery, and at fifteen I would be able to summon another reanimated corpse. Level fifteen was going to be a very large power spike for me no doubt. I was looking forward to it greatly.

I made sure to not resummon my skeletons in case there was some issue with the bow. When Jessica used the bow, it spawned arrows when the bowstring was drawn but I wasn't sure if that would be the case for my skeletons. It would be a tragedy if I resummoned to lock it in with the bow, only to find the warrior suddenly did nothing.

Fortunately, the next enemy we encountered allowed me to test its archery. The bow-wielding skeleton had no issue chaining attacks together with endless arrows, albeit at a fraction of the speed Jessica could do so.

"Hey, do you see that?" Jessica suddenly asked while looking at the sky.

I turned in the direction she was looking and could make out a faint column of pale light stretching from the horizon up into the sky, "Sort of...what is it?" It was so unsubstantial I couldn't really tell. The fact that Jessica had spotted it at all must have been a side effect of her perfect vision.

"I think it's getting brighter," she said. We both came to a complete stop and watched as the light became somewhat more solid. It was about half a block in width and beaming straight up into the sky. "Isn't that...where the center of the city is?"

"I think we should go inside." I said, "I'm getting a bad feeling about this." We both looked for a building to hold up in and Jessica found an office block which had good visibility in all directions from its open plan first floor. From time to time I kept looking out at the mysterious white light. Slowly, the white color of the column grew brighter and more distinct.

After what felt like fifteen minutes, even in broad daylight, the light was so vivid I was sure it could be seen from miles away. The brighter it got, the more intense became the bad feeling I felt. As if it had reached a crescendo, it suddenly exploded with a nova high in the sky.

A pulse traveled across the land outwards from where the column had been, like an explosive shockwave that I could feel even from inside my body. Something in the world had changed in that moment, and it surely wasn't good. "What…just happened?" Jessica seemed completely bewildered.

Truthfully, I was as well. "I'm not sure." I had felt the pulse, but there was no new system message, and nothing visibly had changed. As if on cue to provide me with an answer, the situation outside changed. Mobs began to spawn.

"A forced respawn?" I wondered aloud. This was my first thought, but it was quickly proven wrong. The enemies that spawned outside were not just ogres and banshees. There were also a variety of new enemies instead, as if the spawns had been scrambled.

Mixed in with the mobs we were familiar with were those snake-like demi-humans as well as a new monster that I called an abomination. These were bulky humanoids, with a thick muscular torso that was more like a bull's than a human's. Their heads, however, were like that of a tyrannosaur, flatter but with just as many sharp

125

teeth. It was then that I realized we had been surrounded. We were now trapped within this building with new mob types we had never fought before just outside.

Walking outside would surely cause groups of these mobs to aggro. We would, one hundred percent, pull at least one demi-human, one abomination and an ogre by leaving the building by the main entrance. Looking at them however, didn't increase the prickling on my neck. There was something worse out there.

My nerves were a wreck and the hairs of my neck were standing and I couldn't pinpoint why. I scanned the area repeatedly until I noticed something out of the corner of my eye. It was a person clinging almost inconspicuously to the side of a former hairdresser's building.

I felt indescribable fear when my eyes locked onto the figure. A single word continued to pass through my mind over and over: death. The creature was pure black and humanoid shaped. It reminded me of Venom from *Spiderman*, except there were no eyes at all on its face. The teeth though, the teeth were things of nightmare.

If it had eyes I felt that we would have locked stares. Death sat perched on the corner of the hairdresser's for a moment, almost as if it was waiting for us to come out. I pointed directly at it and made sure Jessica had seen it, before shaking my head.

No words could convey my horror of this monster. We watched it in silence for what felt like a dozen minutes but was probably only one before it rocketed off the side of the building and disappeared. The strength of its limbs must have been incredible for it to be able to propel itself hundreds of feet in a single push.

My body relaxed momentarily as the looming danger disappeared. I realized that my face and back was covered in a thick layer of sweat. "Did you feel it?" I asked her.

"We need to avoid the monster at all costs," Jessica replied, face so pale it was almost green. "The feeling it gave me...was endless. Like a dark pit that had no bottom—pure terror. I won't forget that, ever."

I nodded to agree and changed the subject, "Lucas and Rebekah, I hope they're okay," I said. They were out in the open somewhere leveling, but with things becoming scrambled, were the outer rings still safe? I hoped they had made it inside somewhere.

"We have our own problems to deal with." Jessica said with a gesture towards the creatures just outside the building entrance. We now could see our opponents from up close, and it was clear they were a serious threat.

The trident held by the snake-headed monster was longer than my entire body and the abomination held a cleaver as thick as my torso. They towered over us in terms of size, and their exact capabilities were unknown.

We needed to get back to Lucas and Rebekah, or it was possible we would completely lose track of them. The idea was to always regroup at their apartment, but if they weren't able to continue killing mobs, they might starve before we could assist them.

Jessica and I had enough rations for four or five days, and that was only if we didn't hunt at all and stayed cooped up inside. The situation wasn't ideal, but we could make do regardless. "I will lead the front with my skeletons; you stay safe and out of range. Take no risks at all," I urged her.

I knew that Jessica had put some points into VIT, but nowhere near as many as me. I decided it was time to commit to Bone

127

Armor. A trident of that size would put me on death's door at the very least, and quite possibly kill me in a single hit. There was no doubt in my mind it could pin me to a solid concrete wall with a single toss.

I pulled out the skill book and then used it without hesitation. The skill populated my stats window and I could now see a better description of the ability.

Bone Armor: Covers the user in an armor of bone that greatly reduces damage from physical and magical attacks. Armor value is based upon thirty percent of the Users maximum HP value. Seventy-five percent of damage taken is absorbed by Bone Armor before reaching the User.

If I understood the wording correctly then a hit of 100 damage would deal 75 to bone armor and the remaining 25 would be dealt directly to me. Besides that I also had 6 stat points saved, which I decided would go best into VIT and WIS.

Name: Mike Reynolds (27) Class: Necromancer Level: 11 EXP: 1%
HP: 475/475 MP: 191/230
STR: 5
AGI: 2
DEX: 1
VIT: 15 +2
WIS: 15 +5
Available: 0

Skills: [A]Summon Skeleton LV. 5 |[A]
Decay LV. 1| [A] **Reanimate Dead LV.** 1 | [A]
Bone Armor LV. 1 | [P]Sixth Sense | [P]
Bravery LV. 2 | [P] **Mutated** | [P] **Pain**
Resistance | [P] **Skeletal Mastery** | [P]
Intimidate Living

With my current HP, Bone Armor would have a value of about 140, which wasn't bad at all. Ideally, it would absorb one attack at the very minimum, which could be the difference between life and death.

"Aim for the eyes first. Once you've removed their sight, you're free to maneuver into a better position. I will be mixed in with my skeletons to avoid any ranged attacks to start. Focus on getting a Quagmire down: it doesn't have to be activated via trap,"

Jessica nodded and I could see her resolution. She'd come a long way since I had met her.

I cast Bone Armor for the first time and felt a small weight added to my frame. A thin layer of bone formed around my body with flexible hinges at each joint. Looking down, the new armor was hard to see, as my body was already mostly covered by Demonic Garb, and my face had Skull Mask over it.

The only truly visible parts of my body were my neck and hands, and it was hard to discern that the white of my skin really was bone. There was a white layer around my fingers that could easily be mistaken as a pair of gloves. As I moved my legs and hands to test whether there was any restraint on me, I was surprised at how smooth my motion felt. There was no chunkiness and movement felt natural, which was unexpected and very welcome.

My hand grasped the door and I gave one last look to Jessica, she nodded quietly and I pushed it open. My horde of skeletons rushed out into the open and I hurried to blend in with them. The demi-human, abomination, and ogre noticed my pack all at the same time and the three enemies turned in my direction.

A rattling hiss and the sound of dragging chains grated against my ears. My heart was in my throat for the first time in what felt like days. There could be no holding back at all in this situation and my minions immediately surrounded the demi-human enemy.

From behind, I could hear Jessica cast Quagmire and the enemy banshee bolted it repeatedly, greatly slowing its action speed. I sent my skeleton general on his own to intercept the abomination and hold him for as long possible. The two clashed: with my skeleton general being the underdog.

Again, Jessica cast Quagmire, this time under the abomination to assist the skeleton general and then she began to release arrow after arrow: each one pelting the demi-human enemy in its snake face, specifically targeting the eyes, and I instructed my undead banshee to shift casts between each enemy, so they all remained chilled.

I followed up with a Decay that rapidly withered the scaly exterior of the demi-human and something that I hadn't considered came to me in the moment my warriors pummeled the decaying flesh. Decay also reduced the enemy's defense by softening their natural armor. Blow after blow plowed off dead flesh and revealed the fleshy interior.

Jessica had managed to pierce one eye and yet the trident rained down blows against my summoned undead. Just two hits were all it took before my skeleton warriors exploded into a boney dust. The skeleton general was still off to the side deflecting as many blows as possible.

With so many battles happening at once, it felt like a lot of time had passed. The reality however, was that we had been fighting for just a few seconds only. Everything was happening so fast and the stress of battle was building.

The abomination's cleaver rained down like a clock tower chiming twelve. Still, my general held strong with every blow and did his best to concentrate on pure defense. The sword he normally wielded was already on the floor as both hands grasped the shield and he braced himself for each impact.

The demi-human was hemorrhaging blood, which sprayed from each wound it had received. By now though, three of my four melee warriors were destroyed. A single one remained and then I would be dependent on my two ranged summons. "Finish the ogre!" I yelled to Jessica. Until now, the ogre was the enemy we had been ignoring, and it was currently attacking my last melee skeleton beside the much tougher demi-human.

I focused all my fire power on the ogre as well, as I badly needed a new corpse to respawn my summons. The new strength of Jessica's bow could hardly be seen against the demi-human, but it completely blew the brains out of the brutish monster. Its head nearly exploded as it collapsed to the floor.

My last melee skeleton fell as the ogre died, and I was left exposed. The demi-human began to race towards me while I rushed forward to get in range of the corpse: an ominous feeling washed over me that I had no choice but to ignore.

There was a gurgling sound from the demi-human's mouth as it sprayed a viscous green liquid through the air. I instinctively dived forward to try and avoid the spray. Yet I heard the splatter as a decent chunk of the mist landed upon my back and back legs. I prayed in that moment it wasn't lethal as I rolled forward.

My HP began to rapidly fall as a searing pain raced along my skin. Bone Armor was melted rapidly away until the entire layer disappeared completely and I was left exposed. It felt as if a boiling liquid was poured upon my skin and I let out a howl of pain.

The corpse was in range now, and I cast Summon Skeletons again. My skeletons spawned on the spot and then immediately rushed around the demi-human once again. I backed away while enduring the terrible sensation that was now burning across my skin.

The acid attack had completely removed Bone Armor's protection and dealt another 150 or so damage directly to me. The functionality of my body was fine, however, and with gritted teeth I pushed on through the pain and moved to a safer position.

My renewed skeleton general began clashing again with the abomination while Jessica and I targeted the demi-human. Soon it was convulsing in its death throes: there were no more surprises and no longer any avenue for its survival. Jessica had fully blinded the snake eyes of the monster and continued to put arrow after arrow into its damaged eye sockets.

Her arrows dug deeper with so much power they cracked the creature's skull and eventually went directly into its brain. It collapsed into a heap after taking two more skeletons with it. I didn't hesitate to rush over and cast Reanimate on it. It was clear we needed a bulky melee to back up my general else the abomination would run freely over us.

Fortunately for us, the abomination was a much easier fight. It continuously plowed into my General over and over again without stop while being pummeled repeatedly. I couldn't cast Decay on it, but the reanimated snake-headed human spat acidic venom on the large creature that melted its outer flesh.

As the abomination's hit points became lower and lower, it also used a special ability. Noxious gas poured out from the openings all over its decaying flesh. Fortunately for us, the poison seemed to have no effect on my undead army, as they simply ignored it and continued to lash into the monster.

The fight with the abomination was straight-forward compared to the snake-headed creature: I considered it a tank and spank, purely a stat check encounter. The relief I felt when the monster died made me want to fall on my ass, but I rushed over and reanimated it instead.

It was definitely the tankier of the two enemies, and the noxious gas it expunged intrigued me. I had a good idea for this ability that I wanted to test at a different time: as soon as we could get out of here and back to base.

Name: Mike Reynolds (27) **Class: Necromancer Level:** 11 **EXP:** 43%
HP: 338/475 **MP:** 121/230
STR: 5
AGI: 2
DEX: 1
VIT: 15 +2
WIS: 15 +5
Available: 0

Skills: [A]Summon Skeleton LV. 5 [[A]
Decay LV. 1 [[A] **Reanimate Dead LV.** 1 | [A]
Bone Armor LV. 1 | [P]**Sixth Sense** | [P]
Bravery LV. 2 | [P] **Mutated** | [P] **Pain Resistance LV.** 2 | [P] **Skeletal Mastery** |
[P]**Intimidate Living**

I opened my stats and took a look at how I'd fared in the battle. I had lost 137 HP and 70 MP during the encounter. On the brightside we had gained a ridiculous amount of EXP. These new enemies gave five or six times the amount of EXP of a banshee or brute, which was incredible.

If we didn't have to fight two at once, I figured we could dispatch either type with relative ease; it would just cost a bit more MP per encounter to do so. There was also a new surprise: Pain Resistance had reached level two. I was happy for that, but definitely not happy about the pain I went through to level it up.

"Let's do our best to avoid the snake-heads and move back to Lucas and Rebekah," Jessica said. "If they were lucky, they also took cover and we should be able to find them."

Her suggestion was definitely easier to state than deliver. With the mix-up of spawns, it was no longer a leisurely walk through the city and back. We had wandered some 8 or 9 blocks away before finding the second elite and getting a second class changing stone.

In the end, we decided to move towards the outskirts only to find they still contained abominations and snake heads, just in a slightly less volume. It seemed the ring-like stratification of the city had been destroyed when that light exploded. Also, the situation outside the city was a complete unknown.

Then too, there was that mysterious death-monster we saw on the building exterior. I had absolutely no doubt in my mind that it could kill Jessica and I in a matter of seconds. This was just a feeling, but I didn't want to test it at all.

The mix-up of enemies seemed so completely random that some streets were just goblins and zombies and brutes and banshees all mixed together. The idea I wanted to test later was going to be tested now instead.

I tasked Jessica to lay a Quagmire trap and then sent my reanimated abomination out. He wobbled and the fat flaps and bubbles of pus jiggled as he rushed forward, gathering every mob in sight. As soon as they were chasing him, I pulled him back.

He led them directly over the Quagmire trap and then stopped, causing every pulled enemy to enter into that slowing zone. There were about fifteen enemies around him attempting to swing at him in near slow motion.

Once there, I had him use his noxious gas ability. Fumes of green and grey poured out from the pits and holes and pustules on his body and quickly infected everything around him. The goblins and little aliens melted in place as if the most toxic poison had afflicted them.

The brutes and banshees started to dissolve but clearly lasted longer. In the end, however, everything died to a single cast of his bilious poison. "Jesus Christ..." Jessica said. I felt the same way. It was like the most toxic release of gas you could possibly imagine: in my head the smell of that attack was so bad that everything alive within range simply died.

Zombies were the only enemies remaining, which confirmed that undead enemies were immune to his ability. That suggested to me that the abomination's ability was some form of spell similar to Decay. Clearly, dead enemies couldn't exactly decay any further.

The abomination hacked the remaining zombies into pieces before returning to my side. Just out of safety, I made it stand far enough away from us that an accidental emission of poison wouldn't reach us.

"Good idea," said Jessica earnestly. "I don't feel comfortable anywhere near that guy."

What was clear though, was reanimated corpses retained at least some of their strength and ability from when they were alive. The same skill level had been used for the abomination as I'd used to

135

summon an ogre and banshee, and yet it did more damage and had considerably more HP. Even so, it certainly couldn't go one-versus-one against the living version of itself.

I was pleased with the success of my AOE idea, and the quick burst of EXP we received. For the lot of fifteen monsters we got around 22% of our level. It seemed goblins and zombies gave almost nothing, somewhere below 1% at least per kill. Unfortunately, not a single item dropped.

We cleared the area of any immediate danger and took shelter for several minutes. Our regular food store was depleted, and we broke into our stock of Rations and decided to try eating one each. It was actually my first time trying it, and I was very curious.

There were only five rations between the two of us, so I gave three to Jessica and kept two for myself. "I'll take the next one that drops," I assured her. Each Ration had 3 uses, and I wasn't sure exactly how it would affect us.

Was one entire Ration considered a day's worth of food? Or was one use of a Ration a day's worth of food? I bit into it as if I was eating a piece of bread. The spongy texture was nice, but the flavor was clearly lacking, it was bland almost. It wasn't inedible, but definitely wouldn't be my first choice if I could avoid it.

It was gone in merely a few bites, and yet any hunger or thirst I felt completely disappeared. In fact, after a few minutes had passed I even felt bloated—stuffed even. "I think if we ate one of these in the morning we would be good all day."

"Agreed," Jessica said with a burp. If I was right, we had around fifteen days' worth of food between us. I felt a bit better now about how few of them had dropped. Given their strength, we might be able to feed ourselves through grinding.

As we kept moving with slow progress through the mobs, I realized that reaching Lucas and Rebekah would probably not be possible before sunset.

They would need to survive the night, and the next morning too. It would be afternoon before we could probably reach them.

Chapter 13: Take the Skills that Drop or Hold Out for a Better Build?

The next morning Jessica woke me from a dream in which I had been walking through a desert, burning sun on my back and legs. It was almost a relief to be back in the world, devastated though it was. Finding I didn't need any breakfast and nor did Jessica, we set off in the hope that Lucas and Rebekah had managed to survive.

We continued forward pulling mobs at a steady pace and avoiding the snake-headed monsters as best as possible, occasionally stopping to regenerate a bit of MP. Each fight saw one or two of my summoned undead disintegrating as collateral damage. Which meant each new battle cost me around 10 MP.

I also kept Bone Armor up whenever we were going into a new encounter. The fear of that mysterious deathly creature was fresh on my mind: not that I believed for a second Bone Armor would make a difference if it locked onto me.

After nearly two hours of slow grinding Jessica and I both received a welcome message.

Congratulations, you have reached level
121

The constant re-summoning of skeletons had also raised my level of Skeletal Mastery to level 2, which was a greatly welcome improvement.

Skeletal Mastery LV. 2: Minions deal 20% **increased damage and have** 15% **increased maximum HP per level.**

The damage had increased by 5% and so had the maximum HP, a decent buff per level. There was also a skill book that dropped as well, a very interesting one.

Book of Preliminary Inspection LV. 1:
Allows the user to see the level and tier
of a monster.
Cast Time: Instant
MP Cost: 1
Distance: 10 **Meters**

This was something we were badly missing. Up until now, all we had to go by was the fact that I could look at a monster and make a guestimate of how good or bad of an idea it was to fight it.

Jessica still had a slot remaining for an active skill, but I felt that Preliminary Inspection didn't synergize with her trapper abilities at all. I said so.

"I feel like I should learn this," she replied. "I know it might not be the best I'll find...but I already am good at gathering enemy locations, why not spot their difficulty as well?"

In order for us to take advantage of this skill without her learning it, we would need a new group member, someone who willing to use a precious skill slot on Preliminary Inspection. That probably wasn't too likely to happen soon. On the other hand, taking this felt like a wasted active skill for us right now considering we knew which enemies around here were dangerous and which ones we could currently deal with. I mentioned my thoughts but Jessica countered immediately.

"It won't always be like this though. We saw it just yesterday. It's been merely a week and a half and there's already been a big tossup in what we considered normal. What happens if tomorrow it's tossed around again and there are new monsters? Can we say for sure we could identify the threats? The elites?"

Her point was valid, but I still felt badly about it. She was gimping herself to a more supporting role than if she waited to gain an offensive skill that enhanced her archery.

"Is it fine with you? To give up your active skill slot? You know what you're sacrificing?" I said.

She thought for merely a few seconds and then took the book and learned it without hesitation. I guessed that was her way of answering me. "Let's try it out then." I gave a wry smile.

As we encountered enemies she Inspected each of them:

Goblins were level 2, zombies level 1, and the weird alien creature was level 3; they were all rated normal mobs. The ogres and banshees were both Level 7 and considered normal as well. The abomination was Level 13, and the snake-headed demi-human was Level 15, and they were both showing up as normal as well.

Across the whole day, we didn't run into an enemy that might have been an elite, to see what Jessica's new ability made of it. The sun fell and it was our cue to call it a night. We ended the day with around fifty percent of our next level.

I had told myself that I wouldn't be sleeping on anything but a bed, but clearly the world had a different plan for me: I spent half the night wrapped in the torn-up carpet of an office, the other half I was on watch. I took the first watch, because whenever I slept, all my minions despawned. I think it was just a lack of consciousness that broke the connection between us, causing them to disappear.

The following morning I had the appetite for another Ration charge and Jessica did too. Very soon we were on our way and pushing hard towards the apartment building. "What if they aren't there when we reach it?" Jessica suddenly asked.

It was a negative thought, but understandable given the circumstances. There was no survival for them if they had been forced to engage with an abomination or a snake-headed type enemy. Those monsters were nearly twice the level of our friends and would strike them down in seconds.

"We'll deal with it as it comes." I said, trying to not dwell on that scenario too much. What we did now might be the difference between their life and death. My focus had to be on traversing the fastest route back. This wasn't necessarily the geographically quickest path but the one with the mobs that were easiest to kill.

We departed in an early fog without my having any summoned skeletons. I needed a corpse, and we were having trouble locating one.

At last, Jessica found us a goblin, allowing me to summon my core troops. I felt a lot more reassured, but I wanted to find another abomination to reanimate and decided against fighting and raising a banshee that was available. We weren't lacking for damage at all, partly because Jessica hadn't been saving stats like I was.

She had been steadily pumping STR and DEX ever since she hit 10 VIT. The arrows she shot were like bullets, and the damage was incredibly brutal to see. The arrows often ripped directly through the banshees and ogres like they were cutting through paper.

Sometimes an arrow tunneled through a monster's skull, and it wasn't even possible for my skeletons to reach it before it died. Her killing efficiency was impressive, and her tracking was just as good.

We allowed ourselves a slight detour to find an abomination as soon as possible, because that way we could continue to mop up the enemies in our path and increase our pace. It was relatively easy going, as we skipped all the snake-headed demi-humans we encountered.

The EXP was steadily climbing closer to Level 13, and when we were 90% of the way there, Summon Skeletons leveled up to 6. I was expecting the new benefit to another skeleton warrior, but what I got was a second skeleton general.

Summon Skeleton LV. 6
Cast time: Instant
MP Cost: 14
Distance: 4 Meters
Summons 4 skeleton warriors and two skeleton generals to fight for you.
Skeletons can now be summoned without a corpse. If skill is cast with no corpse available, only one skeleton is summoned, chosen at random.

I now summoned 5 skeleton warriors and 2 skeleton generals. My army of undead was steadily growing, and I felt I had come a long way from the two that I started with.

By constantly using the skill, even when she knew the information it would give her, Jessica had also improved Preliminary Inspection to level 2. It had a cost of only 1 MP, and since we weren't utilizing her traps currently, she spammed it on every enemy. It was a good idea, and also demonstrated that the more you used abilities, the faster they would level.

I wasn't sure if it was the same for my Summon Skeletons though, as the skill had leveled up even after my summoned warriors had been alive all day. I had only needed to recast it a few times, and not that often as of late. My belief for summoning skills, or mine at least, was that it gained EXP through the kills of the skeletons, or maybe skills simply leveled up by completing the purpose of the skill.

My minions' purpose was to kill enemies and the purpose of Inspect was to provide information: they leveled up in different ways. Regardless, the morning was progressing smoothly for us, and I didn't feel like any one of my skills was falling behind.

Admittedly, I wasn't using Decay enough, but it didn't work on the abominations, and we were skipping each snake-headed demi-human for speed. It would level when I found the time to work on it, which wasn't a priority right now.

There were down sides to Jessica leveling Preliminary Inspection to Level 2 though. The cost went up to 2 MP, which wasn't so bad. She could still spam it. An irritating issue was that I was now getting constant pop ups. It seemed that Level 2 of the skill allowed your party members to see the information you received on each cast.

Jessica reveled in the fact I had to endure the suffering alongside her, and somehow I couldn't voice a complaint. She had leveled it against my judgment, and was probably hoping that something amazing would come out of it.

We hit Level 13 merely ten minutes after finding the first abomination. We ended up pulling an abomination plus around fifteen more enemies. The weak addons merely died to the toxic bile while we put our full focus into downing the abomination.

It was unfortunate that my own reanimated abomination died during the fight, but I simply re-summoned with the new corpse. We gained a hefty haul of loot though, perhaps the best drops of any battle that I'd been in.

There were two Bandages, a Ration, a weapon, and also a mysterious coin. I took the Ration as agreed and split the Bandages between Jessica and I. The coin...I wasn't sure what it was.

Survival Medallion

That was as all that the message said, and there was no flavor text or indication of what it was for. Jessica suggested I hold onto it so I stored it in my inventory. The weapon that dropped was a two-handed sword.

**Zweihander: A long sword originating from the Middle Ages. It has incredible range and destructive capabilities.
STR +5, VIT +3, Attack Speed -10%
Grants the user Break Defense.**

I looked at the passive ability it granted.

Break Defense: Pierces 25% of an enemy's armor.

This seemed like a way better item than any of our starting weapons, which prompted me to assume it must have dropped off the abomination. I looked at Jessica with puppy eyes, and it took her only a moment to realize what I wanted.

"Go ahead. I don't care if you put it on one of your skeletons." She laughed and I enjoyed the moment. We were getting a good understanding of each other and, more importantly, how to work as a team to best effect. There was also now the perfect recipient to receive it: my second skeleton general.

I passed the magic weapon to him and marveled in all his glory. The large sword held in his two boney hands looked absolutely terrifying, and if he was my enemy, I would run for the hills immediately. My only curiosity was if the passive ability of Break Defense would work for him or not? It was highly likely that my minions couldn't receive benefits meant for users.

Regardless, his destructive capability must have jumped considerably, and I was itching to try it out. I let him play with the next goblin we encountered, and watched him split the little menace clean in half. I was so proud in that moment, like a father watching his son.

"We're close," Jessica said. "The apartment is directly west. When we left them, they would have come directly to here." It was discouraging that according to Jessica there were no downed monsters in the area as we walked slowly through the streets with their clusters of spawns.

"Wait, there are people here," she suddenly said, turning her bright eyes to mine.

"Is it them? Are they alive?" I asked excitedly.

"I don't know, it might be. They're just around the corner." And we made a beeline for their location, hardly pausing to smash through the mobs in our way. We entered an abandoned clothes store, and hurried up escalators that no longer moved. It wasn't Lucas and Rebekah, but there were three people backed up against a counter.

Chapter 14: More Survivors of the MMRPG Apocalypse

Three young men stared at us in bewilderment. They looked dirty and ragged, and for a moment I didn't know how to even interact with them. I was black garbed with a skull covering my face, probably not exactly the friendliest looking person they'd met.

After several seconds of silence I raised my hand, "Friendly," I said. They looked back and forth from Jessica to me; from their expressions it seemed that my skeletons and I were more alarming than Jessica was reassuring.

"Are you three aware of what has happened to our world?" Jessica asked.

There was a pause before one of them spoke up, "Somewhat."

"Well, don't mind his mask. It's just part of the system we have to deal with. Let's start with your names. I'm Jessica and this is Mike."

"Robert."

"Thomas."

"Alan."

As I looked at them, none of them gave me any bad or negative feeling, "How do you three know each other?" I asked.

Robert started to speak, "Thomas is my cousin. We were together when it all went down. Alan is a family friend."

"So if you know a little bit, you know there are monsters," said Jessica, "do you know about levels?"

It seemed Robert was the leader of their little troupe as he spoke again, "We do, and we're all level three."

"Skills, items?" I asked.

"We found one skill but it wasn't good and none of us wanted to learn it. No items," Robert took a step forward and looked more relaxed.

"How have you been surviving till now?" Jessica chipped in from the side.

"Well, we actually came from outside the city. The encounters out there were pretty scarce, mostly the green fellas and some undeads. They were easy enough to deal with."

I noticed that each of the men had a spear by their side.

"We entered the city yesterday," Robert continued, "and when we got here there were actually no monsters around. We started looking for something to eat and then we saw this incredibly bright light. We were more interested in the hunger in our bellies and continued to break into the stores for food.

"Before we knew it though, the light was gone, and monsters spawned in all around us. We darted for this building and been cooped up ever since. Was no way for us to get out."

"Have you seen anyone else?" I asked.

"No one else."

I turned to Jessica and started to whisper in her ear, "The area was probably clear because of Lucas and Rebekah. It pretty much confirms they were here yesterday."

"Most likely," she whispered back.

"Alright, I have a proposition for you three," I said. "We can help you survive, help you level, gear, and even change your class."

"But what's the catch?" Robert spoke before I could even finish my sales pitch.

"Your loyalty. You become an ally of ours, someone that we can call on. When things are rough and you are needed, you turn up and you follow our orders. Otherwise, you are free to do what you want. It's like being in a guild; if you know about that from gaming."

The three of them thought about it for only a moment, and then Thomas spoke, "I agree. Can't really refuse either way, y'kno? We'll starve soon."

"Same," the shorter one, Alan said. And Robert simply held out his hand, which I shook.

It seemed they were already reaching the breaking point with a lack of food and water. I pulled out a Ration and passed it to Robert. "There's three uses in this. Each of you can bite a third and you'll be satiated for at least the day ahead."

Robert took the ration curiously and then consumed one of the charges before passing it down the line. Their unshaven faces showed a smile for the first time. I guessed not being starving and thirsty was a good incentive to join a guild.

"Right now we don't have any skills available for you," I said, not wanting to give away Heal. "What we can do though is assist you in killing some enemies. There is almost no risk involved. We'll help you get started and then it will be up to you to show initiative," I continued. "As long as you do that, Jessica and I will find Class Changing Stones for each of you so you can pick a class.

"Gather everything you need, we may as well get started right away," I said.

"We can go now. We just have these spears and the clothes on our back." Robert said.

Jessica and I walked out to the already cleared street; our destination was still what we now considered home base. The possibility that Lucas and Rebekah had managed to return before the entire light incident took place was slim, but there was still that chance. If that was the case, they were safely inside waiting for our return.

Robert, Thomas and Alan joined us outside a moment later and I could hear them marveling at the lack of dangerous monsters. Here too, I was keen to show them how much more formidable my army of undead was. It was hard to get an idea when the skeletons were all clumped together in a room.

"We'll deal with the dangerous enemies on the way, and leave goblins and zombies specifically to you three. There's a kind we call ogres and another type we call banshees that we'll assist you with, which should give you a good boost of EXP. Have you three made a party already?" I asked.

Thomas seemed to be gaining in confidence. He said, "We are partied; we had a lot of free time to explore and discovered that menu option and a lot more."

I nodded and led the way with Jessica. The ogres and banshees were the most numerous enemy type now by far, which slowed us down a lot.

Originally, when we leveled Lucas and Rebekah we only subdued ogres as we were afraid of the ranged casts from banshees. It became clear though that a banshee couldn't cast without access to her hands. If my skeletons overpowered her and kept her hands restrained behind her back, there was no risk to the three young men.

As soon as a mob was held down by my skeletons the three newcomers came forward and fearlessly pierced it with spear stabs.

With three people attacking so ruthlessly, the mobs were dying in seconds.

It was obvious watching them that Robert, Thomas and Alan weren't completely inexperienced. They showed a lot of caution when dealing with the goblins so as to not get in the way of a thrown spear. Their own thrusts against zombies were powerful and Alan especially could down a zombie in a single blow to its chest or head.

Watching the newcomers, I'd have thought they were even higher level than three. Had Robert lied to me about that? I didn't think so. The thing about people who lived in the country was that they had a lot of outdoor experience. Hunters, typically, knew what they were about when it came to dispatching animals, and that probably extended to these enemies as well.

Even with having to share EXP, at the speed we were moving, they reached level 5 in fewer than thirty minutes. We were merely two blocks away by now from home base, and several items had dropped. One of them was a crude short bow, and since we also gained the skill Sharp Shooting, Robert decided he would take them both. "Already have experience hunting with a bow, so it just feels right."

There was also another Banshee's Wail that dropped, which I took. The remaining items were another skill book and a Ration. The skill was a new one:

Book of Shield Reflect LV. 2: Covers your shield in a protective layer that absorbs damage. After a certain threshold of damage is met, the damage is then reflected to the enemy.
Reflects 50% of damage absorbed back to the enemy.

Duration: 30 **Minutes**.
MP Cost: 7

It was an ability made for a tank, and surprisingly, Alan showed interest in it. The issue was that we didn't have a shield, but that could be fixed. "The skill says shield, but it doesn't say it needs to be an item. A lot of things can be used as a shield," I pointed out.

I turned to a destroyed minivan about fifteen feet away. It was merely the frame of the vehicle as the minivan had been completely scorched by fire. Both of my Skeleton Generals approached the side door and then ripped it off.

"What about this?" I asked, while they carried it over. Alan attempted to hold the van door and evidently found that it was surprisingly heavy. "Try casting Shield Reflect," I suggested. "If it works we can find something better for you to use."

The shorter and stockier of the young men took the skill book and then learned it, which was a gamble in itself. If it didn't work, then he would have a completely wasted skill. He grasped the doorframe again and then cast Shield Reflect.

To my surprise, a thin layer of light formed over the doorframe that gave it a glossy and polished look.

"Great!" Jessica clapped. "I suggest you put points into STR until you can wield that…thing effectively. You'll need STR anyway for your attacks."

Honestly, the entire thing looked comical. The doorframe covered a majority of his body, and as for a shield, it seemed like it would do surprisingly well. The next ogre we encountered I allowed Alan to tank and discovered another added benefit to using the door. The window frame that was now empty allowed him to safely stab from behind the protection of his shield. He pushed his spear through the hole several times and finally struck into the brute's neck, all the while blocking attacks.

Eventually, a light blasted from the shield and smashed directly into the ogre's chest. The force was so great that it cracked the enemy's ribs and sent it tumbling backwards and onto the floor. Alan rushed over and repeatedly pierced the ogre's neck until it perished.

"Not bad," I said from behind him. I had been poised the whole time to send the skeletons in, but it hadn't proved necessary.

Alan's face was red with excitement as he straightened from the body of the ogre.

Robert gave his friend a slap on the shoulder. "You couldn't have done that just ten minutes ago."

I heard a light cough from behind me and when I turned to look, Jessica beckoned me away to talk. "I think you should tell them we have Heal. Let Thomas decide if he wants to take that role. They seem promising, and if Alan is going to be playing a tank, he will be taking damage regularly and they will need a healer."

I didn't disagree with her, and I had come to form a positive outlook on all three of them. It seemed they were accustomed to surviving outdoors and scraping by with their wits. "All right, I'll ask him." We both returned back to the three newcomers who were now chatting cheerfully. It seemed we had given them a new lease on life.

"I do have another skill," I said. "It's called Heal, and if you want, you can have it Thomas. You are the only person who can still learn it."

Thomas, Robert's cousin, seemed conflicted, "I did want a role that was something more hands on…"

This time it was Jessica who spoke up, "Mike and I are strong now, but we went through a lot of pain, sweat, and blood to get here." She gestured towards me, "He nearly died two or three times, and we barely managed to scrape by. That was with him having his summoned skeletons to tank for us and me being ranged. Neither of us are close to the mobs we fight when we manage it right.

"In your group, it's clear now that Alan will be tanking, and that will put him at considerable risk. And suppose you go for a ranged option of some sort, that doesn't mean you are safe, either. As you've seen, goblins have ranged abilities, and so too will other mobs you face." She looked at him. "If I had the option to learn Heal when I started, I would have chosen it in a heartbeat knowing what I know now."

Her words seemed to sink in deep and caused Thomas to reflect. "Can I see it?" He asked. It was important he understood the requirements of the skill, anyway. Jessica looked at me and I removed the skill book from my inventory and passed it to him.

Thomas held it in his hands for a few moments and then looked at his two companions for confirmation.

"I think it's a good idea. Not having a way to reliably recover HP is going to set us back," Robert said.

Alan didn't say anything, but the stare he gave Thomas was pleading.

"Alright, I'll do it," Thomas said. The book in his hand vanished and that meant he'd learned Heal.

I found myself feeling pleased. Having a healer and a solid camp had to be a good choice for them. Deeper down though, I also felt some anxiety and hoped that nothing untoward happened to Thomas as a result of this moment. Skills that dealt damage seemed to be a dime a dozen, but good support skills were incredibly rare and sometimes carried a real risk of attracting aggro. In some systems, the role of healer required real expertise, to keep the tanks in the fight without overdoing it.

"Let's keep going. We're probably only about fifteen minutes out from our destination," I said.

We didn't need to baby them as we walked on now. Alan seemed eager to get a feel for his new role as a tank. Jessica and I made sure they kept a good distance away from the abominations and snake-headed demi-humans, though.

When the three men saw the intensity of our encounters with those mobs, they became a lot less cheerful, and it was clear we didn't need to warn them to stay clear. In fact, Alan went distinctly pale when he witnessed the abomination slamming a cleaver down over and over against my Skeleton General. I looked over at him, "The more damage it deals, the more damage you'll deal back, right?" I asked. It didn't seem like my remark made him feel any better.

"There's someone up there." Jessica said when we reached the apartment building.

"Just one person?" I asked.

"…Yeah…just one." Jessica said in an ominous tone, causing a grim feeling to well up in me. We raced up the stairs to the third floor and found ourselves in front of a room with a closed door. Jessica knocked but there was no answer, and not seeing any other option I beckoned the Zweihander-wielding Skeleton General to break down the door.

There wasn't the slightest response from inside when the door exploded into a mess of debris. Jessica raced through and into the bedroom only to find Lucas laying on a bed in a pool of sweat and blood.

A wound on his chest was wrapped in blood-soaked clothes and a large circle of blood had spread around him. "Quick, get that out of the way," I said to Jessica while pulling a Bandage from my inventory.

Jessica rushed to the side of the bed and removed the makeshift bandage Lucas must have applied to himself and exposed the deep gash across the side of his chest. It was an incredibly horrible looking wound, and from the smell alone I reckoned it was infected.

Even if I threw the Bandage on, I felt the chance of his survival would be nearly zero. And I didn't want to just cover up that mess and leave it festering underneath.

"Thomas, in here!" I yelled. The countenance on Lucas's face was bright red and the thick layer of sweat on him suggested he had a high fever. This was a flashback to my own previous infection.

Thomas entered the room and then was suddenly taken aback by all of the blood. It could have easily been mistaken for a murder scene.

"Heal him quickly," urged Jessica.

Thomas took another step forward and cast Heal. A bright, blue-tinted light covered Lucas and the red of his face receded slightly. Even the wound seemed to change color and looked much better. Despite that, it still needed to be bandaged.

The open wound closed after I applied the Bandage, but I reckoned there would be a deep, permanent scar there on his chest. Lucas's anguished face seemed to return to calm as he slept on the bed. "Heal him once more please. After that you three are free to go level. I recommend staying in the area though. We will be here," I looked over at Thomas. He nodded, cast Heal again, and left the room.

It seemed they were eager to level, as they left just a few moments later.

"Where is Rebekah then?" Jessica asked in a low voice. I didn't have an answer, and silent anxiety was all she received as her reply.

A part of me felt guilty. If we had stayed with the two of them for a bit longer, perhaps this might not have happened at all. As if Jessica could tell what I was thinking, she said, "It's not your fault. They also agreed to split up. You should get used to this, because it won't be the first time."

What she was saying was true, but I was being an idealist. In a perfect scenario, none of my guild would ever be hurt, be killed. I needed to harden my resolve; people were going to come and go: that was the nature of this new world we found ourselves in.

Chapter 15: Once More Into the Post-Apocalypse Streets

We sat and talked for about two hours before Lucas awoke. His eyes opened and he groaned as he sat up. His hand immediately reached for the now closed wound on his chest. I passed him a Ration which he took with a confused and almost lifeless look.

Jessica and I watched him eat in silence before she asked the question that was at the front of my mind too, "Where is Rebekah?"

Lucas held the ration in his hand as he stared off into space for a few moments. Tears began to fall and pitter onto his chest, "She...she didn't make it." His light crying turned into a full-on sob, "She is dead. Rebekah is dead!"

"What happened? Was it the blast of light?" I asked.

"The light..." he said. It almost seemed he was a bit confused still, "It was the light...monsters spawned around us. There were so many and we tried to run. Rebekah...she, she was hit by a bolt of frost," he looked at the ground as he recounted what occurred.

"I turned to help her and started to fight off the enemies closing in. There were so many ogres though." One of them dug its hook directly into my chest. His fingers traced the now scarred flesh. His voice cracked as he started sobbing harder.

"It was possible, maybe it was possible to save her! There was an abomination coming, it was going to aggro us! I fought as hard as

I could. I had to leave her when it aggroed." He sobbed with deep gulps. "I can still hear her screams." His story wasn't that detailed, but the basic idea came through.

They had been caught in the open when everything spawned. I could picture it: Rebekah frozen in place by a banshee and Lucas fighting to keep the brutes from reaching her, taking heavy damage in the process. Once an abomination aggroed them, however, he could no longer stay. He was forced to run as it approached and leave her behind.

I looked at him, "It's okay, you did your best." I said to him, "it was braver of you to live on then stay and die. I'm sure she would have wanted you to live on." My words only caused his tears to flow without pause, and maybe it was wrong to say these things, but I had wanted to give him some hope to grasp onto.

"I want to be alone, please," he said, looking up, pale faced, "just for a while."

Jessica and I returned to the living room, where I expressed a thought that I had been mulling over. "I want to find some place away from the city we can stay. We can't live here surrounded by monsters."

"What would you suggest?" she asked.

"We shouldn't have to go far into the countryside to find someplace suitable; there are factories, farms, compounds even, with nothing but green grass around for miles, giving us a decent line of sight to any approaching danger. It should be close enough to the city that we can drive in daily, but far enough to be safe from attacks at night."

"And if we can't find somewhere like that?" she asked.

"Then we build a base. Look at the materials around us. We have an entire city of supplies and tools at our fingertips." I didn't fully believe what I was saying, but given time it should be possible. Presumably there were people from all walks of life still alive: engineers, doctors, mechanics, farmers—they just needed to be found and brought together.

Jessica and I didn't go back out that night, and Lucas didn't leave the room. The three newest additions to our squad returned just as the sun was going down. In the end, they had reached level 7 and picked up a new sword for their tank Alan and a rod that gave WIS and boost to healing effect for Thomas.

I felt a tinge of jealousy for Thomas's new magic item, as we had found so many weapons, and yet none of them were caster weapons that suited me. But I reminded myself that persistence was key; eventually Jessica and I would be fully geared, and we'd be even more efficient.

Lucas didn't leave the room until early the following morning. While I slept lightly that night and nearby Jessica seemed to be awake for some of the night too. Although I felt no animosity from our new members, it wasn't guaranteed they couldn't have a change of heart and their presence at the other side of the room made me uneasy.

"How are you feeling?" Jessica asked Lucas when he finally appeared with the light of dawn. She kept her voice low, because the other three were still sleeping.

He sat down at the table and I got up and carefully did the same. Putting her blanket aside, Jessica sat up.

"Lost. Destroyed." This was understandable. He'd lost someone he loved in the most horrific way. I couldn't fault him for it.

"What level did you reach?" I asked. "Alan, Robert and Thomas are all level seven. It's possible you can join them." I had high hopes for him, and didn't want to see him give up now. If he gave up, we would have no choice but to abandon him. Every mouth that needed to be fed had to contribute.

I didn't say that to him, of course, but it would happen naturally enough if things went in that direction. We'd be moving forward while Lucas holed up somewhere. But to speak about this was likely to be counter-productive. His mood was no doubt volatile, and any attempt to point out that it was in his interests to keep fighting could trigger the opposite effect.

"You should go out on the streets with them. It will take your mind off your loss," Jessica came over and took the seat on my left. "It's no good staying inside with nothing but your thoughts, especially right now."

"Right." I was glad to hear Lucas agree, and I passed him another Ration. The supply of around fifteen days Jessica and I had was cut in half supporting these four. But I had promised, so there was no complaint on my end; it just meant we needed to be smarter, more efficient about acquiring them.

"What do you think of finding a safe place to stay? A base outside the city we could call home?" I asked

Lucas looked at me while stuffing the Ration in his mouth, "I say it's a good idea, except we would lose access to the city. And we need the option of levelling and gaining drops. What did you have in mind?"

"A farm? A ranch? There are factories out there too," I replied.

"It could work, but we would need solid transportation. I know of a farm about ten miles south of here: that's more than an hour walk on foot, but merely ten minutes in a vehicle."

"So we need vehicles then," Jessica said, "What else?"

Jessica and I had spent some time during the previous evening talking about this, but I was curious to hear Lucas' take.

"Well, the farmland won't be secure. Not without some tidying up. There's a natural mountain on the east side, but the west will be completely exposed. Barbed wire might deter the goblins and zombies, but anything else will wander right in through it."

"True, so what do you suggest?" I asked.

"We'd want to build up some real defense. Walls made of metal at the very least. The tools we'd need are all here in the city; there's also a steel mill just twenty miles in the opposite direction, but…"

"But?"

"This would require some serious man power," he said. "I don't suppose you have the expertise to use heavy machinery like cranes and a digger?"

I shook my head; Jessica shrugged.

"Then we need a lot of man power to make something like this happen," Lucas continued, "if it's to be at the scale I think you want to achieve."

"Right," I said. "So what we need now most is time. Time to find more allies; time to find vehicles and supplies and a location we could hole up in. Gas won't be a problem. I have access to the main tank at a station just west. Unless it's been ransacked that should last us months."

"So transportation is our immediate concern then?" Lucas confirmed.

"Yeah, I think so. Right now, we're basically holed up here and any chance of moving on is very risky. Once we leave we don't know what we'll run into. I don't want to find myself trapped by a horde of zombies on foot.,

"Agreed." Jessica chimed in.

Lucas went silent in contemplation, "Alright, I know I need to pull myself together and move on. You gave us a chance. I appreciate that. So I'll help you find and build a base. The opportunity to level here is important, but there's no sense of peace. I always feel on edge and danger feels like it's around every corner. People can't live like this and stay sane."

I was relieved to hear he hadn't given up. His effort to bounce back was commendable, and I praised him internally. He had a level head on his shoulders, and I felt that he was worthy of my trust. "Do you want to join the team of three?" I asked. "And get another level or two while Jessica and I search for a decent vehicle?

"I'll join them if they'll have me."

His response was like music to my ears, and I decided right then that Lucas would have my full support from here on out. Anyone that could go through a life-threatening situation, lose the closest person to them still alive, and still make the effort to keep going…I didn't know if I could do the same.

"You have my full support." I patted him on the shoulder, then whispered, "and you can also keep an eye on them, just in case."

Robert woke up around an hour later and his greetings to us woke up Alan and Thomas. To my surprise and joy, they had their own Ration for breakfast. Jessica presented the idea of Lucas joining them and after Lucas gave a demonstration of his abilities, was gladly accepted.

Alan was really happy to have another melee person to fight by his side, as facing enemies from the front alone felt isolating and a bit claustrophobic. As soon as it was confirmed Lucas was on board, I pulled a Class Changing Stone from my inventory and handed it to him.

The other three looked at it with awe, "This is a class changing stone," I said. "Using it allows you to pick a class. There will be generic options, and with some luck, special class choices. From what we understand, it's based upon your skill choice, stat allocation, and quite possibly weapon of choice."

Lucas took it with care and then stored it away. "I'm not quite ready to change yet," he said.

I had another stone in my inventory that had been meant for Rebekah, but I didn't reveal that information.

I could see the looks of envy on the faces of the other three, "Jessica and I will find three more of these for you all as well, but it will take some time. When the mobs all got mixed up, it became harder to find the elite enemies that drop Class Changing Stones. You'll know it when you see them though, and I recommend you don't fight them yet. They are well over five times more difficult than their non-elite counterpart, and that's a low estimate. If you do find them, you can report their location to us."

After I said that, Jessica stepped in to explain our interest in finding a permanent location to live in, and our need for transportation and supplies. I could see by their expressions that the other group were keen on the idea and insisted they would help in any way possible.

They departed and agreed to keep track of any vehicles and supplies we might be able to use for the planned base.

"Shall we go level as well?" Jessica asked.

"We should, but I also want to find a few useful things as well. I'd like to get some maps, up until now we've just been wandering around aimlessly. We need a direction."

I wanted to get away from town and out to a ¾ relatively ¾ safe place as soon as possible. There was something that neither Jessica or I had told the others, and that was to admit we'd seen an enemy we stood no chance against. And that this dark creature might be randomly roaming the city. Maybe the chance of encountering the monster again was extremely low, but it was a ticking time bomb. Eventually it would claim all our lives if we remained here as we were now.

Name: Mike Reynolds (27) **Class: Necromancer Level**: 13 **EXP**: 17%
HP: 525/525 **MP**: 240/240
STR: 5 **Fear Resistance**: 5
AGI: 2
DEX: 1
VIT: 15 +2
WIS: 15 +5
Available: 6

Skills: [A]Summon Skeleton LV. 6 |[A]
Decay LV. 1| [A] Reanimate Dead LV. 1 | [A]
Bone Armor LV. 1 | [P]Sixth Sense | [P]
Bravery LV. 2 | [P] Mutated | [P] Pain
Resistance LV. 2 | [P] Skeletal Mastery LV. 2
| [P]Intimidate Living

I took a quick look at my status before Jessica and I set out. We had reached level 13 on our way back yesterday, and gotten about a fifth of the way towards 14 before we ran into the other group and brought them with us. The 6 available stat points would sit in reserve for an emergency situation if need be.

By now, Jessica and I had a pretty good idea of how to approach each encounter. Even the demi-human enemies were easily defeated; it was just hard to finish them without one or two skeletons dying.

With Summon Skeleton reaching level 6, it was quite costly to have to re-summon them after each demi-human encounter. It made me look forward to levelling even more, as the increase to my mana pool would help sustain our grind, even if we did take on several of the snake-headed monsters.

"Are you familiar with this part of town?" I asked. I wasn't completely unfamiliar with the region we were in, which was mostly working-class homes. For a map we'd want to go to the most popular tourist areas, and those weren't on the outskirts.

"Not too much," Jessica replied.

"There's a district tourists usually frequent, and we should hopefully be able to get a map from one of the gift shops there."

She thought about it for a moment, looking towards the taller buildings of the inner city "Right, but wouldn't we have to get a lot closer to the center?"

"Yeah, I think it's about six blocks, but I won't know for sure until I see a familiar landmark. It's kind of hard with the way things are now." There was a lot of destruction and debris that made everything look out of place.

"We can, but I can say for sure that it's still much more dangerous going in that direction."

"Oh? Did your Tracking level up?" I asked.

"Yeah, it reached level three last night."

"So fast? My passive is only level two." I could hear the note of complaint in my own voice and quickly gave her a smile.

"I don't think my passive is as drastic a power increase as yours…" She shook her head.

Once my minions were set up, we started moving towards 6th and Wallace: the most active street for tourists.

"How bad is the danger then?" I asked Jessica.

"Well, two blocks in that direction and basically every brute and banshee is gone again. It's purely abominations and demi-humans. There's also something else there, too," she added. I gave her a look.

"No, it's not that deadly creature we saw. I said I wouldn't forget to always be on the alert for it and I won't. No, there's a new enemy type we haven't encountered yet."

"I want to push on if you think we can," I said. "Once we have a good map of the area we can make better decisions. We want a map that shows all the small towns, farms, and any construction within a hundred miles."

"So specific?"

"Nothing says we need to make this city our hunting ground. There's always the option of finding a new one. All I care about is that we find a strong base. We build it up. We make a name for ourselves, and people will come to shelter under us."

She nodded in understanding and gave me the signal that it was time to stop chattering. Just beyond this street the easy enemies dwindled to nothing and only abominations and demi-humans awaited us.

Chapter 16: When Deadly Spawns Fill the Streets of Your City

I made a habit of following Jessica's line of sight, as she was usually scouting out our movement plan. She was reliable in that respect and I had learned to leave our route to her and concentrate on watching for enemies. Most of my thoughts were taken up by thinking about the new and difficult encounters and how to minimize risk and maximize efficiency.

"Over there," she pointed to a goliath of an abomination, which surely had to be an elite enemy? The size of the dinosaur-headed monster was staggering; it was about twenty-five feet tall. But it wasn't only the size that was intimidating; the massive abomination was also different to the standard version in other aspects. The elite ogres and banshees were just large clones of the normal type, but this...

I was staring at a monster that had at least six arms coming from its bull-like torso, and all of them held enormous cleavers. "How are we even supposed to fight that? Can you inspect it from here?" I asked.

Jessica tried with success and the information that came back was interesting, albeit worrying. It was indeed an abomination, level eighteen, but it wasn't an elite. It was only marked as an 'exceptional' enemy. If this wasn't the elite form, then what was?

"We can avoid it," Jessica said, "follow me." I stuck close behind her as she pushed across the street and ducked behind a shoe store. Moments later, she nocked an arrow to her long bow and pulled an abomination that was in the alley ahead and we cleanly dispatched it.

I used the corpse to reanimate an undead version to add to our small force and then shadowed my partner as we edged along the alley. She ended up pulling three more abominations from range before it was safe to move across the alley and into an apartment block through the back entrance. From the top of the steps at the far side, I looked up and down the nearby streets: between the downed poles and charred building sides the city was so unfamiliar to me that I couldn't make heads or tails of exactly where we were.

We continued to move as stealthily as possible. I had to admit that Jessica's tracking skill was definitely as useful or more useful than most of my passive skills (except, perhaps Sixth Sense, which had the potential to be lifesaving). On two occasions already, she accurately avoided pulling a pack of enemies hidden around corners that could have wiped us out.

Jessica's skill allowed her to have a sense of the movements of patrolling mobs, and basically watch them move through walls. It was a godlike ability to say the least, and her decision to go Trapper was now showing its worth and then some.

We poked our head out of an alleyway about five blocks in. I scanned each direction as I looked for anything familiar, anything that could put a mark on our location. "There," I said with relief. I recognized a half-burned mural on the side of a duplex. I had come down here before to avoid traffic, and from here I knew how to get to 6th and Wallace.

"You see it? The mural there?" I pointed.

168

"The graffiti with the badly drawn butterfly?" she asked.

"Hey, it's called a mural to the people who live here."

"Right, so what does it mean to us?"

I pointed. "We're two blocks away. We need to head in that direction."

As soon as Jessica looked in the direction I had indicated her facial expression changed. It looked as if she'd eaten a pile of shit, "it's there..." she said.

"It?" I asked, and even before she could answer I realized what she was talking about.

"Run...we have to run," she said in a panic, and before I could even clarify what was happening, she grabbed my arm and started pulling me in the opposite direction. Her eyes scanned in a hurry before she dragged me up the steps of a home. She turned the door-knob but it didn't open.

"Break it down! Now!" she was frantic.

I had never seen her lose her cool this much, so I didn't hesitate. My skeletons chopped open the door and we raced inside. She dragged me upstairs to the second floor and into a bedroom. Her hands frantically locked the door.

I wasn't used to such a reaction, especially when my own Sixth Sense didn't indicate that anything was wrong. There was no prickling on the back of my neck. She inched over to the window and looked out onto the street towards the direction we needed to travel.

I crawled up beside her and looked out as well, waiting for any sign of that evil creature.

"It's here," Jessica suddenly said in a whisper. My eyes scanned the distance and I couldn't see anything at all. "On the wall of that building about three floors up," she added.

My eyes pinpointed the general area, and yet I could see nothing. She wouldn't be toying with me, so I continued to concentrate, and then I saw it. The clouds shifted and a ray of light bounced off the wall, and there was a refraction of light.

For a moment the creature's lizard-like body appeared there, and then it disappeared like a chameleon. My heart picked up speed: this was the creature I feared the most so far. "It can fucking go invisible?" I protested. I wanted to curse the developers of this 'game'.

Her eyes were glued to that spot, and my eyes were glued to hers. I couldn't see the evil being anymore, and when her eyes moved, I knew that it had as well. The top of a tree rattled with a sudden intensity, but there wasn't any wind. It was just a dozen meters away from us now, completely invisible from my sight.

What was it doing? Was it coming for us? Suddenly, its purpose was revealed. The creature launched itself from the tree at a speed hard to track with the naked eye, and landed directly onto to one of the snake-headed mobs. There was almost no resistance at all. Jaws forward, the creature itself, slim and spinning like a drill, smashed directly through the chest of its target: a one hit KO.

I'm sure my eyes nearly sprang from my sockets. That was instant death for either of us if we were hit. Bone armor would do nothing to stop that attack, I was sure of it. "Can you inspect it?" I whispered.

"I...don't know. I'm scared I might attract its attention," Jessica admitted. I didn't have anything to say to that, as it was the reasonable response. Was it possible that it would feel the detection? We had never tried it on any enemy remotely similar in power to this one.

After the snake-headed mob had died, disgustingly, the evil chameleon started to devour the corpse. The difference in size between the two enemies was enormous, and yet chunks of the demi-human disappeared into the reptilian's small frame as though its stomach contained another dimension.

I hadn't urged Jessica to inspect again, but information suddenly appeared before me. It was called a Fiend, level 33, Elite. Immediately after the inspection, the Fiend raised its head for a moment and started to sniff the air.

My heart was in my throat, the creature did not seem to have eyes; what was it using to search with? Scent? After the sniff, its long tongue extended and tasted the air as well. The Fiend didn't react and when it lowered its head to finish the dead monster I felt a wave of relief like I'd never experienced before. As soon as the corpse was devoured, the Fiend took off and moving away from us it disappeared in the distance once again.

We waited at least fifteen minutes before we decided it was best to continue. The faster we finished, the faster we could get out of here. "We should make this as quick as possible," I said.

"Agreed."

We returned to the street and made the most efficient beeline for 6th and Wallace possible. Snake-heads or abominations, we didn't care. They were both on the menu because my MP was recoverable and my life was not.

We ended up dispatching over ten enemies on the way.

Congratulations, you have reached level 14!

My necromancer passive triggered again, and I was able to add one more skeleton to my ranks. Besides that, a weapon dropped for me and armor for Jessica. There were also three consumables: a ration, an EXP UP potion, and an Elixir that increased STR.

Survivors Rod: A staff that symbolizes the hardship one has undergone to survive.
HP +50, WIS +3

There was no passive skill, but the massive increase in HP and 3 WIS was amazing. I happily equipped it.

Sniping Suit: A suit designed with optimal movement in mind.
HP +20, DEX +3, True Strike +7

More critical strike and damage for Jessica was welcome as well. I had to recognize too that the tight-fitting, dark leather suit looked good on her. She appeared lithe and deadly, like a movie heroine. And if I had been a little intimidated by her beauty on first meeting her, that was reinforced now. Looking away before she caught me staring, I checked my character sheet.

Name: Mike Reynolds (27) Class:
Necromancer Level: 14 EXP: 2%
HP: 590/590 MP: 213/260
STR: 5 Fear Resistance: 5
AGI: 2
DEX: 1
VIT: 15 +2
WIS: 15 +8
Available: 9

Skills: [A]Summon Skeleton LV. 6 |[A]
Decay LV. 1| [A] **Reanimate Dead LV.** 1 | [A]
Bone Armor LV. 1 | [P]**Sixth Sense** | [P]
Bravery LV. 2 | [P] **Mutated** | [P] **Pain
Resistance LV.** 2 | [P] **Skeletal Mastery LV.** 2
| [P] **Intimidate Living**

My HP was nearly 600 now, which felt absolutely amazing. It seemed the bar kept getting higher and higher though. At first I had been afraid of the goblins, and then the snake-headed humans, and now it was the new Fiend. I was also afraid of guns in the hands of other survivors. The power of a rifle or shotgun terrified me, and I wasn't sure even now if 600 HP meant it was possible to withstand a bullet to the chest.

**EXP UP Potion: Increases EXP gain by
+50% for thirty minutes.**

Showing the potion to me, Jessica said, "I suggest we save it and if we get another, we can go all out somewhere rich in targets."

I nodded with appreciation at the sentiment. We had a bond between us, and should keep levelling side by side without either of us falling behind if it could be avoided.

Our destination was only just across the street now, and we had dispatched all the enemies that could hinder us from reaching a door that had been torn open.

Having scampered inside, worried that the place might have been smashed up by mobs, I was delighted to see most of the goods were still on the shelves, and immediately in front of me I found a basket with rolled up maps. I didn't hesitate to grab every single one and put them all in my pack. There was a map of the city on the wall with a red dot marked 'You are here!' on it. I ripped that off as well and stuffed it away.

After that was done, we treated ourselves to some candies that were still good. Our bags were completely packed when we left, and there was no doubt that Lucas and the three others would enjoy some of them too.

A journey that had taken us several hours grinding our way through mobs ended with a race back that lasted less than ten minutes. We had our maps, and that was good enough for me.

Chapter 17: Necromancer and Archer: The Best RPG Class Combination?

We spent the next two days grinding and managed to hit level 16. Although the rate of EXP gain had slowed considerably, with an added skeleton and also adding a second reanimated dead to my summoned squad, our kill speed improved significantly.

I had begun the grind by reanimating two of the demi-humans, and they were absolutely killing it in terms of damage. During the first day Reanimate Dead reached level 2, and Summon Skeletons reached level 7; the following day Bone Armor reached level two, and a completely new skill was granted to me as a Necromancer skill at 15. It seemed to me that Summon Skeletons was staying at a little under half my level, maybe falling behind slightly.

Summon Skeleton LV. 7
Cast time: Instant
MP Cost: 18
Distance: 4 Meters
Summons 4 skeleton warriors and two skeleton generals to fight for you.
Skeletons can now be summoned without a corpse. If skill is cast with no corpse available, two skeletons are summoned.

The Skeletons summoned are chosen at random.

Another change to Summon Skeletons at level 7 was that summoning two instead of one without a corpse, not that I used it in such a way very often.

Reanimate Dead LV. 2: Allows the user to reanimate the corpse of a recently defeated enemy. User can only have one reanimated corpse. User cannot reanimate an enemy killed by another User. Cannot reanimate Elite and boss type enemies.
Cast Time: 2 seconds
MP Cost: 30 MP
Distance: 1 Meters
Corpse Efficiency +15%

I was disappointed that levelling up Reanimate Dead didn't grant me the ability to summon another monster to our side. What was new was something called Corpse Efficiency. I thought about this for a while and came up with a working theory for what Corpse Efficiency 15% might mean. Probably, it referred to the extent to which the powers of the corpse matched those of the slain mob. Given that the already reanimated dead were at least half as efficient as when they had been alive, it didn't mean that the undead version was only 15% as powerful as the living version. This was some other scale of progress and I hoped that I'd be able to see the difference in the strength of the newly raised undead. If I kept levelling up the skill, what would happen? Would it cap when the undead mob reached the same strength as the living version or would I able to go beyond the original?

It was a long way off, but I looked forward to finding out.

Bone Armor LV. 2: Covers the user in an armor of bone that greatly reduces damage from physical and magical attacks.
Armor value is based upon thirty-five percent of the Users maximum HP value.
Eighty percent of damage taken is absorbed by Bone Armor before reaching the User.

My Bone Armor upgrade had led to me gaining a bit more absorption based upon my HP and the efficiency went to 80:20, shield: life.

Then there was my new Necromancer skill, which I felt was incredibly useful.

Vast Shadows: Allows the User to hide his minions within his shadow. When cast, minions enter into a state of suspension and cannot attack or defend until Vast Shadows is cast again. Users and enemies cannot see or detect minions hidden within your shadow. Skill can only be used while you have a shadow.

At first, I didn't quite understand the skill, if I needed a shadow, then it was only useful during the day. And what was the point of hiding the undead squad besides when I needed stealth? It was only after having cast the skill and I slept did I understand. Even when I did not have a shadow, for example, when I was sleeping, the minions remained trapped in Vast Shadow.

My fear had been that using the skill in this way could be a double-edged sword. If someone attacked during the night and I had no shadow, I might not be able to find my previously summoned undead warriors if I'd placed them in Vast Shadow. Fortunately, that proved not to be the case. When I cast Summon Skeletons I got new ones and those in the Vast Shadow simply vanished. The real bonus though, was that casting Reanimate Dead was different: it brought the minions back from the Vast Shadow.

This aspect of the skill made it incredibly nice for getting going quickly in the morning. It cost 30 MP to cast each time for a total of 60 MP, but casting two reanimates would have been the same. The difference was we didn't have to kill anything to get me a corpse. Now I could park them at night and bring them out of Vast Shadow in the morning, I realized just how tedious it was having to start the day by finding two new corpses each morning.

It wasn't just Jessica and I who had made big progress over the two days. Lucas and the trio had reached level 10, and because Alan proved himself a very effective tank, they had even risked and successfully downed two of the elite enemies on their own. Both had been ogres, so tank types. Our friends hadn't dared to try a banshee, because of our warning about the fear effect.

That meant that all three Class Changing Stones that we needed had been discovered. I had kept the third so far, not for any particular reason besides thinking that maybe they would obtain a third on their own and mine would then be spare. It was when listening to Alan talk about the battles that I realized there was something else I had neglected.

The wording of Reanimate Dead clearly said the skill couldn't raise the corpses of Elite enemies. I had taken for granted this meant that I could only use the skill on common monsters. The talk of elites reminded me of the large abomination that was described as an Exceptional enemy. Maybe I could raise Exceptionals.

The fact I hadn't thought to try this was an oversight by me, totally, because if it was possible to reanimate an Exceptional snake-headed monster or even an abomination…Well, when paired with Vast Shadows, this would allow me to save really powerful summoned monsters indefinitely: it would definitely be worth the investment of time to find and defeat one and then summon it as my minion.

Along with our gains in levels and skills, we had found three possible vehicles in good shape for exploring the countryside. There were a lot of abandoned vehicles in reasonable condition, but most of them didn't fit the requirements we wanted. We specifically wanted trucks, or SUVs: vehicles which had good storage capacity and space for people, so as to maximize our gas usage.

The plan for Jessica and I today was to attempt an Exceptional abomination and then head to the west city entrance and use my minions to try and move the debris and destroyed vehicles from the street.

We chose the west highway because there were two steel-mill factories in that direction as well as a food production plant. Not only that, there was a large farm nearby as well, which would make an amazing base if fortified properly. I could see from studying the map that there was no doubt it could hold a space for several hundred people.

Name: Mike Reynolds (27) Class: Necromancer Level: 16 EXP: 2%
HP: 620/620 MP: 270/270
STR: 5 Fear Resistance: 5
AGI: 2

DEX: 1
VIT: 15 +2
WIS: 15 +8
Available: 15

Skills: [A]Summon Skeleton LV. 7 |[A]
Decay LV. 1| [A] Reanimate Dead LV. 2 | [A]
Bone Armor LV. 2 | [A] Vast Shadows
[P]Sixth Sense | [P] Bravery LV. 2 | [P]
Mutated | [P] Pain Resistance LV. 2 | [P]
Skeletal Mastery LV. 2 | [P] Intimidate
Living

I had so many extra points still banked and decided it was time to use some. Four points went into DEX, five each into both VIT and WIS and the remaining stat would sit there for now. I wanted some cast speed to start leveling Decay which is why I brought DEX up to 5.

We made our way towards the Exceptional abomination, and before we had fought our first enemy, a nervous excitement covered my entire body. Despite the risk, I couldn't remember a time in my life when I had looked forward to something so much as this.

The sheer amount of power I would have if I could gain an Exceptional abomination and an Exceptional demi-human as reanimated servants. I couldn't even fathom it, honestly.

We found our target at record pace thanks to Jessica's tracking.

"How should we go about this?" I asked. Looking at the huge monster didn't produce any feelings of uneasiness beyond those you'd expect when confronted by a dinosaur-headed giant wielding six massive cleavers. Since Sixth Sense was not warning me of any unpleasant surprises, I was confident we could defeat him, the question was, at what cost? I would probably lose most of my summoned undead, but it was a sacrifice I was willing to make.

From what we knew of Exceptional enemies from experience, it seemed they always had an additional ability. The Exceptional ogre had the ability to use his meat hook as a projectile, the Exceptional banshee had an AoE fear.

What would this abomination do? "I think we just throw your skeletons at him till he goes down," Jessica said. And somehow, that seemed to be the best option. "I'll set a quagmire trap here and leave an ankle snare for a possible retreat. We run if it turns out to be more than we can deal with."

I nodded my head and sent forward both my reanimated demi-humans as well as both skeleton generals. They were going to hold the front, and the rest of my warriors would remain behind the abomination to avoid any collateral damage from its six cleavers.

A tree-lined square in front of a ruined library served as our target area in which we would tank the mob. It had an alley on the opposite side of the direction of the pull, so that if my generals couldn't cope we could run up the alley for quick escape.

Watching the mob thump a heavy path back and forth in the distance, Jessica nocked an arrow and looked at me. Heart beating fast, I gave her a nod. The arrow flew out with incredible force and caused the air to whistle.

It was a direct hit into one of the abomination's eyes, which no doubt would help us greatly in this encounter. Her marksmanship had become stellar, more so than it was before and I felt a flow of warmth towards her. If someone told me to put an apple on my head and stand 50 meters away, I had complete confidence in Jessica that she would hit it properly.

The abomination came stomping in our direction, its pus and fatty tissue oozing while chains dragged along the floor. My minions were waiting just beyond the quagmire trap, and as soon as it triggered, swarmed him.

The monster's six cleavers did not swing independently, but instead came two-together for each of its opponents. Strong blows began to rain down against a zweihander-wielding skeleton general and the other target was one of the two reanimated snake-headed demi-humans, holding shield and trident. This was good news actually, as it wouldn't randomly one-shot one of my weaker skeleton warriors.

Putrid and rotten flesh continued to slough off the abomination with each blow from my minions' attacks. Jessica put all of her focus into damaging the face of the monster and had successfully taken out both eyes. Still, the abomination held its ground and thunderous attack after thunderous attack slammed down.

With such heavy blows, those in front of the monster had to commit to full defense and only one of my snake-headed minions could freely attack. His trident constantly stabbed into the thick but rubbery flesh. Putrid pus and noxious gas would occasionally explode outward in a disgusting mist: perhaps that effect would be poisonous to a human tank, but whether it was or not, the spray had no effect on the undead.

We knew we were making steady progress when the abomination suddenly secreted a noxious bile that filled the air. We'd reached this point of the battle with none of my tankier minions having perished. I could hear the constant crashing of cleaver attacks though and was in no doubts that my minion's bones were being splintered.

The free snake-headed demi-human began secreting a venomous concoction of its own, and sprayed a thick spew of liquid that seared through the monster's dead flesh like acid. So far, so good, but I was worried about what would happen next.

The Exceptional enemies we had encountered so far had used a skill once their HP were brought low enough to trigger it. Whatever hidden ability this abomination had, it was coming soon. And just a few seconds after that thought crossed my mind it happened.

The abomination's dead flesh started to glow a reddish hue and its body became enlarged, raising it up another two or three feet. The blows that it launched now were many times faster and stronger before. The monster clearly had an enrage mechanic and it had significantly upped its damage and attack speed.

My two minions facing the blows of the Exceptional mob started to falter, and they quickly dropped to their knees. The zwei-hander minion was the first to fall, and then the demi-human. The shield-wielding skeleton general braced himself with bended knee as blow after blow rained down upon him.

Four cleavers collided with the shield of the skeleton general and slammed him into the concrete. I could see the bones of his arm shattering and fracturing until they exploded into a white mist.

The cleavers didn't stop there and smashed the helmet upon his skull and then shattered his corpse. Now only my reanimated snake-head remained in front of us while the five skeleton warriors pummeled it from behind.

There was also my one ranged skeleton that stood near me and Jessica constantly nocking arrows, but I doubted he was dealing a significant amount of damage. My reanimated demi-human raised his trident and tried to block attack after attack from the six cleavers.

"We don't flee," Jessica said without taking her eyes off her target. It was clear that the monster's buff had made him incredibly fast, and I was afraid it might well be able to outrun us on foot. Jessica was right. We had to stand and give it all we had. I drew heart from the incredibly battered appearance of the abomination: he had to be on desperately low hp.

My snake-head only lasted another three blows, which in reality was actually nine, before he collapsed and disappeared. The five skeleton warriors continued to fearlessly hack away only to be immediately clobbered to pieces.

Having readied myself for this, I cast Summon Skeleton and spawned two skeletons to slow the monster's advance towards us as Jessica continued to put arrow after arrow into his skull. These new minions could only survive a single blow, but at least the monster stopped moving in order to swing all six blades to get rid of them. And so I cast my summoning ability again, and again.

I was at the point where my MP would run out in moments with this spamming, and the enemy was still not dead. I could only use the ability three more times. "Two casts left!" I shouted. "Last one!" Then I was out of MP.

Beginning to panic and furious at not having spawned a single skeleton general, I thought it was time to run. Jessica had already preplaced traps in the alleyway, so we had a good chance of escape. "Run!" I cried and was relieved when Jessica gave a nod. I had been worried she was so carried away by the battle and how close we much be to winning it that she'd miscalculate and get herself killed.

As we ran, Jessica fitted a single final arrow to her bow and even though the sounds of its pounding feet were getting closer, looked back over her shoulder, released the arrow into its eye socket and downed it.

The Exceptional abomination collapsed to the floor, causing the ground to quake. I wanted to fall on my ass right then and there, but instead rushed over to the body and immediately cast Reanimate Dead. Everything that had happened so far, none of it mattered to me as much as this moment.

Except nothing happened. I needed 30 Mana. "I have to rest up," I explained to Jessica.

"Lie down, close your eyes, do what you have to. I'll take the drops and keep guard. And Mike?"

"Yeah?"

"Good fight. We were at our limit there."

"You too."

It was hard, when my heart was pounding so much, to relax and encourage my natural mana regeneration to tick upwards. Were we going to lose this opportunity? How long did corpses last before they couldn't be reanimated?

At least we had a decent chunk of EXP, nearly 70% of a level. And the information on the drops that Jessica shared with me was encouraging.

Meat Cleaver: A butcher's cleaver used for dealing with large animals.
STR +7, VIT +3
Grants the user Overpowering Strike
Overpowering Strike: Strikes against enemies always inflict Bleeding.

Survival Medallion
Corpse Runners: A pair of boots made from the skin of a cadaver. They offer small protection but put you closer to death.
VIT +1, Movement Speed +10%

Grants the user Skeletal Mastery.

Now that was an interesting development. The boots granted an ability that I already owned myself. I wondered if that meant they would have no effect or perhaps they would add to my existing ability. "Mind if I try the boots on?"

"Go ahead."

A moment later I equipped them and checked my character sheet. "Good news, they have leveled up my Skeletal Mastery." I noticed that the color of the number showing the level of the skill had changed, presumably to indicate it came from an item.

"You keep them. I was almost disappointed because I'd like that movement boost. But extra hit points and strength for your skeletons is just great. At least I have that medallion. That's one each now."

"Any idea what they do?"

"Not a clue." She laughed and I opened my eyes to look at her. "It's probably just the game playing a joke with us, like giving us a collector's item for after all this is over."

At last, my MP reached 30 and immediately I cast Reanimate Corpse. A beautiful and gigantic abomination appeared in place of the body. There was just a singular skeleton remaining, my archer, and then this wonderful creature. Seeing the strength of this undead monster firsthand, I honestly believed this minion alone was stronger than all of my skeletons combined.

Chapter 18: Ghost Hand

The Exceptional abomination was all that we came for, and having obtained it, we completely changed directions and began heading west.

I allowed the newly raised undead to run ahead and completely wreak havoc on everything. It was so powerful as a minion that it could kill the snake-headed enemies entirely by itself. I only tested this once though, in fear that something unexpected might happen and I'd lose him.

I didn't have enough MP to fight another Exceptional enemy today, although the goal was to get a second one. Jessica and I agreed that if she could find an Exceptional snake-headed type we would keep track of its location and kill it at a later time.

By the time I had re-summoned my minions and a second re-animated corpse, I was already depleted of mana again, which by my standards was dangerous. Difficult battles were absolutely something I wanted to avoid today.

Because of that, we skirted around the outer edge of the city as we moved, and the added distance made it take around two hours of walking to reach the main route west. Fortunately though, we did manage to hit level 17 off the brutes and banshees and a few of the stronger enemies before finding the western most exit. The level up didn't refill my mana bar, unfortunately, but I got a small boost and came back up to 45 MP.

As we looked at the thoroughfare, my heart sank. It was a mess. Abandoned vehicles lay in all sorts of positions, some on their sides and some upside down. Driving west along this highway was likely to be an arduous and slow process. I was, however, underestimating the strength of the Exceptional abomination; it only took only twenty seconds or so for my reanimated corpse to move each vehicle. He simply shoved it along the road and out of the way, sparks flying.

Even if there were no tires on the vehicle and it was just frame, metal scraped along asphalt as he used brute force to move them out of the road. The undead abomination on its own was enough to move a single vehicle, and I could group together the remaining summoned undead to work as a team to move another.

Although this made progress a lot faster than I had first expected, the reality was there were hundreds upon hundreds of vehicles in the way. If we wanted to create a clear road out of the city, it had to be done. So systematically, we set about the task. It felt like a grind, except one without any EXP gain.

Something happened around thirty minutes into our cleaning session though. Jessica suddenly stopped and looked west, "There's people coming…four of them."

The road westwards wasn't purely flat, it rose slightly, which meant the horizon was not that far away. Not far enough away to be comfortable. "In a vehicle? On foot?" I asked.

"They aren't moving fast enough for it to be a car. I think they're running."

I immediately moved my minions to behind a building and out of sight. If the approaching people weren't hostile, they might take one look at the squad of undead monsters and just end up turning and hauling the other direction upon seeing us. We found a spot to hide and observe as we watched the furthest point we could see down the road.

Only seconds after settling into the second floor of a ruined office, four figures appeared on the hill, and from what I could tell, they were all women. Their faces were red and frantic as they struggled to not trip over their own feet.

"There's people behind them," Jessica said. "Two people moving fast, probably in a vehicle."

Was it our business at all to interfere in whatever was happening? The look on the faces of the women told me they were terrified for their life. Whoever was chasing them didn't have good intentions. "Let's help," I said.

A grim-faced Jessica nodded, and we ran back down the stairs and ducked into a side alley where I gathered my team. According to Jessica, the women would not be caught until after our position, which would give us a chance to see what the situation was. None of the approaching women triggered a warning feeling from Sixth Sense, or seemed dangerous at all. It was completely possible none of them had leveled up even once.

As the women reached the stretch of road we had cleared, I could see a jeep coming over the hill at a fast speed. There was a man driving and another man standing up hollering into the air, "Stop running and you won't be punished!"

Once the women were close, Jessica stepped out and waved her arms overhead to intercept them. They were spooked and if they hadn't been exhausted, I think they would have scattered rather than give her a chance. But Jessica kept up a steady, calming introduction, "Come here; come here quick. We're not going to harm you; we'll protect you. It's okay, stay behind me."

All of the women were red-faced; one was crying, and another put her hands on her knees and threw up on the spot. All of them were breathing so heavily I wondered if any of them were close to collapse. But they needed to keep moving and get into the shelter of our alley. Since I couldn't shout without scaring them, even with my skull mask tipped up onto my forehead, I left it to Jessica and this worked, one by one the women came up to us.

With a roar followed by the shriek of its brakes, the jeep arrived at the cleared road, where it came to a stop about fifty feet from the alley. The two men leaped out and started to walk forward, checking the side streets.

When they were just a bit away from where we were hiding, Jessica and I stepped out of the alley. My minions didn't show themselves and remained hidden, as I didn't want to reveal any of my cards. The men noticed us, faces caught in a look of shock before they adjusted to try to assume looks of haughty confidence.

When they were barely twenty feet away, they noticed the women standing behind Jessica and I.

"There you are, come over here," the driver said. "You won't make this hard if you know what's good for you." He was dressed in a black leather jacket and jeans, as was his companion. It seemed to me like a uniform.

"What's happening here?" I asked, pulling down my mask. "It doesn't seem like these women want anything to do with you."

The two men looked at me with a bit of hesitation, no doubt affected by the Skull Mask's Intimidate Living.

"Listen, this is none of your business. It's also none of our business either. They're property of our boss, Ghost Hand." It seemed that the man—the passenger—was hoping this name would have a bit of deterrent.

190

"Never heard of him." I turned back and looked at the four women behind, "Is that right? Are you the property of Ghost Hand?" I asked with sarcasm in my voice. As far as I was concerned, I didn't care what the men said. Humans were never property.

The women shook their heads frantically emphasizing how completely they disagreed, but none of them dared speak up. "It doesn't seem like that's the case. You can leave now," I said to the two men.

"You don't want to do this friend. It won't end well for you…" The driver said.

"I'm not your friend, and you can leave. I won't tell you again. Stay a little longer and I'll kill you both." Their expressions showed that the pursuers felt stuck between a rock and a hard place. "Tell this Ghost Hand whatever you want. He can find us here whenever he wishes," I added firmly. I was confident I could easily kill both of them, but I didn't want to unless I really had to.

The two men's faces turned red, but neither of them dared to attack. I could tell they wanted to test me, but I really wasn't kidding. Perhaps they were terrible people worthy of death, but who was I to make that kind of judgement and act on it? I didn't have the full story either, and maybe they were just pawns for this Ghost Hand character.

They started whispering to each other and then turned to leave. That was when Jessica raised her bow and released an arrow. It flew out with pinpoint accuracy and went directly through the keychain in the driver's hand. The car keys were pinned into the ground, "The vehicle stays. You two can walk," she said.

It seemed that this entire situation was pissing her off to no end. When she was quiet and reserved like this, I knew she was bubbling inside. The men turned to complain, but she pulled her bow back and nocked another arrow. No doubt she was prepared to put an arrow directly through a skull right now, and I wouldn't blame her.

Whatever words they were going to say caught in their throat and they started to sprint into the distance. Only when beyond the horizon and beyond the point that Jessica could feel them with her detection did she dare lower her bow.

At her nod, I lifted my mask and turned towards the four women.

"Are you okay?" Jessica asked.

The nearest of them immediately grasped Jessica's upper arm with both hands, "Thank you...thank you so much. You can't imagine what we've been suffering." She was wracked with sobs.

"Let's stop for today and head back," I said to Jessica, then looked towards the women. "This is no place to have a conversation."

"We have somewhere safe we can stay," Jessica explained to them. "It's at least an hour walk away though. Can you all make it?" Jessica was already in her pack grabbing leftover candy and handing it to the women.

They nodded and Jessica whispered to me, "stay back with your undead. You'll spook them otherwise." Then she set off with the women while I waited. I couldn't afford the MP to use Vast Shadows and then remove my minions from it if there was a dangerous situation, so they would just have to accept that I was acting as a rearguard.

We hadn't gone far though, when one of the women looked back and caught sight of the Exceptional Abomination who was slow to duck aside. She screamed.

"It's okay. Those undead have been created by Mike. They will obey him." Jessica said. It took at least three minutes of constant soothing before the women resumed walking again. And it seemed to me they were distinctly less enthusiastic than before.

Even after I showed them everything was okay, and that the minions were fully under my control, the women constantly looked my way with fearful stares back in my direction. *C'mon…I just helped save you…*

I stayed back and allowed Jessica to talk to them, as they seemed completely uncomfortable being anywhere near me. We had cleared all the spawns around here, and because of that the journey back was safe. They hadn't seen a single enemy at all.

The other group were nowhere to be seen when we returned to the apartment, which I thought was for the best. It would definitely be less intimidating with just us two there to ask questions.

Once we'd given the women drinks and they had refreshed themselves, I let Jessica do all the talking and we heard the entire situation. According to these women, someone called Ghost Hand had occupied the very farm I'd identified as a promising place for a base, and he had been gathering people.

The problem was he wasn't a good person, or a good leader. There were only four of five people close to him that had any levels and abilities, but around thirty people stayed there: the rest of them being either unleveled or extremely low level.

The problem arose when it came to women. Besides being required to do menial labor, they were treated as prostitutes. Refusal was not an option, and apparently two women had already been killed for refusing to play that role.

According to them, the farm was in good shape and had remained relatively unaffected by the apocalypse. Crops were harvestable and there were animals to be tended. Ghost Hand had already started to fortify the farm as well.

The men of the compound that he trusted were able to level and learn skills, and those that he didn't trust did hard labor. Apparently, Ghost Hand's trusted men regularly searched in all directions to recruit survivors, whom would unknowingly end up in this slave-labor type situation.

The four women had managed to steal a vehicle and drive towards the city in hopes of escape. It was the one direction that Ghost Hand was afraid to explore because of the density and difficulty of the monsters. Unfortunately, about a mile out from where they had met Jessica and I, their car broke down and they were forced to continue on foot.

As I heard their story, I had felt a growing anger towards Ghost Hand, and Jessica was visibly livid by the time we had all the information. Ghost Hand and his trusted little group were essentially luring in women with the promise of safety, raping them, and forcing them into slavery.

I looked at Jessica and knew what she was thinking.

"We have to go there," she said.

"I agree, but we'll have to convince the others." Our task was clear. To overthrow this Ghost Hand. He had already prepped the farm and recruited people to his cause but was abusing the situation instead of helping humanity survive.

We asked what they knew about him, but they didn't know the extent of his abilities. Just that he had some sort of telekinetic power or invisible hand. They had been grabbed by it, choked by it—it was some sort of invisible force.

Ghost Hand and his men also had a few guns as well, which I expected but was a concern all the same. Although guns were not as dangerous to me as when I'd been low level, it seemed likely that a high-powered sniper rifle shot to the head could kill me. Hopefully, my HP could absorb a body shot and make it non-lethal.

It was mid-day and with my MP already being dangerously low, I stored the summoned undead away in Vast Shadow and decided it was fine to call it an early night. The women were completely exhausted, and after explaining their situation, just wanted a place to sleep.

Maybe Jessica had caught their names but I didn't know them. It didn't matter for now, that would come in time. Jessica set them up in the bedroom we usually slept in and put her own bedroll by the door to be sure that no one would bother them.

I didn't know how to deal with this situation. It was obvious these women had been abused, and that could go several ways. In a whispered conversation though, Jessica convinced me that once we took the farm, there would be opportunities for all of them to begin the path to levelling up, regardless of how their experience had altered their perception of the world and the people around them. They could be valuable members of the community we wanted to build.

Chapter 19: It's a Dog-Eat-Dog Post-Apocalypse World

It was nighttime when Lucas and the young men returned, but there was something odd about them today. Looking at Robert gave me an ominous feeling that I recognized from Sixth Sense. I'd never before experienced such a feeling coming from him. I tugged on Jessica's shirt and flicked my eyes towards Robert to give her a bit of an early warning.

Jessica played it off naturally, but she sat slightly behind me and her bow appeared in her hand. Her actions didn't look like anything out of the ordinary, and no one paid her any mind.

I asked myself whether I should confront Robert, but that sense of danger was nagging at the back of my neck with such insistence that I knew it would be a mistake to ignore it.

One of my biggest concerns was that if something went wrong and I had to recall my squad of summoned undead, I wouldn't have enough MP to recast Vast Shadows. Still, I had to find out what had changed and why it had changed in a way that spelled danger for me. "How did leveling go?" I asked, not looking at anyone in particular.

"It was good." Lucas said. "We all hit level eleven and a few items dropped. We didn't get our third Class Changing Stone yet though."

"Did something unusual happen today Robert?" It was such an out of the blue question that it took him off guard. While he stared at me in surprise, I had an intuition about what the issue might be. "Did you gain anything special today?"

"Ah…not really, just leveled," he replied curtly.

It was then that Lucas spoke up, "Oh right, Robert got an interesting drop. He found an item, but it was actually a gun, with bullets."

"An item that was a gun? And it came with bullets?" I asked. Almost immediately after Lucas revealed that information the feeling of danger emanating from Robert pressed down on me even more powerfully.

"What kind of gun was it Robert?" I asked.

"A shotgun and it works with my sharpshooting, too." The way he looked at me was odd, almost as if articulating a threat.

The reality was that I didn't feel safe knowing he had a gun. The warning from Sixth Sense must mean his opinion about our relationship had changed for the worse. "I'll be honest," I said, "for now I don't want anyone to have guns."

His face tried to hide his annoyance, but I could tell that he wasn't happy with my comment. "I know it's your item, but I hope you'll understand and hand it over to me for safekeeping for now," I said.

The entire atmosphere in the room took an odd turn, almost an awkward one, there was a mix of surprise and embarrassment on people's faces. But they couldn't feel the presence of an intense threat. In trying to understand what that threat was, I decided it had to be this new weapon, and the fact that he was radiating such danger meant he was not afraid to use it.

To make matters worse, our conversation had woken the women next door, who now poked their heads out in curiosity. As soon as Robert saw not one, but four scantily dressed women his eyes widened with intense interest.

When he looked back at me, I could almost see the calculation running through his mind. What with the fact that my Minions weren't currently spawned, it probably seemed to him this was his most opportune moment to make a move that might get him control of the group and these women. He took the shotgun out and held towards me, almost as if to give it to me. Instead of passing it to me though, he suddenly cocked it back and aimed the barrel directly at me.

Lucas immediately moved to my side in confusion, "What are you doing Robert?"

"What does it look like? I'm pointing a shotgun at Mike."

I looked at both Alan and Thomas who seemed completely shocked and conflicted. From their uneasy expressions it was clear that this was not planned, and Robert was going rogue.

"What do you want?" I looked at him, "Do you just want to leave and bail on your promise to help? You can do that. No one is stopping you."

It seemed that I'd challenged Robert before he'd thought this through, so it took him a few moments before he shook his head, "I want your magic items and your supplies." Then his eyes shifted to the women who were looking on in pure horror. "And I want those women."

Jessica had already stood up behind me; her bow perched just beside my shoulder fully drawn. It seemed this wasn't going to end peacefully. With hand motions behind my back, I cast Bone Armor and I didn't think Robert had noticed. He was staring at me with the shotgun aimed at my face.

"Put the bow down Jessica," he said. I glanced at his companions: up until now, Thomas and Alan hadn't made a single move.

"Don't put your bow down. Kill him if he fires," I said over my shoulder, "probably, his shot won't kill me, but for certain he'll definitely die."

Robert's face soured when he heard the defiance in my voice, and maybe a seed of doubt had been planted in his mind. I honestly didn't know how much good it would do; but he also didn't know the extent of my abilities.

"I assume you two aren't in on it?" I looked at Thomas and Alan.

The impression I got from their reaction made me think their desire to survive this apocalypse by working with us was now conflicting heavily with their loyalty to Robert. Neither of them spoke, to either confirm that they had been making plans with Robert or to deny it.

Robert was angry. "Look at the women we can have you idiots. We don't need Mike anymore. Has he supplied us with a single Class Changing Stone yet? Or any more food than what he gave us originally? We're level eleven now. We can go it alone."

"You two can still make it out of this room alive," I said, "Robert is already a dead man though. If you side with him you'll lose and even if you escape, Jessica can track you as far as you can run, and she will kill you. If you stand aside, staying out of this, then that's fine," I said to them, "we won't have a problem afterwards."

The two young men didn't make the slightest movement, and it seemed like this meant they were leaning towards my side. And the truth was that if Jessica was hunting them down, they wouldn't get a moment's rest.

It was impossible for them to move through the city as fast as Jessica and I. They wouldn't have a single peaceful night.

"There's no way out for you anymore," I said to Robert and could see from the deepening frown lines of his forehead that it was dawning on him that his hand was played out.

After he got the shotgun, Robert must have cooked up the idea of taking me out. Probably, it would have happened when I was alone and off guard, but my questioning had forced his hand. With Jessica already having her weapon drawn and arrow nocked, he was as good as dead regardless of his actions.

"Can I leave?" he asked. "I'll leave and not show myself again." He slowly started to lower the shotgun, "You can even have the gun." I almost believed him for a moment, and then he raised the gun rapidly and shot directly at my head.

My hands were already outstretched in an attempt to grab the shotgun, and I managed to cross them slightly over my face. The Bone Armor covering my body instantly disappeared as a burning sensation covered the back of my arms and hands.

There was also a burning sensation on one side of my cheek as well, but I had survived. I wasn't dead even though he had shot me at pointblank range.

Jessica didn't lower her guard for even a moment, and the instant Robert fired she let her bow string loose. The arrow ripped right through his neck and completely destroyed one side of it. There wasn't the slightest chance he could survive the injury without magical help.

Robert's legs gave out beneath him and he dropped like a sack of sand. Blood was pouring from the gaping hole in his neck as his eyes grew wide as saucers. One hand reached out for his cousin Thomas, whose face showed absolute horror.

Jessica was already in front of me with a bandage pulled ready to patch my wounds. It seemed Thomas had made his choice as Healing Touch was cast on me despite Robert grasping for aid from the floor below him. I was on 275 out of 750 HP. Robert, however, dropped his hand and stopped moving, blood spreading out in a pool around him. He was dead.

The shot had actually done a considerable amount of damage. Without Bone Armor, the blast would have come close to killing me, and maybe would have killed me regardless if my hands hadn't blocked the blazing pellets from mutilating my face.

The Healing Touch from Thomas soothed a good portion of my pain while Jessica pulled back my sleeves, revealing my bloodied hands and forearms. There were obvious chunks of flesh missing, but somehow I was coping okay.

It seemed a mix of shock and pain resistance did wonders. It still hurt like shit, but it was manageable to a level where I wouldn't pass out. I felt the bandages cross my arms and then the bleeding wounds slowly closed.

The scars, however, would probably always remain. The restored flesh in those areas was white and uneven. It was obvious from looking that I had suffered serious damage to them. Luckily, there was no nerve damage or mobility issue.

"I swear we didn't know!" Alan said from the side. Oddly enough, I believed him. The feelings they gave me hadn't changed even though a long-time friend and relative died right in front of them. It seemed Alan was afraid he and Thomas would be killed next.

"You two are free to leave if you wish." I said, "I won't make you stay after this. Give me the gun." I looked at Lucas, who picked it up immediately and passed it into my hands. I stored it away and knew that I wouldn't be giving it to anyone that I couldn't absolutely trust. Getting shot by something so powerful from close range was not a fun experience.

Still, I had learned something valuable from this. Even a shotgun—an item even, that was probably more powerful than an actual shotgun—couldn't kill me in one hit despite the close range. A rare sense of triumph surged up inside me.

"If you're staying," I said. "These ladies are from our future home. I'm really tired, so Jessica can fill you in." With that I went to one the spare bedroom and lay down on the bed. I felt incredibly tired, but before sleeping noticed a new Passive that showed in my skill list.

Chapter 20: Planning a Way to Start a Post-Apocalypse Community

It must have been afternoon when I woke up. Alan, Thomas, and Lucas would have left to level several hours ago. They each needed to get a new skill after hitting level 10, and for that we still needed one more Class Changing Stone.

The situation last night had been so intense that I just hadn't wanted to deal with anything else other than sleeping and recovering. If the others returned today without having gained a stone, I would give them the one I still had in my inventory.

"How are you feeling?" Jessica asked from the other side of the room.

"Better, surprisingly." My HP had recovered to full while I was sleeping, and the aching in my hands had disappeared. My lack of MP was starting to be a problem, though, as even after being asleep the entire night, I had only regenerated to around 150.

It had always been clear that I was going to reach a point where my MP could not keep up with my casting expenditure; it had just come earlier than I expected. This poor MP regeneration told me it was best to put the remaining 4 stat points I had available into WIS, in an attempt to increase my overall MP regeneration. That brought my WIS up to a natural 24, with plus 8 from magic item bonuses. My mana pool had a potential maximum now of 320, but currently I was on 179.

"How are the women holding up?" I asked. "Yesterday's events must have come as a shock to them."

"They are doing better than expected, actually," Jessica laughed. "In fact, what shocked them most was that you survived that shotgun blast. It seems to have given them some inspiration. One of them even asked if we would consider getting revenge on Ghost Hand."

"So they have faith in me now?" I gave a smile, and no doubt Jessica could see it was a wry one.

"I guess."

"Have any of them expressed interest in leveling up?"

"Only one of them, Maria—the youngest. The older ones are more interested in finding a place of safety with a secure food supply. They'd like to live on the farm, if only it was free of Ghost Hand."

"Interesting. That would work to build a successful community, don't you think? A farm where some people work the land and others like us fight off enemies and level up."

"Are you thinking what I'm thinking?" she was serious now.

"I'm thinking that farm has as good a setup as we could want for a base. And that the people there might stick around and build the community if we free them from Ghost Hand."

Now Jessica smiled again, her perfect white teeth making her whole face seem enlivened. "That's what I reckoned. We'll need to scout it out and figure out their strength but if you and I are several levels higher than Ghost Hand, we should take it off him for the food possibilities and the defenses around there."

"Right. Even though enough rations seem to drop to keep you and I going, other people aren't going to survive this apocalypse without a steady supply of food." I wondered about what level Ghost Hand was and that motivated me to get moving. "We should probably head out soon; it's already gotten quite late." I crawled from the bed, fully dressed from having fallen onto the mattress exhausted both mentally and physically.

Jessica walked towards the door to the women's room. "Alright, I'll see if Maria is willing to come with us and start levelling up and if the others are okay to remain here on their own. We have food for everyone for several days, so there's no need for them to risk going out until our return."

I nodded and then started to stretch. All the walking and moving really put a strain on my muscles and frame. Bones cracked as I twisted and bent. After I finished using the bathroom, I returned to find Jessica was waiting in the living room with the youngest of the four women. She had dark hair and deep tanned skin. If I had to guess, she was most likely Hispanic. "You are Maria?"

"That's right. And you are Mike?" she answered.

I nodded. "We're going to return to where you met us yesterday. Jessica tells me you're interested in leveling, is that true?"

"I do want to learn. The other women are much older than me and they don't feel they have a chance with a game-based system. But I played enough to understand what we need to do."

"Right," I said. "How old are you?"

"Sixteen."

"Okay, if you're serious then take that spear right there and follow us," I said. Her eyes followed mine before landing on the nearly blood drenched spear. There was a moment of hesitation followed by resolve. She grasped it and then put on the most forced angry face I'd ever seen.

I could only let out a light chuckle and then start making our way downstairs. "It's quite late so we'll take the jeep back." We took to the streets that had already been partially cleared by Lucas and the other two men.

Having parked the jeep, we walked for nearly thirty minutes before encountering any reasonable enemies for Maria. Her tough façade had dropped and I could see in her posture that she was nervous. I casted Vast Shadows to summon my army of undead and then gave a brief description of what was going to happen.

Maria understood that all she needed to do was stab the enemies that my squad would restrain for her, but it was clear that no matter how much Jessica and I reassured her, Maria was anxious. We weren't in any rush, and so just to make things easier for her first battles, Jessica and I decided to restrict our pulls to Zombies.

Zombies were just a one hit kill if stabbed in the head, and I had hoped that a few good critical strikes would boost her confidence. When the first one lumbered into the trap of my skeletons, I was pleased to see that Maria wasn't afraid to use the spear, she ran in after Jessica shouted "go!" and began jabbing. The problem was just that her technique wasn't great. Her first zombie took three stabs, mainly because she repeatedly missed the lethal blow on the head.

"No problem." Jessica said when she apologized. "You'll get better in time."

Looking pleased with herself, Maria wiped the sweat from her brow. Her first kill put her at Level 1, and as we continued to walk in search of the next Zombie, Jessica explained to her the ideas behind class changing and stats.

It was up to her to decide what type of role she would feel comfortable in. "I would like to use a bow, like you." Having been silent while Jessica was speaking, it was a surprise when she suddenly blurted out her choice. It seemed she was in awe of Jessica, and it was easy to see why.

A strong female figure that would have no problem soloing all the mobs around us was someone to look up to. Even without me, Jessica would be able to get by in this world. It wouldn't be easy for her to level up off the harder monsters, but I was sure she could find a way, probably some kind of kiting strategy.

Jessica looked at Maria with a serious expression. "If that's the case, you should distribute your first few levels between DEX and STR. It will make this go faster as well." Maria nodded happily and must have taken the advice. After that, she didn't miss her strikes anymore.

Jessica and Maria seemed to get along well, and their conversation sometimes led to a pull that brought along a second mob. It wasn't a problem though, as my Exceptional Abomination ran over every additional enemy we encountered.

With him as a minion, I didn't need any assistance in taking down any enemy in this area. But because we wanted to power level Maria, it took us another forty-five minutes of walking before we returned to yesterday's destination, and by then Maria had reached Level Five.

The early levels that Jessica and I had struggled with went so quickly when all you needed to do was poke the enemy in the neck. Oddly enough, there was no jealousy on my end about this. I didn't feel any resentment towards our newer members who received a silver spoon in their mouth. I was just glad to see some people around me gaining strength.

I thought of Robert's words and how foolish he had been. He didn't realize just how difficult and dangerous it was getting on top of this system; when any serious encounter could result in your death; and when your resources were almost non-existent.

When we arrived at the ruined offices on the western highway where we had encountered the women and their pursuers, I could see that the men's Jeep was still there. Looking to where Jessica's arrow had dug the keys into the ground, I could see them too. No one from the farm had found the vehicle, and none of the res-pawned mobs had damaged it. Good. That would make our trip back much faster.

As was routine now, I got to clearing abandoned vehicles with my minions, working on making a wide path westward. The mobs that were triggered due to the sound were Ankle Snared by Jessica, and it seemed even without my squad holding them in place my teammates could deal with the pulls.

Ankle Snare worked on these monsters every time, allowing Maria to stab them from out of range of their attempts to swipe at her. While the snarls and roars and groans of the mobs were intimidating, Maria wasn't daunted and her confidence grew with each kill. Even better, we got lucky and another Crude Short Bow dropped, which Jessica handed to Maria immediately.

As I watched the two women systematically clear the mobs around us, I felt like I was watching Jessica level up all over again, but this time Maria had the knowledge we acquired previously, and it seemed Jessica had every intention of taking Maria under her wing.

After a non-stop afternoon of clearing and fighting I made sure to cast Vast Shadows as night rolled around and we took the abandoned jeep around the safer, outer edge of the city and left it parked about a ten-minute walk from the building we were using as our camp. Because we had wanted to make the most of the daylight, our timing was slightly off. The sun set and there was no light at all due to a cloudy sky covering the moon. Fortunately, Jessica didn't need to see to know where we were, and we made it back safely.

Everyone, even Robert's friends, greeted us warmly. Their day had been productive but not in regard to a Class Changing Stone, and so I gave the one I currently had to Thomas.

Having explained to us his options, Thomas chose a class called Bishop that had some interesting abilities. His passive gave him a natural resistance to undead and demon enemies, as well as a 25% resistance to status ailments. I wasn't sure exactly what that entailed, but Fear was most likely one of them.

Besides that, he received an AoE heal called **Healing Rain** and then a single target shield called **Holy Shield** that absorbed a flat amount of damage.

Alan and Lucas had both used their Class Changing Stone during the day. Alan had ended up taking a generic class known as knight and was confident in his defensive powers, he had focused his choices on improving his defensive ability.

Alan's active abilities were **Charge**—which allowed him to close the distance between him and an enemy with a quick burst of speed. It stunned the enemy and reduced their attack power by ten percent—and **Battle Cry**, a ferocious shout that increased the attack power of his party members by fifteen percent and increased their resistance to Fear by fifty percent. His passive ability was called **Never Give Up**, which caused him to lose stamina fifty percent more slowly than before, and also reduced incoming damage taken by thirty percent when he was below half HP.

209

Lucas had felt his best class option was one called Shogun. His skills were very interesting. The only active skill was called **Dual Strike**, which, as it indicated, let him strike out with both weapons at the same time. One of his two passives were **Dual Wield**—which was needed so that he could wield two swords at once and bring Dual Strike into play. It was very promising that Lucas could combine Dual Wield with Wind Slash, and this would launch two wind projectiles instead of one.

Perhaps even more interesting than both of those skills was his second passive, **Ruler**. Ruler gave Lucas plus 10% increased stats per nearby enemy. Which right now was nothing at all of course, but if he had five enemies nearby that would bump him up to around 30 STR or AGI. As he explained it to me, I was encouraged. That was a skill which would scale well and could make all the difference in a crisis.

While we were comparing skills, I took the Meat Cleaver from my inventory and offered it to both Alan and Lucas, neither of them wanted it though. The weapon was much too big and clunky for effective attacking, and so I used it to gear up another skeleton.

Chapter 21: The Sniper Class

We repeated our grinding and clearing for the next three days, Maria coming with us each time. Even at a pace that erred on the side of caution she soon reached level 9. A skill book that fit her perfectly had dropped as well.

Book of Strafing LV. 1: Allows the User to fire three arrows in quick succession.
Cast Time: 0.2 seconds
MP Cost: 3
User must have a bow equipped.

My progress in clearing out a path through the city was basically completed, and by the end of this third day it was possible to drive directly from our apartment complex to the west highway beyond where there were abandoned vehicles and regular spawns. Jessica was passionate about Maria and her progress, and insisted we find her a Class Changing Stone as soon as possible.

I was interested in acquiring another Abomination as well, so the idea sat well with me. What I wasn't expecting though, was that she wanted Maria to join us for that battle. I wasn't sure it was the best idea in regard to her safety. Any failure on our part to control the aggro of the elite and she would die.

In the end though, Maria insisted on being a participant and Jessica thought it was a good idea. I wasn't going to fight them on it, but I made Maria promise safety would be prioritized over maximizing her damage contribution. With Jessica being the more effective in ranged combat, then Maria should be third on the monster's aggro list should my undead squad lose control of it. I just had a slight fear that some unexpected event or Maria's use of the Strafing skill at the wrong time might bring about disaster.

Given that plenty of time had passed, the Exceptional Abomination we had previously fought should have respawned by now and that was our destination. Even though Maria wasn't grouped with us Jessica gave Maria the green light to join in any of the battles once we started fighting and the mob was clearly locked down by my undead squad.

As we cleared our way through the abandoned streets, it didn't take long to see that Maria was getting massive amounts of EXP. Unlike some games, where ungrouped players got nothing for kills they did less than 50 percent of the damage to, here it seemed Maria was most likely getting a split of the EXP before it was divided between Jessica and I. Our EXP had been stagnant for the past three days anyway, so even the small amounts we were getting now were welcomed by me and I didn't complain about Maria taking a share.

Moving through this part of the city was stress free for Jessica and I, which was both a blessing and a curse. I wanted to move on to something better for us, EXP wise, but that would have to wait till after we carried out our scouting of Ghost Hand and his set up.

It took us around two hours of searching to find the Exceptional Abomination, as it seemed he was on the farther point of his route. Again, the sight of the dinosaur-headed monster, wielding six massive cleavers was intimidating. It was repellent, too, how the fatty tissue oozed pus as it dragged chains along the floor. All the same, now that we had our own undead version in the summoned squad as well as Maria for her extra DPS, I wasn't anxious about the coming fight. Nor did Jessica feel that we needed a special strategy other than slow its movement with Quagmire, surround it with my minions and hit hard.

All the same, we weren't complacent, keeping Maria at a distance and clearing an escape route through a ruined garage in case anything went wrong.

The pull was clean, Jessica's arrow made the Exceptional Abomination spin around and lumber towards us without any adds. Then another arrow set up Quagmire trap and next my minions intercepted the roaring monster and brought it to a halt. There were no surprises as the fight progressed, and instead, it progressed incredibly quickly.

Within five seconds of the encounter starting the abomination's noxious bile was released, and merely three or four seconds after that the monster went into his enrage status. Our DPS was insane and we were literally tearing strips from him.

By the time the boss fell I had merely lost a single Skeleton General only. That was just how much faster we downed him compared to the previous fight. Sharing a triumphant look with Jessica, I quickly reanimated him. There was nothing else that I needed to do to prepare for testing ourselves against Ghost Hand, at least on my end.

I had two Exceptional reanimated dead in my squad and enough supplies for at least a week in the wilderness. Besides that, everyone in the other group was racing towards level 13 and even Maria was gaining on them.

Apparently, she had gained two full levels when the abomination died, which to me was absolutely incredible. That put her at level 11, which really wasn't far off from Lucas. It probably made sense for Maria to join the others from now on, but I wasn't sure how Jessica would feel about that: she seemed to be enjoying Maria's company and I couldn't blame her, Maria was much more talkative than me.

The Exceptional Abomination dropped three items, one of which was the Class Changing Stone that went directly to Maria. Besides that, we got another **Survivor's Medallion** and a **Large HP Potion.**

Jessica and I had begun to discuss whether it was worth Maria waiting for a second skill or whether changing right now was the best option, when Maria announced that in her excitement, she'd already made the decision. She had been given the option of a bow class called Sniper and taken it at once.

Like most classes we'd seen so far, she had two active skills and a single passive skill.

Entangling Shot: Causes vines to sprout wildly from target's wound. Restrains an enemy in place for at least five seconds and deals damage over time.
Explosive Arrow: Shoots an arrow with a fuse that explodes two seconds after hitting its target. Deals massive damage physical and fire damage.
Clear Vision: Grants the user perfect vision.

Interestingly enough, Clear Vision was the same passive Jessica had received from her Geloas' Eyes. The difference was that it was possible for Maria to level her passive up, and Jessica could not. In the future, Maria should gain something beyond perfect vision and I wondered what that might be, night vision perhaps?

Full of good cheer and with a sense of mission accomplished, we returned to our base and when Lucas and the others returned, looking rather more tired and worn out than us, we joined with the women in discussing if we were strong enough to take on Ghost Hand and his gang. They believed so, and while I wanted this to be true, I knew I couldn't put that much weight on the opinion of someone who hadn't been trying to level up and didn't know the ins and outs of the game system.

From what the women told me, he spent most of his time on compound and wasn't really putting the effort into leveling. Now this was an important fact that I could use to speculate about his power. Ever since the arrival of the game system on Earth, I'd been levelling with hardly a break. It was hard to believe but this was only day 12 since the apocalypse. As far as I knew, I'd made good choices and my squad of summoned undead was as strong as anyone could have made it in the same time. In this light, Ghost Hand might be merely level 7 or 8, which would be enough for him to dominate most people, especially if he had access to guns.

The other consideration was grouping. In Jessica I had a very smart—talented even—DPS and pulling partner who complemented my skills. Would that have given us an advantage over Ghost Hand though? The report of the women was that he had three other men in his gang who also were levelling up. The fact he only allowed a few close people to level up meant he was cautious of someone growing stronger than himself. It was likely he had allowed the women to be abused to appease these closer members, in hopes they would be satisfied enough to not overthrow him. In other words, it didn't sound like he'd been building a team the way Lucas, Thomas and Alan had, let alone Jessica and I.

Even if Ghost Hand was level fifteen, I didn't think he would be able to deal with the force we were coming with. So, while Lucas was recommending, we scout from a distance and try to pick off one or two of the others who had levels, it seemed to me we were more likely to catch them by surprise with a direct approach. "I kind of think we should just show up during the day with my army of minions in Vast Shadows," I said, "claiming to be survivors who have heard about the farm and are looking for safety. That way I'll get an understanding of how dangerous he is and possibly what their members are like."

"And if Ghost Hand tries to kill us right then?" asked Lucas.

"I think we'll win the fight and by some distance." And I explained my thinking, getting the women to confirm again that most days Ghost Hand and his entourage did not go out of the compound. It just did not seem possible that they were near our level.

"What about us?" asked one of the women.

"You had best stay here, except Maria. She can hide in one of the vehicles and guide us. According to the map it should be about an hour drive."

"And what happens if Ghost Hand is friendly. If he acts like he's happy for us to join the farm?" Lucas asked.

"Kill him anyway," said Maria, eyes full of fire. "Kill all four of them. You've no idea."

There were nods and mutters of agreement from the other women.

I shrugged. "If we get the opportunity to jump them, we do. If they then surrender, I'm not going to kill anyone in cold blood. Otherwise, as far as I'm concerned Ghost Hand and his crew are scum so I'm hoping things go south. And if there are guns around, no one should show any mercy as it might bite you in the ass. So, to reiterate: we go to their gate as survivors hoping to join. If we get inside the camp, I'll drop my squad on Ghost Hand when I think we have the advantage."

"Let me do the talking," said Jessica, her voice grim. "Sounds like they will underestimate a woman."

I glanced at and had to agree. That would be the smart move. Their own attitude might work against them and cause them to lower their guard.

"All willing to try this? It's volunteers only. I'm not holding anyone to our deal on this. But I would remind you that it's not just about revenge. It's about building a place that can be a beacon for all survivors to gather at in safety."

"I'm in," said Alan.

"Me too," added Thomas and Lucas nodded. All three of them looked determined and I was heartened.

"Is anyone close to levelling?" I asked. "If so we can delay a bit, otherwise I'd like to go tomorrow or the next day at the latest."

Jessica and I were merely 40% through level 17, so not exactly close. We could definitely hit 18 with a full day's grind, but as our next active skill wasn't likely to be until level 20, it didn't seem worth giving Ghost Hand any more time. If, as I suspected, he and his gang hadn't yet reached 10 the sooner we made our move the better.

Our abilities took us well beyond the snake-headed mobs and abominations that were nearby, and I wanted to hunt stronger enemies. The issue was that moving deeper into the city was too risky. The Fiend could stumble upon us and wipe us out in an instant.

We were stuck between a rock and a hard place, the hard place being long and arduous grinding with minimal reward. Enemies that took a bit of finesse to kill were what I was looking for. Good

EXP and good drops were the dream. Until we had that, we were at something of a plateau. And while it didn't sound like Ghost Hand and his crew were concentrating on levelling, they could certainly progress faster than us if they wanted to.

I was pleased then, when no one wanted to delay.

"We leave tomorrow morning after a good rest. Think about what you may need, if anything. We'll be driving straight from here to the farm," I said.

No one had a complaint. I was expecting some pushback, but perhaps the others shared my calculations. Perhaps too, they felt like I did: that already we were leagues above our former selves. We were all well above super-human strength, even Maria.

If we worked together, maybe we could even kill the Fiend. Obviously, I wouldn't take that gamble any time soon. The biggest uncertainty that troubled me was not Ghost Hand but was what was to come for humanity? We were probably only at the start of whatever challenge this was. The mysterious blue light that had mixed up spawns came around a week after the apocalypse and so what might we expect at the end of week two? Or the first month? Or the first 100 days? For now, I felt we were well ahead of the curve in terms of levels, at least I imagined so. But I remembered how easy it would have been in those first few days to fall behind and never even be able to start progressing against zombies and goblins. Another steep curve might come our way at any time.

Sleep didn't come easy that night as I turned my thoughts to Ghost Hand: there were three options. Ghost Hand would prove to have an unexpected trick up his sleeve and we would be killed; my companions and would kill him and his followers; or he'd surrender. From what I'd heard about him, that last option didn't seem likely.

I had already killed two men before in self-defense, but that didn't make it any easier. *They're bad people.* I told myself that over and over.

Chapter 22: The Secret of Ghost Hand's Powers

We slept in late, and it seemed like I was having more anxiety about the coming expedition than the others. They were almost treating it like a vacation day from the constant grind. The most excited though, were the four women, three of whom weren't even coming.

Their enthusiasm and conviction that we would triumph over their former oppressor gave me a bit more resolve: Ghost Hand was scum, and I was doing this world a favor by taking him on. Thinking about it that way made the thought of dispatching Ghost Hand much more pleasant, we were delivering justice.

At Lucas's suggestion, we all squeezed into the one jeep—not the one from the farm—and fortunately it had enough gas that no detours were needed. I expected to drive, but it seemed Lucas wanted to and he actually insisted, which allowed me to sit in the back and relax as much as possible with Jessica jammed up against my left arm and Thomas on my right with Maria squashed tight behind him.

It was incredible just how normal the world still looked once we left the destruction of the city. If you could ignore the roaming zombies and goblins you had to avoid on the road then it was like a pre-apocalypse drive through the countryside. The fresh air rushing past my face felt nice, and for the first time in a while I realized just how draining living in the city was.

Waking up every morning to monsters, torched cars, decaying bodies and massive destruction took a toll on you. It was exactly as Lucas had said; this wasn't a place to live. It was impossible to forget the danger for even a moment. The stress was endless.

As we pulled off the main road and onto a dirt road, I couldn't help but think the good road had ended too soon. The smooth countryside road compared to the rocky and bumpy gravel we traveled now woke me from my relaxed stupor.

The farmland could be seen in the distance, about a mile off. A slender fence raced from both sides of the road and off to the horizon. The only thing keeping the zombies and goblins out were three strips of barbed wire. The fencing was a bit sturdier at the road, where a large metal-wire gate stood closed, barred and padlocked, with a man standing behind it, leaning on his spear.

"Should I stop here?" asked Lucas.

'Stick to the plan,' replied Jessica. 'Go right up there and see if we can get in.'

The man gestured with his spear when we arrived, showing the jeep where to pull over. "Who are you with?" He asked as Lucas leaned out of the window. The expression on his face was one of puzzlement more than hostility.

"No one, we're just here to speak with Ghost Hand," Lucas answered.

"We don't accept visitors," the guard said flatly.

"We've got women, we want to trade." This was an improvisation by Lucas and it was perfect. The man looked interested and was peering towards the interior of the jeep, where Jessica was visible but Maria had her head down.

Lucas got out and opened the passenger door beside Jessica. "Get out. Show him you're a beauty." Lucas should have been an actor in his former life; he sounded the part of a callous slaver.

Leaving her bow lying at our feet, Jessica fixed her face in a scowl and got out to stand beside Lucas. Should I get out too? I didn't want to spook the guard yet so I just edged the bow with my feet so the end was poking out and an easy grab for Jessica.

The guard let out a long, low whistle. "She's hot all right. Ghost Hand will want to see her. But I can't let you all in. Just you and the women can drive on up.

"Fair enough. Everyone else out," said Lucas.

Leaving my mask behind, Thomas and I got out behind Jessica, while Alan stepped from the passenger seat beside the driver. Jessica then took hold of the door as if going back inside the jeep. Back behind the wheel, Lucas revved the engine while the guard undid the padlock and the bolt.

Once the gate was open, instead of returning to her seat Jessica pulled out her bow and an arrow from her quiver, drawing it tight and pointing it directly at the man. His face grew dark, and he moved his spear so the tip pointed towards us. "What's going on?"

Jessica loosed the arrow with incredible force and it exploded forward. The air twisted and whistled as it passed within inches from his ear and pierced into a dirt bank beyond him with a loud thunk. "The next one won't miss."

The man looked over his shoulder at the hole a single arrow had created in the ground, as big as if an explosive was attached. Pale now, his spear was wavering and looking at the evidence of his own trembling with disgust, he threw the weapon down. "I don't know what you are up to, but you're out of your depth. Ghost Hand will screw you up."

We drove up a long, winding road through ploughed fields to a farmhouse without anyone stopping us. Once parked in a large yard between two barns and a cowshed, Jessica and I jumped out with magic items on, weapons in hand, started walking on foot towards the only residence, a large two-story building with whitewashed wooden walls and a steep roof of grey slates. In the patio before two closed wooden doors were two men sitting in chairs and talking. As we got closer and they realized we were strangers to them, both stood up. The older man, bearded, rushed inside while the other— clean shaven, twenty-something—faced us, nervous and angry, "Who are you?"

"We've just come to speak to Ghost Hand," said Jessica calmly. "We have a trade to offer him." A moment later the older man came back out with two rifles. He passed one to the younger one and they stood there at the ready.

"Now, strangers," said the bearded man with a sneer. "Fuck off."

"I was just telling your friend," Jessica replied. "We are here to trade. We found some good gear out there, but we need food."

The young man leaned close to the older one, never taking his eyes off Jessica, and whispered something. The older man grinned and nodded and the young man went inside, careful to close the door behind him with a click.

Keeping his rifle up and held across his chest the man waited, his eyes drawn again and again to Jessica's curves.

"You okay?" shouted Lucas from the jeep. Neither Jessica nor I turned. The bearded man, however, scowled and shifted the rifle to his shoulder. "You stay in that vehicle."

While we waited for whoever the young man had gone to fetch—hopefully Ghost Hand—I got ready to drop my squad of undead. Really, there was nothing more I could do to prepare for the outbreak of a battle, so I studied the farm. My eyes scanned the area, and I could tell that the farmland would need a lot of work. There was plenty of land, but more than half of it seemed to be uncultivated.

A motion caught my eye, but it was only two women peeking out from behind a barn door.

"You two. Get back inside," the bearded man growled at them.

Is that where the women lived? Or worked? Either way, it didn't seem to offer much protection. Barbed wire on a thin fence wouldn't be enough to keep the goblins and zombies out if they came this way. So, on top of abusing the women, Ghost Hand wasn't even properly protecting them.

The more I read the signs, the more I disliked Ghost Hand. Farm tools were just lying around the yard, some were rusty. A washing line was hung inefficiently between barns, where they would be in the shade for most of the day. And there were cow pats all over the yard.

We waited over five minutes for any development.

It seemed that the man with the rifle enjoyed making me wait. He wore a smirk as he held my eyes with a long stare until I looked away.

At last, the two entrance doors were thrown wide by the clean-shaven guard and from behind him four men strode onto the porch: three bearing rifles and a bald, stocky man in a checked shirt who was unarmed but whose pose—with hands on hips—said that he was in charge.

As I looked over them carefully, none of them struck me as having powers that triggered my Sixth Sense. Admittedly, there was a risk facing anyone wielding a gun. Yet both Jessica and I were high enough level to absorb several shots. Nothing about this gang was special at all. I was confident looking at them that as soon as I removed my minions from Vast Shadow, Jessica and I could easily deal with them.

"Are you Ghost Hand?" I addressed the fleshy, unarmed man who took a few steps forward.

"What do you want?" he asked.

Middle-aged. Clothes fraying. Tattoos visible through the sleeves of his shirt and collar. And still nothing screaming at me that I was in danger, other than from bullets. "Are you Ghost Hand?" I asked again.

"That's me. What's your business here?"

I could tell from the man's demeanor that he wasn't worried. Did he have any idea of what levelling meant? Of what humans could achieve if they worked the system? "I've come to take control of the farm. You're being evicted." There really wasn't any way to put it besides as blunt as possible.

Everything went still and quiet. I could hear only the faint buzz of a fly. And then the silence was interrupted by laughter. All six men started laughing as if I'd told the funniest joke. Good. They just couldn't grasp that it was possible for two people without guns to defeat six. That meant they had no real idea of how levelling scaled up our abilities exponentially.

A jeep pulling into the yard from our left interrupted their laughter. It was the two men—still dressed in black leather jacket and jeans—who we had chased away when we had helped Maria and her friends escape them. They got out of the vehicle with a swagger but their faces soured when they saw us and they hurried to Ghost Hand's side and began whispering in his ear. Glancing over my shoulder I signaled for Lucas and the others to get out. We were on the cusp of battle, I was sure of it.

"It seems you two stole a vehicle from me, and four girls?" Ghost Hand suddenly asked.

"We stole a jeep, yes. The four women were never your property," Jessica said. His eyes looked past us at the jeep that Lucas was driving.

"I'll take that as payment for the vehicle but what of the girls?" He asked and looking at Jessica, slowly licked his lips. Beside me, Jessica slotted an arrow to the string of her bow and equally slowly raised it to aim at Ghost Hand's heart. He frowned and all his men aimed their guns at Jessica, some cocking them with an audible click.

"Did what I say go in one ear and out the other?" I asked.

"You don't seem to understand the situation." Ghost Hand sounded confident but he took two steps back to place one of his goons between him and Jessica. "It's you who have to pay me that jeep and you and your friends can get out of here on foot. How many girls have you got there? Just the two? Is that you Maria? You dumb bitch coming back here."

"Tell you what…I'll take your pretty new one for three of those ugly ones I was bored with anyway. And I'll let you walk out of here alive."

I felt like we had been talking to a rock, and the downside of Ghost Hand's lack of comprehension of the power available to us was that he would never consider surrendering. Never.

This was bound to end in a fight and I didn't see any more reason to let them shoot first. We might be the good guys but this was no Hollywood movie. For the briefest of moments, I looked to Jessica and taking in her fierce expression, saw the faintest of nods. She understood and was ready.

"I don't know what you are thinking," Ghost Hand raised his hand, "but you seem to be getting set to make a move. A dumb move. Well, it's over." He pushed his upraised hand towards me like a martial arts gesture and I suddenly felt pain on my throat. There was a pressure there, but it was almost completely blocked by Bone Armor. Ghost Hand's attack was dealing constant damage, and to a normal person would probably kill them in around six or seven seconds.

Bone Armor completely blocked any strangling effect, and at the rate my hit points were dropping, it would take over two-minutes to kill me. I started to smile, "So this is it? The reason they call you Ghost Hand?" I asked.

His face blushed bright red with surprise, as there was no struggle on my side. I wasn't grasping for air or scrambling to remove his grip from my neck. I stood there calmly watching him straining to exert as much power as he could.

"Did he do something?" Jessica asked and without waiting for an answer released her arrow, which hit Ghost Hand's outstretched arm so violently, it took off the hand. Blood sprayed his men as their boss reeled around. I immediately felt a release of the pressure on my neck.

"Yeah, he threw the first stone," I said. My skull mask went on and I unleashed my squad from Vast Shadow. A swarm of undead appeared around me in an instant.

Every single one of our opponent's faces registered horror.

"Fire! KILL THEM!" Ghost Hand yelled at the sight of my summoned undead. Jessica and I were now covered front and flanks. I specifically kept my shield-wielding skeleton general in front of Jessica to protect her from stray bullets. She wouldn't die from being shot once or twice, but I wanted to avoid any risk to her at all.

The rest of my squad rushed forward in a frenzy as I reached out and cast Decay on the nearest gun-wielding enemy, the man who had been staring me down as we waited. The bearded flesh of his face started to melt as if acid had been poured over it. He let out a scream and dropped his rifle immediately while swatting at the falling flesh.

Ghost Hand and the two men in black leather were running like hell, eventually jumping into a jeep. Jessica was incredibly quick though and even as the driver turned the key and the engine caught, an arrow smashed through the windscreen directly into the driver's neck. Lucas and company had started running up as soon as Jessica had released her first arrow, but the battle was as good as over in the few seconds it took them to get to us.

My squad was in the faces of the men, causing extreme chaos and preventing them firing their rifles. Efficiently drawing and releasing her arrows, Jessica had the biggest impact and had killed all but two enemies. One was the wounded Ghost Hand, now holding his arm and staggering away between two barns and the other was the man I had cast Decay on, who was on the ground, moaning with his head in his hands.

Ghost Hand found himself alone, and tried to run on foot. There was no way he was escaping as Jessica was merciless and put an arrow directly into the calf of his leg. He collapsed in a heap and started to drag his foot frantically across the stone.

From various windows and doors around the farm, I saw faces looking out, curious as to what all the gunfire was. Although I checked for rifles or other signs of resistance I didn't see any. Some men just ran at the sight of my undead and the bodies strewn about.

Others, the women, strained to get a better look at what was happening.

Soon we had a small viewing party of a dozen women watching as we walked over to Ghost Hand and stood above him. I didn't have any words for him and neither, it seemed, did Jessica. The tough look he maintained earlier had vanished completely as he looked at us, pale and shuddering.

"Wait!" It was Maria rushing over, "please don't kill him yet!" She hurried to our side.

"Then what will we do with him?" I asked curiously. More and more women had come outside, confident now that they had seen Maria that we weren't monsters even worse than Ghost Hand.

"If you want everyone here to follow you wholeheartedly, give them justice," Maria said. I suddenly had a bad feeling about what this 'justice' would entail, but I looked at Maria and shrugged.

It was clear that Maria herself was struggling with a desire to put an arrow through Ghost Hand. He had wronged more than just her and the other women though. Everyone here was a victim of his abuse.

"I'll let you deal with him then," I said. He was guilty of whatever would happen to him, and maybe I was being soft in thinking that he deserved a swift death. I looked at one of the women bystanders, "Can you bring everyone out? I have something I want to say."

Her eyes looked at me with fear and hesitation, and then she rushed away. Everyone was already aware of the commotion, and to get them to all gather in the yard was only a matter of minutes. A group of about a dozen women stood at the front, men behind them as well, continuously taking glances at Ghost Hand who was moaning on the ground below us, blood beginning to pool around him. He wouldn't last much longer without treatment, whatever Maria had in mind.

"Let me talk to them," Jessica leaned into me and spoke quietly. "We need them to stay and help run the farm. That would be better coming from a woman not a man in a freak-show mask with an army of undead."

Taking off the mask, I gave her a nod and did my best to smile at the people before us.

"Hello everyone! I am Jessica. This is Marcus. Lucas. Thomas. Alan. And you know Maria. As of this moment, we are going to take control of this farm. What this means is different for each and every one of you, depending on what you chose to do."

"We will not treat you as Ghost Hand treated you. You will have options, and right now if you wish to leave no one will stop you." She paused. "It's dangerous out there though. We are living in a game system and monsters are everywhere and as there seems to be a design behind this game, I anticipate things are only going to get worse.

"If you wish to level, then we will help you level. If you wish to live peacefully and work on the farm in return for our protection that can also be arranged.

"All we ask is that everyone here contributes so we can build something great. If you contribute, you will be protected and provided for. If you do not, then this place will not be for you.

"Everyone will be treated fairly, and in turn you are expected to treat others with the same fairness. Violence is not something that will be tolerated. Anyone harming another member of the community will immediately be expelled.

"The world may be going to hell, but I refuse to give up my humanity, and I expect the same for you all as well," she finished.

Even though we hadn't discussed this, Jessica had found words that flowed eloquently, and I truly admired her for it. It was a grand speech.

A few of the anxious faces showed relief at what she had said, while others remained skeptical. A woman suddenly stepped forward and addressed Maria, "Maria, is she telling the truth? Are these people decent? What happened to Sarah and the others?"

"Yes! I'm better than ever and the others are fine as well. They're back in the city, but we'll be getting them and returning here with them shortly!" Maria said excitedly.

More and more women broke ranks and gathered around Maria, and as their voices rose in expressions of deeply felt relief I had an insight into what life had been like for them. Probably, all of these women had been taken advantage of and abused.

I turned to Lucas, "will you be able to drive to the city alone and bring our friends back? That will help encourage everyone to stay with us." Unless there had been a major respawn the route was clear and the sooner we brought them over the better. "Also deal with the man at the fence. See what his temperament is like and decide on your own."

"Got it! I'll be back before nightfall," Lucas answered and strode back to our jeep with a spring in his step. It seemed he enjoyed the role of the hero coming to the rescue.

Chapter 23: Making Plans for a Post-Apocalypse Community

"Can I be shown around?" I asked. "I want to see everything." Maria gave a nod and a few of the women followed along with her, showering her with questions. Eyes followed us as we moved from building to building.

Maria wasn't exaggerating when she said there were animals and crops to be tended and harvested. There were at least fifteen cows, a dozen pigs and two chicken coops. They showed me the farmland, and the tool shed, as well as the shed for heavy machinery.

Their faces all darkened when they took me to the last building. It seemed just like another barn for animals, but when I walked in the stench assaulted me. There were random patches of blood on the stone floor and an odd noise coming from inside.

I walked in not knowing what to expect and approached a stall. I reached out for a closed shutter, intending to open it and see what animal was being kept there.

"Careful! If you get bit you will die!" One of the women following Maria called out. I realized the pen had zombies in them. In fact, all three pens had zombies in them.

"…What is this for?" I asked.

"Ghost Hand decided that threatening us with death wouldn't work. The girls that refused…ended up being thrown inside," the woman said. Her words made me nearly want to vomit.

"He was feeding girls that refused to be abused to zombies?"

"Yes…some of us weren't afraid of death, but not one of them could stomach being eaten alive. We thought he wouldn't do it…but two girls died in this way. Even if you survive being attacked…the infection kills you."

I thought back to my own early encounter with zombies, "The infection always kills you?" I asked.

"Yes, even one of Ghost Hand's trusted friends got bit. Rumor said he was level six, and he still died."

There was a passive skill I had called Mutated that had never leveled up even once. It came to me after I was bitten by a zombie and survived. Did that mean? I knew it was a stupid idea—a shot in the dark—but I opened the shutter and leaned to offer my hand to the shuffling monster that came forward.

"Oh my god, what are you doing?" The woman cried, "did you not hear what I just said? Maria! Tell him!"

Maria looked uneasy and looked to me to confirm, "You'll be fine right? You know what you're doing," she said.

"I hope so." Was all I could say in response. There was a sudden pain followed by a clear tingling in my hand as the zombie bit into it. I jerked it back, closed the shutter over and checked my status.

Name: Mike Reynolds (27) Class:
Necromancer Level: 17 EXP: 40%
HP: 709/710 MP: 260/320
STR: 5 Fear Resistance: 5
AGI: 2
DEX: 5
VIT: 20 +2

WIS: 24 +8
Available: 0

Skills: [A]Summon Skeleton LV. 7 |[A] Decay LV. 2| [A] Reanimate Dead LV. 2 | [A] Bone Armor LV. 2 | [A] Vast Shadows | [P]Sixth Sense | [P] Bravery LV. 2 | [P] Mutated | [P] Pain Resistance LV. 2 | [P] Skeletal Mastery LV. 3| [P]Intimidate Living |[P] Inner Calm

Disappointingly, Mutated remained at level 1. And I watched as my HP dropped by 1 point every 10 seconds or so, which meant the infection was beating out my HP recovery, although just barely. There was only the tingling in my hand, and no other adverse status effect.

Worst case scenario I could drink a potion and have Thomas heal me. It should be completely fine.

"What did you do that for?" asked Jessica.

"I gained the Mutated skill in the past from a zombie bite. I was hoping it would level up but it hasn't." Feeling slightly foolish, I gave a shrug but Jessica simply nodded, like it was a reasonable action.

After inspecting my wound, I caught Maria's eye. "Can you gather everyone up again? I'd like to have a better understanding of where we stand. I want to know what everyone's previous professions were, any specialties and special knowledge. I also want to know what they want to do—that is if they wish to remain here on the farm, leave, or level up."

"I don't think many of them will understand what it means to level up."

"You can explain it to them. Point out that we have a system that works. You are level eleven already. You could have handled Ghost Hand by yourself." Listening to this exchange, the other women with us looked at Maria with expressions of admiration before turning away together. Neither Jessica or I set off to follow them and when they were out of earshot, Jessica spoke.

"What will we do with this place?" she asked.

"I'm not sure. Having a food supply is going to be essential but I'm not sure the perimeter can be made defensible."

Jessica nodded. "How about we stay here for a few days and not push anyone to a quick decision about whether to join us. They are going to be nervous and I'd like to avoid anyone having silly ideas. As soon as they see we don't have any ill intentions things will fall into place."

"Agreed." With that we went back to the yard, but Maria was still out getting hold of everyone and there was an awkward silence as the people present eyed us while they waited. Feeling uncomfortable, I went inside the main farmhouse and soon found the room on the ground floor that Ghost Hand had used for his office.

Perhaps it was taking Maria time to explain exactly what leveling meant, and what it entailed. But it was over twenty minutes before Jessica called me out front, to where the people were standing in groups near the porch.

Alan and Thomas walked through them and tallied up the population count. There were 17 men and 10 women. The majority of them were all below middle-aged and looked to be in good shape. There were three elderly members of the farm, but even they weren't so old they couldn't get around or contribute.

Ghost Hand had kept a notebook at his desk, and I brought it with me to write down the information we needed. One by one, as

Jessica did the talking I made notes: names, age, and previous occupation. If Ghost Hand had recorded any of that somewhere, I hadn't found it. It wasn't likely, but I was really hoping that among these people would be a doctor, or an engineer, or an architect. That was the main reason Jessica was asking their former occupations. We wanted to know that.

There was no chance a doctor was going to be mending cows, or an engineer picking corn. We needed people with specialty skills doing what they did best. When all was said and done and the tally was finished we knew what we had to work with, or at least what was immediately useful to us.

Of the 10 women, one was a nurse, one was an agricultural student working her masters, and one of them was a veterinarian. The veterinarian insisted farm animals weren't her practice, but there was some carry over. The other 7 had professions that didn't exactly have overlap with creating a safe base in a post-RPG apocalypse world.

Among the 17 men there were several more professions that could be useful to the community. Two of them were mechanical engineers, one of them having extensive experience working on cars. Another two had been workers at the steel mill just five miles away and had experience handling metal and using the machines in the factory. There was also a carpenter, a man that worked on a farm, and another nurse.

No one was useless, but I was looking for specialties. Having someone with the knowledge of how best to build up the walls, or build up the infrastructure, or when to harvest crops, or how to tend to the animals, were subjects we most needed covered right now. Since we couldn't go online anymore, human memory and experience was precious.

More than half of the people in front of us expressed an interest in leveling. That is to say, they were interested in gaining at least a few levels, and I recommended everyone to do so. Even if you only planned to do manual work for the community, having points in STR could increase your productivity considerably. Not to mention that the extra hit points could be life saving.

When I got a murmur of agreement, I said that was all from me for now, we would come up with a plan for how to level everyone safely.

"Thanks everyone," said Jessica. "I hope you'll all stay but anyone who wants to leave can do so. We're going to build a place where people can be safe and prosper. We'll get back to you soon with our plan."

Talking in small groups, the people in the yard started to disperse. I suggested to Jessica, Thomas, and Alan that we go inside to the chairs in Ghost Hand's office, but Jessica shook her head. "That will look like we are going to do things in the same way he did. Let's bring the chairs out here on the porch so people can see us."

We did that and soon were seated, except for Thomas who leaned on the railing that divided the porch from the yard. The big question was where to find the low level mobs that we could use to get levels for seventeen people. On the way here I had seen individual roaming zombies and goblins, but far too few for efficient levelling.

Would they be willing to come in small groups in the jeep? Jessica wasn't sure they would. Some people had said they didn't want to leave the farm for any reason. And I could understand why someone might resist that idea: if we had ill intentions, they might end up dumped on the side of the street with violent monsters all around. It wasn't a logical thought at all, but I could understand what fear made people think.

"They might be willing to go with us once Lucas is back with the other women," Jessica said.

We put leveling on the backburner and turned our attention to planning how to secure the farm as quickly as possible.

The steel mill workers had said the machinery in the factory was all electrically powered, but generators were put in place to keep the mill running for at least a day without it. As far as they knew, gas was kept on site for that occasion.

Thomas reckoned that it should be possible to get hundreds of pieces of sheet metal with a day's work, which we could use to fortify compound walls built from earth around the core farm buildings. That was where our two mechanical engineers came into play. As long as we had the steel beams and required tools, they should be able to draw up a sketch that would satisfy our defensive needs.

Some of the machinery up at the factory might also be useful. The four of us resolved on an expedition to the steel mills, with Maria and Lucas and two jeeps. It might well be dangerous. According to Maria, some of the people at the farm were refugees from Withersburg, a large city that had experienced a really fast takeover by monsters. If those monsters had pushed on past the city boundary they would be at the steel mill.

Our conversation then turned to the housing situation. It wasn't fair to expect the farm workers to continue sleeping in barns while we had the house bedrooms. That was how Ghost Hand had run the place but we were going to be different. The answer was probably to build new, simple homes for everyone. We had a carpenter and although he wasn't a house builder, he was familiar with the building materials for a simple home. There was no need to be fancy, as one room was enough. Without running water and electricity, a box with a door was basically all that was needed.

In the end, everything came down to transportation and safety. We needed the right type of vehicles, and enough of them, to transport the heavy supplies required for rebuilding the farm in a secure and comfortable way. Those things could be found in our city plus the steel mill.

Our plans were grandiose, and no one could expect us to deliver on it immediately, but it was good to have a goal—to have hope. My spirits had risen as we'd made these plans.

Lucas managed to return just before sunset with the women and the few personal articles we had kept in the apartment. None of us had much but I was glad to see my toothbrush and a change of clothes. He was right to have brought it all. We wouldn't be returning to that apartment again, at least not for anytime soon.

Having waited for her friends, Maria and the other women decided what was to happen to Ghost Hand. A part of me didn't actually want to know, but my curiosity got the best of me and I went to find Maria and ask her. It was a primitive method—death by firing squad.

I could only shake my head, but didn't say anything. The women despised how him and his thugs had abused them. They were all going to put a bullet in him: whether it was the one that killed him or not, they didn't care.

The execution was planned for the morning and I decided to visit Ghost Hand, who was tied to a post near the zombie stalls. It wasn't sympathy that took me to him but a feeling that I should try to find out about his ability. Maybe I'd encounter other people or monsters with it.

He looked at me as I came in, eyes full of anger.

"Tomorrow you're going to be executed," I said to him. "It seems you've really done a good job of making everyone hate you."

"I figured," he replied. "What's the point of coming here to tell me?"

"I want your magic and gear." I said plainly. "I know that you must have built up a decent amount of them taking advantage of all these people."

"As far as I know," he said, "items don't drop when you die. If I don't give them willingly you'll never get them." He had more knowledge than me on this subject most likely. Pair that with the fact that not a single one of his men dropped anything, I could only take his word for it.

"That's probably true," I said. "But do you know that skills that heal people exist?"

"I'd never seen one, but what is your point?" He asked.

"It would be possible for me to keep you alive for an extended period of time tomorrow. I can't say for sure how long, but I'm sure it would be long enough for them to shoot you thirty or forty times."

"Weren't you boasting about humanity just earlier?"

"I was, but I've already resolved myself to extend that humanity to people who are deserving of it. You are not one of them."

"So if I don't give you my items, you will keep me alive as long as possible during my execution?"

I nodded. "Correct. It's not a bad deal for you. A dead man doesn't need items. In fact, I'll make sure it goes quick. As soon as the firing starts you'll take a shot to the head and be done."

"I've a better idea. Let me go and you can have it all."

"The women would never forgive me. And I doubt you have anything that powerful or you'd have used it."

He didn't say anything for several seconds and then started pulling items from his inventory. I was actually surprised at the sheer amount, and it seemed he had been funneling from everyone he could.

There was a stack of over 20 Rations, 10 Bandages, several HP potions and six Survivor's Medallions that I happily scooped up. This would help tremendously with making sure everyone was well taken care of.

"Good enough to let me go?" he asked.

"Nowhere near," I said. "But it's enough that I'm not going to interfere with your execution. It will be instant. It will be a lot less painful death than many of those who died because of you."

He didn't say another word and just quietly sat there, pale and grim.

Somehow the thought crossed my mind that he was lucky they didn't feed him to the zombies. He truly did deserve the karma coming his way.

Chapter 24: Exploring Another Post-Apocalypse City

Spirits were high that night, and soared with the discovery that Ghost Hand had enjoyed alcohol. We found dozens of unopened bottles of whisky stashed away that were passed around. Before I knew it there was a party under the moonlight.

I wasn't much of a drinker, but couldn't resist when Jessica handed me a glass with the amber liquid in it. The rest of that night went by in a fuzz, but I knew a party was a badly needed break for everyone. No one could imagine what was coming. And it was a chance for us to bond. I did, however, make sure that those taking watches as guards over Ghost Hand were sober while on duty.

The following morning I woke early, despite a slight headache. My first thought was that this was the day when Ghost Hand was going to be executed. Searching out Maria, I asked her to make it quick. "Just put a bullet in his head a second or two after the others start shooting," I said. "And take these; pass one each to the women."

I handed her 10 rations, which would be enough food for several days. There was no doubt they were hungry, and at the moment the farm wasn't exactly up and running with everything happening.

The turnout for watching the execution of Ghost Hand was way higher than I expected. These people must have seen serious brutality to want to witness his demise. The former ruler of the farm had his hands behind his back and someone had placed a sack placed over his head, probably with the idea of preventing him using his power. They were sensible precautions, just in case Ghost Hand decided to change his mind last second and try to hurt someone.

In total, there were only six guns available to the community and the women had first dibs. The ones that had been abused the worst couldn't stop themselves from crying while preparing. Ropes were actually placed under his arms, and he was strapped to a tree so that he couldn't fall after being shot.

I realized then that my precaution with Maria was well needed as these people were going to use his body as a shooting target for as long as he would survive. He deserved it...but we weren't savages.

Still, I didn't say anything against to stop the proceedings, and I watched as Maria called out, 'everybody aim.'

The women lifted their guns, some wavering.

'Ghost Hand, you deserve to die. Instead of trying to save people from the apocalypse, you took advantage, you and your cronies, to abuse us and you drove three good women to their deaths.

'I'm not going to give you a final say. No one wants to hear your excuses.'

He did begin to say something, but the hood muffled his voice. 'Three. Two. One. Fire!'

A ragged volley of shots all hit the man's body and as several were in the chest, he probably died right then. But the women reloaded and fired again, while Maria took careful aim and put a bullet in his head.

The sack and ropes made it hard to tell Ghost Hand was dead, and crazily enough even more people came forward to ask for a gun and vent their hatred by shooting at the body. It wasn't a good use of ammo at all, but I didn't feel like saying so. Best that they release their anger and rid themselves of this overwhelming negativity.

The moment Ghost Hand died a new era began for all of these people. It was time to start moving forward and getting back to the activities that needed to be done. Which honestly was a bit easier said than done.

Once we got some levels on people though, they should be able to watch the cows graze and keep out the zombies and goblins. As soon as our fortified walls were erected life here could perhaps go back to semi-normal, depending what new developments took place in the game.

Five men and two women were interested in leveling seriously, and our first stop was the barn with the captured zombies in it. Here was a chance for them to gain their first bit of EXP. By my count, there were ten zombies inside the pens.

Jessica and I got the volunteers into a party together and passed out spears for them to take turns. One zombie kill per person wasn't quite enough to level them, so they each killed one—safely protected by the walls and lower gate of the stalls—and then shared the hits on the other three. By the time all ten zombies were dead, the group had all reached level 1.

Since she was much more sociable than me and understood the system perfectly, I said very little, letting my partner take the lead in explaining stats, skills, items and passive skills. There were several questions, which Jessica answered pretty much exactly as I would have.

They all understood there was risk involved in leveling. We would help them get started, but eventually the decisions they made and the encounters they picked would be their own, and they could only depend on themselves.

The plan was to bring them with us to the steel mill, as well as the two workers and several other men. There were enough vehicles on farm to get everyone whom was seriously interested in leveling there. Getting the sheet metal back was another story, and we would figure that out at a later time.

"We leave tomorrow afternoon. The steel mill is just a few minutes by car away. If you're not here, I'll assume you're not very serious about levelling," I said. "You can drop out now if you like." Although the newly levelled people looked anxious about going to the steel mill, none of them gave up.

They had the entire remainder of the day as well as night to decide if this was what they wanted. Without touching a skill or really gaining a lot of items, it was hard for anyone to get a taste for the game and to really appreciate the difference in power between each level. From their perspective there was probably not much difference between me and Ghost Hand. Fortunately, we had Jessica and her words and example reassured everyone.

After scheduling the expedition for the next day, Jessica and I met up with Lucas to discuss another matter. If we wanted to start building infrastructure for housing, we needed wood. I tasked him to head into the forest and take a look at what might be there.

There was an enormous supply of wood nearby and we just needed to ensure that it was safe to go into the forest to cut the timber. We needed to know exactly what was waiting for us there besides the natural wild-life. Had the apocalypse introduced monsters into the forest? If so, were they higher level than the mobs in the city?

"While you take Alan and Thomas to scout the forest, Jessica and I will be heading into the city and taking a look."

"Sangeal or Withersburg?" he asked.

"Withersburg." I said, "according to what I've heard from the few that made runs there, the monster spawn rate is much more rapid. We'll be able to take a look and see today." It was only around twenty minutes by car from here. "Are you ready to go?" I asked Jessica.

She nodded her head.

"Should we take Maria along?"

"Let her stay. She's busy with the others," Jessica said. "As far as the residents are concerned, we are still outsiders. Maria is someone they trust and she admires us. That will come across to them."

It was good karma for us that we had treated Maria with kindness and respect. If she had anything negative to say about us I would be surprised. I was sure, too, that the other three women we had rescued looked on us favorably as well.

Fortunately for us, Ghost Hand wasn't completely lacking foresight and had secured five vehicles: three jeeps, a GMC Sierra, and a Toyota Tacoma. All had good capacity for carrying large loads. He had secured a decent stockpile of gas as well. Still, as soon as we could find a large tank and a trailer, I wanted to ransack my old gas station.

If I could bring a full tanker here, that amount of gas would last us months. For now, we ended up taking one of the Jeeps. Speed might matter. And the air blowing against your face truly was refreshing. Jessica seemed to enjoy it as well, her shoulder-length brunette hair streaming around her as she turned her head from side to side.

On arrival at Withersburg, we had a problem and Jessica pulled a long way short of the tall buildings in the distance. The mobs were densely packed. Behind their lines, the destruction and mayhem could be seen clearly from a distance. Hardly a building seemed to have an intact window, and many were stained dark with the aftermath of fires.

In front of us were the typical zombies and goblins we were familiar with, but also new enemies I hadn't encountered before. Jessica took the time to inspect each one so we weren't blindsided.

Savage: Level four. Normal. It was another little humanoid like the goblin, except it looked smaller, had a blue-tinge to its skin and was wearing decorations like long silver earrings and armbands. Most of them were holding two axes as weapons and I reckoned they might be a step up from the little lobster-like alien creatures.

A thought passed my mind: perhaps a larger city meant more population which meant more difficult enemies. The mobs were the same level as their counterparts in Sangeal but better armed. These blue savages, for example, dual wielded axes, which might prove to have more DPS than the spears of the green goblins. If I had to guess which was deadlier, I'd say the savage.

Fortunately, after I summoned my squad of undead we could plow right through these low-level enemies. For Jessica too, they were mostly one-shots. So carefully and clearing a wide path, we took down a swathe of mobs and progressed deeper into the city. Before long we were encountering two new types of mobs, presumably the equivalents to ogres and banshees. These turned out to be higher level too, and it seemed hunting here would be promising. Jessica gave us the information we needed.

Levitating Eye: Level Ten. Normal. This monster was simply a floating eye with no appendages, which led us to deduce it attacked via spell. I sent a skeleton in to investigate, and a beam of blue light exploded from the pupil with great force and speed.

The flash and impact of the spell was almost immediate, which made it several times more deadly than a banshee's Frost Bolt, since that could be dodged by hiding behind obstacles.

The other new mob, which I presumed was equivalent to Sangeal's ogre was called a sickleman.

Sickleman: Level 10. Normal. This was a skeleton that wielded a large scythe. The fact that it was undead meant a lot of my offensive abilities lost their effectiveness against it. Not only that, it had a gigantic distance for its attacks that was even larger than the spears Jessica and I had started with.

If each city had different enemies with varying difficulty based on their population, then the situation here probably was a mild one comparatively speaking, which didn't bode well for the groups of people who were out there somewhere. Even against easier monsters than these, the vast majority of people in my home city had been slaughtered.

Maybe more people had survived than I thought though, and they were living like rats scrounging and doing whatever they could to hide and stay alive. Humanity's resilience was surprisingly high.

Despite these enemies being relatively low level compared to us, there were so many of them that Jessica and I were getting good EXP. Letting my two abominations run forward and gather them up was a sight to see.

Constant flashes of bright blue light shooting from eyeballs pelted into my abominations. My huge undead were slapping left and right with their multiple fists, killing every savage, sickleman, goblin and zombie in sight that hadn't fallen to the noxious bile.

The levitating eyes remained stationary and blasted beam after beam, which didn't have much effect on my minions. Jessica used them as target practice and sent arrows through each and every one. A thick viscous goop dripped from the fallen eyeballs before they dropped to the ground and despawned.

Although each individual mob seemed to have a low drop chance, the sheer rate at which we were wiping them out meant items continuously dropped and our EXP was climbing rapidly. On the downside, I couldn't see how our low-level people could even begin to farm the mobs here: the vast amount of them meant one bad pull would see you instantly overwhelmed.

Jessica and I didn't have that issue. Even when dozens of mobs were triggered and swarmed my skeletal squad, they held the aggro and reappeared in due course after killing them. The abominations were gathering up twenty and thirty monsters at a time as we moved forward. We had found eight Rations and three Survivor's Medallions in a period of ten minutes, which was a record for us.

A wake of destruction was left in our path, and we hit level 18 in such a speed that I almost didn't want to pause to check my character sheet.

Name: Mike Reynolds (27) Class: Necromancer Level: 18 EXP: 1%
HP: 670/725 MP: 260/325
STR: 5 Fear Resistance: 5
AGI: 2
DEX: 5
VIT: 20 +2
WIS: 24 +8
Available: 3

Skills: [A]Summon Skeleton LV. 7 |[A]
Decay LV. 2| [A] **Reanimate Dead LV.** 2 | [A]
Bone Armor LV. 2 | [A] **Vast Shadows** |
[P]**Sixth Sense** | [P] **Bravery LV.** 2 | [P]
Mutated LV. 2| [P] **Pain Resistance LV.** 2 | [P]
Skeletal Mastery LV. 3| [P]**Intimidate Living**
|[P] **Inner Calm**

I was glad I did though, as I could see that my HP was still going up and down. The infection I received from the zombie was still in my system, and yet I didn't feel it. Mutated…mutated had hit level 2 and my heart stopped in shock.

The infection was the cause then…definitely. I quickly went further into the passive skill.

Mutated LV. 2: You are being changed in unknown ways.

The passive skill still didn't give me any information on what it was doing at all, which only increased my desire to know more about it.

It seemed the system enjoyed teasing me. Maybe it was a passive that did nothing until it reached max level, but what level was that? Three? Five? I couldn't be sure.

Based on what I'd learned about the system so far, we each needed to acquire two new active skills before reaching Level Twenty, but unlike gear, the skill drops were few and far between, and when they did drop, they often weren't something we wanted to use. Ideally, I wanted another offensive spell or a second type of minion spawn.

I wasn't sure if there was another minion ability, but there were definitely active spells to cast. Something besides decay that I could use on all mob-types, so I wasn't sitting around doing mostly nothing on particularly difficult encounters.

Jessica was also looking for an offensive ability that dealt significant damage. All she was able to do right now was shoot arrow after arrow. She needed some augmented ability that would bring her arrows to a new height.

There were still several hours of sunlight remaining in the day, and so we kept moving forward, hoping to catch a glimpse of the enemies we would consider equivalent to our snake-headed demi-human and abominations back at Sangeal.

Chapter 25: Two New Post-Apocalypse Mobs

"Just another block and I can feel two new enemy types. Probably what we're looking for." Jessica sounded almost eager and that was my cue to hurry it up and move faster, I guessed that we were both itching to get a look. Nor was I disappointed when I located the new mob types.

Demonic Goat: Level Eighteen. Normal. This monster was a goat man with intimidating horns on his forehead that curled into a sharp tip. The hair of its fur was blood red and tapered off into needle-like points. A black coloration surrounded both of its red eyes, which gave the large satyr a menacing look. The whole threatening effect was topped off with the weapon the demonic goat held in both hands: a gigantic morning star as tall as it was—nearly seven feet.

The other mob was an undead: Blood Lich. Level Nineteen. Normal. This monster was at least ten feet tall and hovered above the ground. The garb it wore was black and red, a cowl that fluttered even without the presence of any wind. A sphere of red swirled between its two hands.

Both enemies seemed menacing enough, but the lich gave me an even worse feeling than the goat did. Most likely, this was because the goat's attack was obvious, he used that morning star, but the lich was a spell caster, and the spells it wielded were unknown to me.

"Goat first?" Jessica asked. It seemed she had the same idea as I did.

"Send it," I replied. I was already prepared, and although these were higher level than ogres and half-snakes, I wasn't expecting any significant amount of resistance from them. Being swarmed by my 10 minions wouldn't allow for much room to counter-attack.

An arrow pierced through the bristly fur of a demonic goat and triggered him to rush us. His hoofs clapped against the asphalt street as the morning star was gripped tightly in both his hands.

My squad of undead fighters rushed out to meet it and the morning star fell upon my skeleton general with a sound like a gong being struck hard. He didn't even flinch or give way at all as his sword came up immediately and slashed against the almost metal coat of the demonic goat.

The new monster was swarmed in a moment and my minions hacked it to pieces within seconds. It fell without much ability to put up a fight, and Jessica and I gained 5% EXP and another Survivor's Medallion.

The lich took a little more thought, and we made sure to find a place where we could hide. This time Jessica placed a Quagmire Trap for it to path through. My minions rushed forward in a zerg-like manner.

Ranged enemies always required respect, because so much of their tactics were unknown. Until the melee attacks of my summoned squad gained its full attention, there was always the chance of a ranged attack against Jessica who had the early aggro from her pull shot. Was there possibly a skill that had a chance of killing you in one hit? Even though it wouldn't be 'fair', the answer was that there really could be.

The lich floated there while changing target from minion to minion casting some blood ability. I couldn't tell what it was doing, because it seemed to have no effect on the skeletons or the cleaver-wielding Exceptional Abominations. Was it trying to suck blood, or absorb blood?

An ephemeral cackle constantly echoed outward from its maw as the lich continuously cast its spells without much care that they were not working. The garb around its body was swiftly being torn to shreds with each hack and slash from my squad.

Jessica pelted the lich near the eyes with arrows to no avail. There was nothing but blood-red flames where the eye sockets were, and arrows didn't seem to have the ability to blind it at all. All the same, the monster's body began glowing red as its life plummeted towards zero.

A circle of blood exploded outward from its body and blasted into my minions, sending them tumbling backwards and onto the floor. None of them had died, but that final attack would probably do significant damage to human fighters attacking in melee.

With a last cackle that seemed to fade into the distance echoing through the area the lich collapsed into a heap on the floor.

To our surprise, there was a Class Changing Stone floating there, which indicated that it didn't only drop from exceptional monsters. Besides that, there was an item floating above the remains of the lich. It was a shield made of pure bone.

Lich's Aegis: A shield made from the breastplate of a lich.

VIT +5. Increases chance to block attacks by thirty-two percent. Blocked attacks deal twenty-five percent of their original damage.
Grants the user Necrotic Vision.

I didn't have a shield yet, and honestly wasn't sure if I could even wield it. My survivor's rod was only one handed, but it was still quite large. The anticipation just before equipping the shield was too much to bear.

A moment later the shield was slotted in my character sheet, and the rush of happiness knowing I'd found another useful item couldn't be described. This was one of the feelings that kept me addicted, kept me wanting to keep leveling, the feeling of constant improvement.

I opened my status sheet to check the skill Necrotic Vision.

Name: Mike Reynolds [27] Class:
Necromancer Level: 18 EXP: 12%
HP: 745/875 MP: 285/375
STR: 5 Fear Resistance: 5
AGI: 2
DEX: 5
VIT: 20 +12
WIS: 24 +18
Available: 3
Skills: [A]Summon Skeleton LV. 7 I[A]
Decay LV. 2I [A] Reanimate Dead LV. 2 I [A]
Bone Armor LV. 2 I [A] Vast Shadows I
[P]Sixth Sense I [P] Bravery LV. 2 I [P]
Mutated LV. 2I [P] Pain Resistance LV. 2 I [P]
Skeletal Mastery LV. 3I [P]Intimidate Living
I[P] Inner Calm [P]Necrotic Vision

It was there in a beautiful yellow, a passive granted from an item. I opened the submenu.

Necrotic Vision: You can see the essence of life itself. Your eyes have a strange glow to them.

I didn't quite understand what seeing life essence meant till I stepped away from Jessica and took a good look at her. There was a faint aura, almost like a flame that twirled near the core of her body. I couldn't see through walls…but this was basically a form of night vision almost.

I took off the Skull Mask, "Look at my eyes, do you see anything?" I asked excitedly.

She gave a deep stare that suddenly made me feel a bit hot, "There's something flickering in your vision. Almost like a little orange hue, maybe a flame?" she offered questioningly. "What's wrong?"

It was actually hard for me to keep my eyes locked on hers as she was so incredibly close, "Nothing, you're just so close."

"Wait, are you blushing?" Jessica laughed. "Hoho, for a while I thought you thought about nothing but levelling up. But I guess that you have feelings after all." Looking cheerful, she added, "I'll have to be careful of those women back at camp."

"Wait, what is that supposed to mean?" I said aloud. It was impossible to not see Jessica as a beautiful woman with heroic qualities of bravery and determination, but I didn't want to complicate our extraordinary fighting partnership. The fear of losing our close comradeship was too scary to take any risks by letting loose the powerful feelings I knew were there in me.

As soon as emotions got involved it was harder to think rationally. Maybe I had been over-thinking her remark as I looked at her back.

"Nothing," she glanced over her shoulder, still smiling. "Let's get a few more kills and then head back."

I couldn't have agreed with her faster. When it came to fighting monsters I felt quite confident, but when I looked at her lithe figure walking ahead of me, I didn't feel anything like firm ground beneath my feet. We spent another hour exploring and even marked two four-wheel drive vehicles that were in potentially good condition. We could come back at another time and retrieve them with our mechanic.

In the end, we found a few more Rations and three more Survivor's Medallions. I had 19 of them in my inventory now, and still no idea what they were used for. Jessica insisted on driving on the way back, which I had no problem with.

She really embraced the saying 'pedal to the metal'. If it wasn't for her foresight from her tracking, I'd question her ability to avoid the enemies along the road. It was such crazy driving I started to question whether my HP would allow me to survive a full-on car crash and subsequent explosion.

I didn't say anything as she was clearly having fun while swerving along the road. I had to admit, she looked beautiful with her brunette hair fluttering in the wind. It was a silent ride back, but I felt a lot of emotions had been conveyed. Should I say something? Instead, I pushed aside hope of romance in a world that was going to ruin and thought about our plans to make the farm into a sustainable and safe base. In the morning we would set off on our trip to the steel mill, and what came after that we could only guess.

On our return without accident, I met with Lucas and was up-dated on their groups experiences of going to the forest in search of timber. Every animal they had come across was extremely aggres-sive, even deer rushed at them with no regard for their lives. There were random zombies and goblins about, but that was the extent to which monsters were present.

They hadn't gone in deep enough to see what else might have spawned in the forest, but all we cared about was working around the edge anyway. According to him, he could down a tree with a single wind slash, which meant chain saws weren't needed, and the only problem we faced was that of extraction, which seemed to be a reoccurring issue for us.

Although it felt like longer, only twelve days had passed since the RPG apocalypse, and I had a nagging feeling on the back of my neck that there were a lot of new challenges ahead. After one week there had been the flare, which heralded the spawning of many more monsters. Would there be something similar at the two-week mark? The pessimist in me couldn't believe it was possible to keep progressing so smoothly as Jessica and I had been.

Sleeping that night didn't come easy as all sorts of high-level scenarios filled my mind. What would be thrown at us next? The last special event could be considered deadly, but in terms of actual difficulty it wasn't really that bad.

If you hid away in a country-side like this one, it would probably be easy enough to avoid new events by staying clear of the many mobs in the city. Was that intended? The nature of the attack on Earth was a challenge, designed to make us fight in the world as though in an RPG game. It was so carefully structured that I really felt in the long run, or even the medium run, hiding out would not prove to be a successful option. Even now, Jessica and I and the others could not afford to fall behind in levelling, given the possibility of some event that raised the bar higher than we could jump.

I don't remember when I fell asleep, but I absolutely didn't feel rested that following morning. Not only did I have a slight headache but I was starving. From the scents coming into my room it seemed breakfast had been cooked: eggs and some bacon which was from on site, a welcomed treat.

This was the first time I'd eaten something that wasn't a ration in many days or straight out of a baggy in two weeks—an actual cooked meal. Coming into the kitchen, I found that Alan had cooked the bacon and eggs, and sitting at the table with a full plate was Jessica.

"Here, Mike, enjoy some fresh food," said Alan proudly.

I thanked him, ate breakfast, and then I realized there was something terribly wrong.

"I'm...not getting full," I said. "This feels like I haven't eaten anything." I looked at Alan, then Jessica, a feeling of anxiety settling over me like a dark cloud.

"Me too." Jessica's face was filled with confusion.

Alan scooped some scrambled egg out of the pan with a spoon, blew away the steam and ate it. Then some more.

While he tested his own response, I wondered aloud, "Could it be...we can't sustain ourselves on anything but Rations?" If that were the case...then a peaceful life was impossible. Rations were dropped from enemies, and as you killed them and leveled, Rations became more and more rare a drop from the lower level ones.

"I think we're being forced to continue killing monsters to survive. But the Level Ones don't seem to have had this issue at all. Is this lack of energy from real food happening because we have been eating Rations or is it because we've reached a certain level?

"Should we say something to the others who want to level?" Jessica asked. She was right to think about that; if it was levels, then they deserved to know before leaving the relative safety of being able to live off natural food. Yet was access to natural foods really enough of an incentive to leave your life to the mercy of others? You had zero power or control of your own fate as a Level One.

These people had experienced that already anyway, and the ones coming with us absolutely didn't like that. Ghost Hand was the perfect example. He wasn't even particularly strong and yet had thirty people at the tips of his fingers. What about months from now, a year from now?

"I don't think we can say for sure it's the levels. If it isn't food, I have a hunch that the post-apocalypse system will find some means to stop them simply retreating from the game."

Jessica gave a nod to me. "All the same, they should understand the possible consequences of levelling."

While Alan finished his breakfast—no longer quite so enthusiastic about it—Jessica and I went outside to the vehicles. The sun had merely risen an hour ago and the temperature was still cool, albeit humid. Everyone was outside waiting for us already, including the two steel mill workers and three men they deemed necessary for helping them.

Not a single one of the seven that had already expressed interest in levelling backed out. They were all here and waiting, eager to grab their own thread of destiny and ensure no one could cut it short against their will.

"Do you need any special gear or can we go?" I asked Will, one of the two mill workers.

"I think we're good like this. Hopefully the mill is intact."

"Good then. We'll take three vehicles. Jessica and I will each drive one, and one of you will drive the third, any volunteers?"

"I'll drive," Will said. "You can follow me so there's no getting lost." I nodded and let him leave first, Jessica followed directly after, and I drove the last of the vehicles in our small convoy.

They weren't kidding when they said the steel mill was merely a five-minute drive. We pulled onto another off-road for about thirty seconds and then the mill was there right up against the forest. It was a huge hangar-like building with giant doors for equipment to come through.

Chapter 26: The Enticement of a Special Shop in an RPG

Before we could pull up in front of the mill, I could see mobs in every direction, and I honked at Will, leaning out the car window to shout, "Stop here and get back!" The vehicles came to an abrupt stop and Jessica and I rushed out. There were several mobs, but not an overwhelming amount.

They weren't difficult encounters: mostly sicklemen and floating eyes, but we needed to take care for the sake our of low-level members. On the plus side, I reckoned that after we'd cleared the mobs, our novices would be level 3, maybe even level 4. I pulled my army of minions from Vast Shadow and sent them forth to trap a sickleman.

We couldn't let Jessica pull anymore, as she one-shot these enemies with every arrow. Instead, my summoned squad were ordered to pin a target and press its arms to its side so it couldn't fight. I had assured the new comers there would be no risk as they levelled and I intended to keep that promise.

Unlike the captured zombies though, all these mobs were free roaming, and the enthusiasm the new recruits had shown from the day previous wasn't as strong now as when they had gained their first EXP. It was obvious to me that a few of them were even questioning their decision to participate in the game. "If you can't deal with enemies that are helpless, give up," I said to a man and woman who had not yet gotten out of the car. "If you can't fight, leave the party so there's more experience for those who can."

My words were intended to be a harsh wakeup call. I wasn't going to allow half the group to be carried by the other half, not this time. Both of the people in the car immediately hardened their resolve and got out to join the action. Soon they were all stabbing away at my pull.

If anyone could see past my mask, they would see a smile on my face. It was the first kill that was the hardest, that foreign feeling when stabbing into flesh was like nothing you'd ever felt before. But once you felt the effects of levelling up, you never wanted to stop.

"Good job, let's keep going." We methodically cleared the entire steel mill. In the end, all the new volunteers reached level four, which was good news and the confidence they had gained was evident in their smiles and banter.

Everyone on the raid had already been given a mini-lesson from Jessica on how to increase their stats based on what they wanted to accomplish. We had a few items drop as well as five skill books. I checked them all to see if there was anything useful for the high-level people, but they were more of the same skills we'd seen before.

It had become clear to me that support skills and abilities like Summon Skeleton were few and far between. The drops at the mill were all simple skills with no depth, like Energy Bolt or Fireball or simple augments to weapon-type attacks.

The new players weren't exactly fighting over the skills presented to them, but more than half wanted either Energy Bolt or Fireball, which was to be expected at least. Ranged abilities kept you away from the danger, but it didn't necessarily make them safer.

Once it was clear there were no more mobs, Will brought his squad in and located the generators and the materials we needed to get our power supply up and running. Fortunately for us, no one had ransacked them before we got here.

The workers were there for heavy lifting only. Sheets were fed and then forcefully grooved for stability, after that a large machine cut them to the perfect size. The workers we brought were meant to carry these off.

"How long will this take?" I asked.

"It will take about four hours to get enough sheets for the walls. The main difficulty I can see is the matter of finding the means to transport them," Will said.

"What about the truck in the back?" I asked. There was a particularly large vehicle on site, and although I didn't know what it was called or what they used it for, it did have a bed in the back.

"It's meant for solid metal, not sheets, but it could work."

There was nothing for the seven players to do for the moment so I proposed they helped the workers. "Load what you can, it doesn't have to be neat. Those who ended up putting points in STR can lift them into the truck," I said.

Every time a sheet came off the press, we grabbed it with a collective strength that was extraordinary compared to previous times and then we carried it to the truck. Being of a uniform size and shape, the sheets stacked tightly like puzzle pieces, so they actually didn't take much space when loaded standing upright.

When we'd maximized the space in the truck with sheets for the walls of the compound, there was still a little more room. "Will it be possible to get some support beams?" I asked.

Will shook his head. "Not before dark. There's plenty of rebar on site but we can't melt it down. It's unfortunate but rebar is all we'll be getting."

"It'll have to make do then." All-in-all we ended up spending five hours at the mill. Bringing some spare gas we'd found, Will drove the truck back. I wasn't sure if we had enough metal sheeting to build a good barrier, but it was all the sheeting in the factory, and there wasn't going to be another shipment.

Besides that, there were no beams on site and we ended up taking as much rebar as we could. It wasn't ideal, but we could supplement the construction with wooden spikes. This wasn't a short-term project by any means, so there was no rush to finish it immediately.

The metal was unloaded from the truck by everyone, despite the complaints of those who had only come along to level up. It was back-breaking work, but we had solved our transportation issue. This truck would be able to bring lumber back as well. It was just a matter of working with it.

As I added up the amount of metal pieces that we'd fashioned and tried to calculate the quantity needed for a wall around the farm buildings, I couldn't help but get a headache. My hands rubbed my head vigorously in frustration. I felt a hand rub against my back, "Are you okay?" It was Jessica.

"I'm fine. I just didn't really understand how much work this will actually be," I confessed. Somehow or another I had this fantasy idea that once we had the metal sheets, we could put them together like Legos.

Creating a sturdy defensive barrier required so much more work than that, frustratingly so. Holes needed to be dug; we needed concrete; and we needed to weld or find some way to attach the walls

265

to each other. Everything needed to be moved and placed meticulously to fit into one cohesive unit.

This was going to take hundreds upon hundreds of man hours as well many more expeditions to gather materials. We didn't even have all the tools needed. We knew where we could find them though—either Sangeal or Withersburg.

A nagging feeling on the back of my neck told me this task was urgent: it made me impatient and it continued to cause my head to pound. "Let's go inside," Jessica said. I gave a nod and we made for the farmhouse. It was then that something was transmitted to my brain directly.

It was a map, a blank map with a location clearly marked with a red dot. I looked at Jessica who locked eyes with me. It was clear we were both experiencing the same phenomena.

A Special Shop containing valuable skills and items has spawned 231 miles away from you. Defeat the guardians of the Special Shop to gain access to the Special Vendor and make purchases with Medallions. Monsters within 500 miles of the Special Shop will continue to grow stronger until the Special Vendor is accessed.

"A special shop?" I looked at Jessica.

"What does the Survivor's Medallion say now?" she asked. I checked my inventory and pulled up the coin that had previous said nothing at all.

Survivor's Medallion: Allows the User to purchase skills, items, and other consumables from the Special Vendor.

"It's the currency for the special vendor!" I said excitedly.

"How many do we have now?" she asked.

"Twenty-six of them," I said. "It doesn't seem like much."

Jessica remained enthusiastic, "Maybe, but they didn't drop that often. Twenty-six could actually be a lot." We had killed a shit ton of monsters to reach our current level no doubt, plus there were the ones we'd taken from Ghost Hand, and he had been funneling from several people.

"Monsters will get stronger overtime. I wish they specified exactly what that meant," I said. At least there was some form of warning this time. They could have just put a dot on the map and waited for you to go find out why everything started kicking your ass.

"Do you think one spawned every set number of miles? A thousand say?" Jessica asked. "We can't be the only area that got one."

"Probably...I wish we knew more about what was happening to the rest of the country. All we can do is our best here and maybe in time we'll be able to travel, or hear from travelers. For now, let's focus on getting to see what the Special Vendor has to offer." Two-hundred and thirty-one Miles away was a few hours by car, and we did have the vehicles and gas required to make that move.

"I don't think this will be simple. The message referred to guardians, and if they are guarding valuable skills and items they will be correspondingly tough."

"Difficult enemies then," I agreed. "Also, we don't know where exactly that place is. It could be in the middle of a city for all we know, which would make it extremely hard to reach." If the shop was in the middle of a city with a lot of spawns, then it would take a lot of man power to reach it.

As I thought about how everyone in the vicinity of the store would be coming together, I felt no excitement or enthusiasm at all. Rather, the prospect of meeting other groups terrified me. Anyone who could make the journey would have at least some combat capability. Not all of the survivors of the apocalypse were good people, and nothing said the Special Vendor was accessible by everyone.

The possibility existed that it was first come first serve, and even if it wasn't, the Special Vendor probably wouldn't sell an endless amount of valuable skills and items. The other problem was what 'grow stronger' meant.

Were enemies growing stronger by the second? The minute? The day? The week? The message was so vaguely worded that it induced anxiety all on its own. How much time did we realistically have before we were hiding from every goblin and zombie we saw?

It wasn't just those that had leveled at least once who heard the message either. Everyone seemed to go into an uproar over it. This was only the second time the 'system' had retroactively spoken to anyone. It was different than getting a message for leveling up or obtaining an item.

This was a change happening in the world that affected everyone, and given the state of the world now, it was reasonable to assume that if it wasn't dealt with in a timely manner, the change was going to wipe everyone out.

What other goal could be seen from this new development besides someone, somewhere gaining pleasure from watching us lesser beings struggle? Whomever or whatever caused this was taking enjoyment at our expense, and what better way to watch us squirm than to turn up the heat?

When I thought about it that way, I realized this was a pressing issue. Monsters were going to be getting continuously stronger, maybe even by the second. Anything longer than a day per incremental strength increase was unlikely to keep up. Here, violence happened on a whim with no forewarning—the post-apocalypse world wasn't forgiving.

The problem was: what to do about the farmland while the best fighters went to look for the shop? It wasn't possible or feasible to bring everyone out that far from safety, nor would the low-level people even want to accompany us. On the other hand, it was likely that Alan, Thomas, Maria and Lucas would want to be part of the raid, and they probably should be.

Doubtless other groups of survivors would show up at the shop too and they might pose more danger than the local mobs. Anyone who was capable of getting in a car and defending themselves would make an appearance. I felt that the shop would be a place to make allies and possibly enemies, but more than anything, it would be a place to grow stronger.

A decision had to be made: who would take control of the decisions on the farm while we were away? Jessica tasked Maria with finding someone suitable and who had the support of all the farm workers. Maria kept it simple, calling everyone to the main yard and making it a public vote.

To my surprise, there was no great fuss, no battle for the responsibility of running the farm. In fact, by unanimous agreement of the crowd, they wanted an elderly gentleman in his seventies to take charge.

The name of the newly elected leader for the farming community was Charles, and he struck me as the type of person who was kind to absolutely everyone. Nor was there any sign that he would change with the responsibility of the role. A frailty in the way he was standing fitted with the fact he wasn't interested in levelling and I just couldn't see him bullying anyone.

Probably, he had only one ambition: to live out the remainder of his life comfortably, which suited me fine as it meant his goal was to build the farm into a safe place to live. It wasn't as if he was made a king either, there would be others on hand to help make decisions and any difficult decisions could be decided by vote.

Once that was resolved, Charles went around shaking hands then gestured to me to address the crowd.

"We'll leave in three days, before then I'll do my best to gather as much food and other supplies as I can," I said. "That's all I have to say."

Although I hadn't said much, my promise to help the farm stock up before we left was met with a smattering of applause.

We had all the metal we could possibly get from the Steel Mill, and after taking a tally, the engineers told me there were enough plates that we could reinforce about sixty-percent of the wall. This news was slightly disappointing, but it was going to be a lot better than the flimsy defenses we had now.

Lucas was going to be coming with us to the shop, and he devoted his three days to taking five workers into the nearby forest to build up the timber supply. His entire day was spent cutting trees down and sectioning them with Wind Slash.

Sean, the carpenter, gave Jessica and I a list of things he needed and several addresses. They were shops we could visit to gather the supplies he needed in Withersburg. He even marked them on a city map for us.

For Jessica and I most of the three days were spent in Withersburg grinding and gathering the necessary supplies. We didn't hold anything back in terms of leveling and each used one of the two EXP UP potions we had.

When the three days were up, Jessica and I had reached Level 20.

Name: Mike Reynolds (27) **Class:**
Necromancer Level: 20 **EXP:** 0%
HP: 905/905 **MP:** 385/385
STR: 5 **Fear Resistance:** 5
AGI: 2
DEX: 5
VIT: 20 +12
WIS: 24 +18
Available: 9

Skills: [A]**Summon Skeleton LV.** 8 I[A]
Decay LV. 2I [A] **Reanimate Dead LV.** 2 I [A]
Bone Armor LV. 2 I [A] **Vast Shadows** I
[P]**Sixth Sense** I [P] **Bravery LV.** 2 I [P]
Mutated LV. 2I [P] **Pain Resistance LV.** 2 I [P]
Skeletal Mastery LV. 4I [P]**Intimidate Living**
I[P] **Inner Calm** I[P] **Necrotic Vision**

Summon Skeletons hit Level Eight granting an extra minion, Skeletal Mastery reached Level Four. Besides that, my infection had calmed and Mutated was still Level Two only. It didn't seem there would be any time in the near future to continue investigating it.

I had nine available points to spend, but wasn't feeling any pressure to do so. Once we arrived at the Special Shop, I would decide then. The same with a new Skill slot that had opened at Level 20. Jessica and I decided that rather than equip any of the Skills we'd found, we'd wait to see what was available at the vendor.

As a result of levelling up, I had 10 skeleton minions and two reanimated dead for a total of 12 undead in my squad. Eight of my skeletons were granted from the skill itself, while two came from my Necromancer passive. It seemed that one was added for every seven base levels, in which case I'd be due a new skeleton next level.

Reanimate dead didn't grant base levels but instead monster efficiency per level. At level fourteen I had been granted the ability through my Necromancer passive to summon a second reanimated dead.

Three of my eight skeleton warriors were currently equipped with special weapons: A morning star, a meat cleaver, and a crude short bow. Of my two skeleton Generals, one was default kitted, which was just a shield and sword, while the other wielded a Two-handed sword called a Zweihander.

Both of my Reanimated minions were Exceptional Abominations. Their attacks weren't varied, but they dealt an incredible amount of single target damage with the six cleavers they wielded. Their AoE wasn't bad when Noxious Bile was released and I hadn't seen them get low enough yet to find out if Enrage was also an ability they could use.

Jessica had leveled up Anomalous Trap to Level Three, which granted a 35% increased effectiveness of skills used in this way. Quagmire had reached Level Four as well, which increased the duration slightly. Besides that, there was still no change to her inspection ability. We found four more Survivor's Medallions, which put us at an even thirty, but no new skills or items worthy of equipping or using.

A massive pile of lumber had been transported onto the farm and Jessica and I had gathered more than enough materials for construction to begin on the new wall.

Hammers, nails, handsaws, and three chainsaws—there was also table saw and generator that had both been absolute hell to transport back to the vehicle. These would have to make do for Sean's new tools, and our carpenter couldn't have been more grateful for the table saw and generator. He said that he could use the chainsaw to cut out boards, but it would be nowhere near as fast, efficient, and accurate as the table saw.

Besides that, I gave those remaining behind at the farm the keys to the gas container at my old workplace and marked it clearly on a map. They wouldn't be low on gas if they regularly took trips there: and with the generator and chainsaws there would be a constant expenditure for the foreseeable future.

Before we set off for the vendor, I left behind fifty-percent of the Rations Jessica and I had accumulated in case of an emergency, as well as a few Bandages and Minor HP Potions. There was no indication of how long this would take.

Lucas, Alan and Thomas had all reached level 16 and Maria was close behind them at 15.

Over the three days, it had become clear to me that Jessica and I needed to guide the farm indirectly and allow others to make decisions in our stead. It was too time consuming to micromanage the place when we could better spend our time leveling. As long as we secured supplies, those that weren't interested in leveling could carry out the tasks involved in growing our own food supply and keeping the place safe.

On the dawn of the fourth day after the announcement, the expedition team gathered in the main yard, with a surprising number of farm workers gathered to cheer us and bid us good luck. We were finally on our way to find out about the special shop and what it contained.

Chapter 27: Who Dares Approach the Gateway?

"Does everyone have everything they need?" I asked, shouldering my pack onto my back. This was truly the first real journey we would take together as a group.

"We're good to go," Alan replied. It was fortunate that there was an actual inventory for items like weapons and armor as well as other drops from the mobs. As long as an object was considered an item it could be stored there, and the stack size seemed indefinite as far as I could tell.

The inventory did have a counter showing you could only hold a hundred different types of items, but that seemed like a distant limit, one that I wouldn't reach for a very long time, if at all.

Nothing was more pressing than what lay ahead. The special vendor was clearly a critical event for the fate of those people who had survived this far. The fact that we'd been collecting Survivor's Medallions also underscored the significance of this opportunity. If we didn't take it, these drops and all the fighting that went into getting them would be wasted. But were we strong enough? For myself and Jessica, I had few reservations. We had done as much as we could to maximize our strength. But perhaps this was a raid event that needed a hundred people of high level to overcome whatever guardians there were between us and the shop. In which case, we'd be unable to get there and even trying would mean death for us all.

The fate of our community depended on all five of us above level ten to come along and take up this challenge, but the rewards could be transformative. "Alright, let's go," I said. We hopped into the only SUV on farm and Lucas gladly drove.

After skirting around Sangeal, we would be heading east for about two hours, and then from there would have to play it by the map. Our goal just showed as a dot where the Special Shop was, and the map also showed me as a dot. Neither the obstacles between us, nor exactly where the shop was were shown properly. The only other information on the map was our distance to the shop, which was 231 Miles. We routed around Sangeal and then kept on the road for around another 200 miles, passing the turnoff for Perchane, which was another fair-sized city, and small farm town.

Eventually, the map showed that the shop was just north of us, and as we turned off the highway. I could see car tracks were already evident on this seemingly ancient pathway. This seemed to prove a point that others would be showing and it made me uneasy. Other groups could be allies to get into the shop, but they could also consider us rivals for the rewards. The new road didn't look natural at all, and as we drove for about thirty minutes, I realized it wasn't. The land around me seemed to have become completely flat.

"Something changed! Wasn't there a mountain on our right just now?" Alan asked.

"Yeah, there was. Coal mining used to happen there," Thomas replied, but there was no mountain now. All the way to the horizon was just unbelievably flat land that made me think we were traveling through a desert. It stretched away for such a distance that it almost didn't seem to follow the curvature of the Earth.

We could see our destination up ahead. A blue light beamed upwards into the sky faintly and would pulse just as faintly every couple of minutes. As we drove closer, I could see that thirty-foot walls surrounded a towering structure, but whatever was hidden behind the walls couldn't be discerned. A minimarket? A town perhaps? They were big enough.

There were other people already there as we approached, maybe a hundred or so standing around their vehicles and looking up at the behemoth of a monument.

A single opening was visible in the walls, and beside it were two incredibly large statues looking like something straight out of Egypt. They were two sphinxes, standing on either side of an open arch. "Can you tell anything about the statues?" I asked Jessica. There was no glowing fire visible from them.

She shook her head, "I can't scan them. They are inanimate objects."

That didn't make any sense to me. There was nothing beside them or behind them or anything but free real estate once you crossed the threshold of the entrance. Why was no one going in? I got out of the SUV and walked closer to get a better look.

People around started looking at me, and I could feel their piercing stares. One foot in front of the other, close and closer, and yet I couldn't see anything out of the ordinary about the sphinxes. Was there another entrance on the other side of the walls?

I put my foot down and suddenly my sixth sense went off like crazy. My eyes immediately bolted to the sphinx statue in front of me, and even though it was fully an inanimate statue, its eyes...The eyes of the statue followed me with such murderous intent that I could feel it.

This was dangerous, and it was only second to the Fiend. The fiend was on another level completely in terms of threat. My senses were telling me though, if I stepped a few more feet forward I would be attacked, and the battle wouldn't be an easy one.

If it was only one statue, then my feeling was that we would be able to control the fight and dispatch it, but there was a second. Were there more mobs besides these statues waiting as well? I didn't want to be the guinea pig of this group.

In the hope someone would give me some information, I looked around and most people gave me unfriendly stares. In their defense though, I didn't look welcoming either. My skull mask and black garb paired with my bone shield gave me a demonic look. In their eyes I was probably a total bad guy.

I reported my findings to the others and the consensus was to wait and gather information about earlier attempts to go in. Unfortunately, no one gave me a single welcoming look. Fortunately, we had a beautiful woman with us whom was attracting as many stares as I was but of a very different sort.

It didn't take long for Jessica to find a running mouth, "About a day ago someone walked too close, and the sphinx statues attacked him. He was doing okay running away, but just when we thought he was going to get clear they simply shot a laser from their eyes. His body just turned to ash." The man shrugged ruefully. "After that, no one has gone anywhere near the arch."

Probably the crowd had hoped that I would trigger the sphinxes, so they could learn more about them. It wasn't the most generous of thoughts but if so, I felt the same. It would be very useful to watch someone try to go in. Only when the sphinx was animate would there be a chance Jessica could scan them and at least find out their tier and level.

What also became readily clear was that many of the men here were too full of themselves, "Hey beautiful, why don't you hang out with us?" This came from a young tank-type, probably younger than me, catcalling Jessica.

She looked him up and down then gave a condescending laugh, "Not interested."

The youth's eyes scanned us as a group with ill intent, "Are these people even able to protect you?" Confident words, but as far as I could tell there was nothing special at all about this person in front of me. I was sure he was even weaker than Ghost Hand, and that if she wanted to Jessica could dispatch him with a single arrow in one swift motion.

"I'm taken already. Get lost!" Jessica barked at him before walking over to me and grabbing my arm. I was suddenly stunned in place and didn't know how to react. She was able to take care of herself no doubt, so why did she have to go and drag me into it?

The arrogant young man looked at me with uneasy eyes, "This ghoulish freak?" Somehow his comment didn't make me annoyed at all. It was actually useful in deterring any others from getting involved. The more I came across as disturbing, the less someone would want to risk taking me on.

"How about this," Jessica smiled sweetly, but without any warmth, "if you can take out a sphinx for me, then I'll change my mind. I'll be all yours."

The guy looked at the sphinxes there for a moment and then turned back with a sour face. "No you won't; I'm not stupid!" He turned away and strode off. When he was about halfway back to his own group he turned around and gave me a double middle-finger.

Now that actually made me annoyed. WTF did I do? Jessica could only laugh at the entire situation, "Are you gonna end up being trouble?" I asked.

"Hey, I almost had someone to go animate those sphinxes for us. I could then have got us some useful info." And she wasn't wrong. If a new group came along, maybe she could convince someone to walk through the gate. I caught myself right there. Had I become so used to this that I would knowingly allow someone to die for the sake of getting through to the shop?

After an hour of finding out very little else, a group of four— two men, two women—rolled up and all of them had serious sticks up their asses. They scornfully mocked everyone and referred to us as weaklings for sitting around and not walking directly into the special shop. This was exactly what we needed and my morals did not have to be tested.

Despite that attitude, someone was still kind enough to warn them to not get too close to the sphinxes, that they would be attacked with lasers from the eyes of the monsters. Yet in a serious case of overestimating their abilities, the four of them walked up and both the sphinxes attacked simultaneously.

The new group weren't just bluster: they definitely did have some ability, as they survived for over a minute fighting. Just as I was wondering whether we should come in and help, despite a lack of information, their tank was smashed under a stone paw and turned to meat mush.

Realizing they had bit off more than they could chew the other three immediately tried to run. Just as the reports said, lasers shot from the sphinxes' eyes and vaporized each and every one of them without fail.

Once you started the encounter, you could not leave. Watching that sight for the second time, many people immediately decided this battle was well past what they could hope to defeat and started to leave.

Jessica had managed to get valuable information though. Each Sphinx was a level 22 Elite enemy. "What level do you think those people were?" I asked everyone in the group.

I honestly couldn't tell, as none of them fought like Jessica and I did. Lucas was the one to speak up, "I'd say they were right around our levels: sixteen to seventeen."

"How hard do you think those sphinxes are hitting?" I asked Alan. He had upgraded his shield from a car door to a tower shield now. He was a tank, and could get a basic idea from just watching the other person struggle.

"Pretty hard. I have one thousand four hundred HP and I think they would be doing around twenty to twenty-five percent of my HP per hit."

"You have Block?" I asked.

"I block thirty-five percent of attacks and take fifteen percent of damage from blocked attacks." Over the course of several hits, Block would account for around a 30% reduction from damage over many hits, which made sense for a tank. He also took another 30% less damage while below half HP.

"So are you confident you can tank one on your own for an extended period of time? It won't be attacking that fast and you'll only have to deal with one." I said. We would double Quagmire on pull and my minions would tank the first one.

"Do you have some sort of plan?" Maria asked. She had been silent for a while now. I thought perhaps that she felt out of place here as she was the newest to our group.

"I do, but it's a basic plan," I admitted. We hadn't seen any special skills from the sphinxes as the other group hadn't managed to deal enough damage to trigger one. They had merely survived, but their efforts had only lasted so long. "I focus a sphinx down as fast possible—the one my minions are attacking. Alan will tank one sphinx alone with Thomas healing him." I looked at Thomas, "How long would you be able to keep him up?"

"If he is under fifty-percent HP and taking thirty-percent less damage, probably several minutes, but that comes with risks."

"Right, we don't know if they have any special abilities," I said. "but in my experience, enemies don't really use them until they've lost HP. We won't be attacking the target Alan is on until we're ready to kill it. There's no way he can deal twenty-five percent or more of its HP alone.

"Once we are on his target, you'll cap him off so he's never too low on HP."

"Okay, this all sounds good," Lucas said, "But how can we be sure we'll be able to defeat the first sphinx before Thomas runs out of MP? If we can't, the second one will kill us all." It was a good point to make.

"How long does it take you four to down an exceptional enemy?" I asked.

"Like the banshees or brutes back at Sangeal?" Alan asked

"Yeah, those, how long?" I would have preferred to measure their performance against the abominations or demi-humans, but at least this would allow me to explain where Jessica and I were at in terms of DPS.

"About thirty seconds, maybe a bit shorter, why?"

I couldn't help but look at Jessica, who also looked back at me. "Those enemies take me alone about five seconds to kill," I said without trying to brag.

"This is no time to exaggerate," Lucas said with a frown.

"I'm not—alone it's in seconds, almost feels instant." I added, "Maria, you were with us when we killed one of these Exceptional Abominations, tell them."

"Ah, I was. I think that fight took around eight or nine seconds only? It used its abilities pretty much back to back and then died."

"...Seriously?" said Alan and he, Thomas, and Lucas all gave a look of 'impossible' on their face.

Jessica strung her bow. "It's been a long time since you've seen us fight."

Lucas turned to her, "So...you kill a level eighteen exceptional enemy in about ten seconds?"

"Around that, yes," Jessica replied.

"Okay, so we have the damage, but how much stronger and more HP do you think these have then? Fifty-percent? One-hundred percent? More?" It was a good question. No one could be sure just how much a difficulty rise Exceptional to Elite was.

Despite the failure of the previous group, this wasn't an impossible encounter. Whoever designed this encounter at least understood that it was in reach of the more experienced players. And if they guessed that human mistrust meant people weren't going to just band together on a whim and fight the sphinxes, they were right. It would take someone with a lot of charisma, or with a track record of building a community to organize those standing around the high walls. This event had come too soon for our farming group to be known or to prove itself as a hope for survivors. We were unknown and probably looked off-putting.

No, people were going to attempt this encounter with the groups they had. Could we go away, level up some more, and come back? The difficulty of the encounter here was likely to rise, after all, we'd had a warning with the system-wide alert that monsters within 500 miles of the Special Shop will continue to grow stronger until the Special Vendor is accessed. The blue pulses of energy coming from the light every few minutes felt to me like a timer of some sort. A countdown? Or a pulse strengthening all the nearby mobs?

It was possible that this whole set up was designed to force large groups of players to come together. That the designers of the system hadn't anticipated one group could rise to the challenge. The formation of a large raiding party seemed like an obvious development. Was that the intended situation? What had they wanted to happen? Well maybe another time Jessica could try to rally people. For now, I believed we had the measure of this.

Chapter 28: "Hell or Victory": The battle with Two Sphinxes

"This isn't going to get any easier if we wait around," I said making eye contact with the group. "Does everyone have bandages and HP Potions?" There was a small moment of double checking, and while Alan, Thomas and Lucas were all set, Maria didn't have either. Jessica and I both gave her one of each, which would be enough for the fight, hopefully.

I took out the STR and DEX buff potions we had found and passed them to Jessica. "Use these as soon we start fighting."

"Which sphinx will we be focusing on?" Alan asked me.

"Tank the left and we will kill the right first. Try to move it away from the other at least a few feet." I said. "Hold nothing back at all. Use your potions, and any abilities that may help. If I recall you have Entangling Arrow right Maria?" I asked.

"Yes!"

"Use that on Jessica's pull after the Quagmire Traps go off. It goes without saying, prioritize living over anything else. If you take damage—use a potion or a bandage—don't wait. If we can survive as long as that other group did we should be able to down them both."

Everyone gave a nod and I felt a nervous excitement start to creep up my spine. This was a fight to the death, and the first that I truly could not run from. I opened my stats.

Name: Mike Reynolds (27) Class: Necromancer Level: 20 EXP: 0%
HP: 905/905 MP: 385/385
STR: 5 Fear Resistance: 5
AGI: 2
DEX: 5
VIT: 20 +12
WIS: 24 +18
Available: 9

Skills: [A]Summon Skeleton LV. 8 I[A] Decay LV. 2I [A] Reanimate Dead LV. 2 I [A] Bone Armor LV. 2 I [A] Vast Shadows I [P]Sixth Sense I [P] Bravery LV. 2 I [P] Mutated LV. 2I [P] Pain Resistance LV. 2 I [P] Skeletal Mastery LV. 4I [P]Intimidate Living I[P] Inner Calm I[P] Necrotic Vision

I had nine stat points unspent and now was the time to use them: I opted to put every single one into VIT. It was only a guess, but it was likely Decay wouldn't have much of an effect on a non-living object.

If I were to get aggro, the extra hit points would give me the best chance of survival. Nine more VIT increased my effective HP pool to 1040 through flat HP. And this also made a significant difference to Bone Armor: my armor value when I activated that skill was based on 35% of my maximum HP. So I'd added nearly 40 HP to that layer of defense.

Although I had previously made WIS my main stat for the MP, I did not anticipate running out in the short space of time this fight would last for—one way or another—even if I spammed summons.

"Let's do it," I said trying to muster enthusiasm. But everyone looked worried, and I felt the same. I took a good hard look at each teammate by my side—Alan, Thomas, Lucas, Maria and, of course, Jessica—it was possible this was our last few moments together.

As we walked towards the sphinxes, the other groups of players noticed our purposeful movement. Hushed whispers raced through the crowd as all eyes were on us. No one tried to alert us to the danger ahead, as it was certain we had witnessed the fate of the group just a little earlier.

Jessica walked as far forward as she felt she could without triggering either sphinx and set two Quagmire Traps; she hurried back and then quickly drank both the STR and DEX potions, back to back. We got into a formation with me at the very back.

I cast Bone Armor and then Vast Shadows. My army of undead appeared behind me in an instant. The sound of gasps and shock sounded out around us, and in that moment, I truly felt like a superhero, or super villain, from a comic book.

Looking around, I found the guy that gave me the double middle finger, and he wouldn't meet my eyes now. It seemed he was regretting his earlier actions.

"This is it," Jessica said, "here comes hell or victory."

Thanks to the boost of the potion, she drew back her bowstring with more strength than ever before. The wooden longbow creaked before it twanged, and an arrow rocketed with enough force to distort the flow of air around it. It was impossible for Jessica to miss.

As soon as the arrow hit the sphinx on the right of the entrance, both statues looked directly at her and rushed in our direction. The earth shook with each step of their massive stone legs, "Hold!" Jessica yelled. The two sphinxes needed to trigger the Quagmire traps first and foremost before Alan ran in.

Time felt as if it slowed down as I watched the two enormous monsters come at us like hungry dogs. "Now!" Jessica said. I was used to this tactic, so my minions were already there and ready to intercept the right Sphinx. Alan charged the left on her shout and then immediately cast his Battle Shout, buffing everyone, including my squad of summoned undead, by fifteen percent.

Maria let off two Entangling Arrows to further slow the sphinxes while Lucas joined the ranks of my skeletons. Double Wind Slash after Wind slash was thrown out, leaving shallow grooves on the deep stony exterior of our target, the right-hand one.

It was immediately clear that these sphinxes had incredible defenses, and yet powder from chunks of stone being plowed off by swings from my abomination streamed into the air. Every attack caused an explosion of debris.

My skeleton general held the front, despite every stomp of the sphinx's massive feet threatening to crush it in place. Somehow though, it continued to take attack after attack without falling. With my squad all engaged, I paid attention to the other battle, where Alan seemed to be holding up and his guess for how much damage he would take was pretty accurate, around twenty percent from each hit.

Thomas carefully allowed Alan to fall below fifty percent and then cast his Barrier on him. Before now, I had never noticed how experienced Thomas had become. I watched him begin casting his heals immediately after completing one, but sometimes canceling the spell at the last second, when he felt it was going to over-heal if it landed. In this way Thomas avoided wasting his MP.

Out of all of us, Jessica was having the most trouble, and the frustration was visible on her face. She didn't have any offensive skills to augment her shooting, and against a stone target her arrows merely left a small indentation before ricocheting away. Often, she leveraged her extraordinary accuracy to target the eyes of our opponents, here they were no more vulnerable than any other part of the Sphinx's body.

Fortunately, Maria was having a better time of things as Entangling Arrow proved incredibly effective. Even the damage from Explosive Arrow was blasting fist-sized rocks off its body. The damage we were dealing was accumulating fast.

Merely ten seconds had passed when suddenly there was a development in the fight. The right sphinx paused his attack for a moment and instead lifted its two front paws into the air. It seemed in that moment that there was nothing but complete silence all around us.

The paws came down with a thud and the entire earth shook. An instant pulse of damage hit everyone, including my summoned undead. It was like the sphinx had summoned an earthquake here in this arena that we couldn't leave.

The shockwave wasn't enough to break my Bone Armor, but I saw everyone lose at least ten percent of their HP. That wasn't alarming. What was alarming was that the sphinx didn't stop at that. There was a second pulse, and then a third.

Luckily, our target stopped after the third pulse and didn't continue. Thomas started to glow with a white halo of light as he cast his AoE healing ability. Everyone gained back half of the thirty percent they had lost. "Drink a potion!" I yelled and then recast Bone Armor. The combination of a group heal plus a potion allowed everyone to bring their HPs back above ninety-five percent.

This was the first ability hurdle we needed to get over, and it was clear it wasn't aimed at inflicting a killing blow on one person, but it was designed to wear down the whole group. Alan was concentrating on defense, so at least the same special attack would not come from the other one until we had switched targets. But with the right sphinx at only twenty-five percent down, I felt there was bound to be a second ability in due course and maybe a third.

Fortunately, none of my summoned squad had fallen to the AoE attack but they were all seriously damaged. My skeleton minions definitely weren't getting out of this alive, and maybe even my abominations were doomed.

I started to count the seconds in my head. The special attacks might be on a timer rather than be triggered by HP loss. The first ability demonstrated by the sphinx had come at around ten seconds into the fight. I was up to ten now…nothing special. Eleven, twelve. A giant stone paw came crashing down and smashed my skeleton general to his knees, and then the next attack crushed him into powder. My second general stepped in and started to parry with its Zweihander. Maria and Jessica continued to pummel the monster with arrow after arrow; nor did Lucas relent from repeatedly casting Wind Slash.

He was focusing on specific spots on its body and building damage. I'd nearly reached a count of twenty seconds when thanks to this damage a huge chunk of stone dropped away from the chest of the sphinx.

Exactly as my count hit twenty, the sphinx paused from stamping at the undead around it and again raised its two front legs in a repetition of its previous attack.

"Second ability is coming!" I cried, mostly for Thomas's benefit as he was concentrating so hard on Alan.

This time, however, the pulsing didn't stop. It continued past three and kept going. Panic was evident as Maria and Lucas cried out and even I felt a sudden urge to run from the deadly waves of damage, despite knowing that lasers would then cut me apart.

It was clear the pulsing wouldn't stop until us or this Sphinx was dead. Thomas recognized this as well as he was casting his AoE healing over and over again. There was nothing better to do with my MP so I continually cast Bone Armor every time it went down.

"BURN IT!" I yelled. Everyone needed to put as much effort into killing the Sphinx as they possibly could before we all died. Despite Thomas healing constantly, everyone but me was losing HP at a steady rate.

Skeleton after skeleton started to fall and then my abominations cast Noxious Bile. No one held anything back as we pumped skill after skill into the sphinx.

The monster was casting one pulse every second, and by the seventh pulse every skeleton minion had died. All that remained of my squad were the two Abominations now spewing endless bile into the air. Stone and dust was spraying into the air from our bombardment. Another two pulses went off and…all at once the right sphinx collapsed, dying with deep cracks all through its stone body.

Immediately I rushed to the corpse, heart pounding with anxiety. It had just occurred to me that being a special mob, it was possible that I couldn't spawn fresh skeletons from its body. If so, then this fight might prove to be a massive and fatal mistake. It was possible we were all going to die for my over-confidence.

Fortunately, Summon Skeletons did land, and my minions re-populated in an instant. My abominations had survived the fight and we could reset the fight on the remaining sphinx. Now I had just one concern: Thomas would be on much lower MP than when we started the fight and might not be able to cope with the AoE pulses at the end of the second battle.

The party menu allowed me to see that everyone but me—who was on full—was around forty-percent health in the party window, and Thomas cast several more AoE heals to bring them to a comfortable eighty percent.

"Bandage and use another potion," Jessica called out. "Cap your health."

As soon as everyone was near full HP, we went all in on the second sphinx. Alan was faring well and had gained considerable aggro on it. My shield skeleton general could deal a bit of damage now, and with a fight this close, that might make a difference.

The background voices around us were growing more and more animated, as it was the first time anyone had seen a skill cast by the sphinx, let alone seen one of them killed. There were cries of encouragement, although no one seemed brave enough to join in. It was impossible for me to block out the noise, but I forced myself to focus.

The second battle was progressing much like the first, and the three pulses came with the mob at seventy-five percent as I had expected. Thomas kept Alan under fifty percent by casting his Barrier and only healing after it went down.

His micromanagement was superb, and I realized that Jessica giving him a chance back after his cousin Robert had tried to ambush us was quite possibly one of the best decisions we ever made. A worse healer would be out of MP right now, and we'd probably wipe.

Jessica still had a look of confidence on her face, while Maria seemed incredibly nervous. I couldn't see Lucas's face, but it was no doubt the epitome of effort. He had been putting in his all non-stop since the fight started.

His muscles must have been absolutely killing from swinging the Nodachi over and over against solid rock. Still, his swings never stopped, and instead seemed to increase in frequency. The first hurdle had been passed, and we were smooth sailing until the 'enrage'.

"We need to burst it at the end, or we all die," I said. "Getting there faster won't help us much; we need to kill it as fast as possible as soon as the pulsing begins." No one said a word, but I knew that everyone heard me.

Maria stopped shooting Explosive Arrows and Lucas ceased from using Wind Slash. Alan hadn't complained a single time despite the constant battering he'd been receiving from the stone paws for over a full minute. It was like a machine press was pushing down against him over and over, and only his will power was keeping him standing.

"It's coming!" I said. My counting was perfect, but my comment had lulled our damage by three or four seconds. The sphinx raised its hands and then slammed down again.

I could hear the people around us, "They're gonna die this time."

"It's over."

"There's no way they survive it a second time."

"Join in!" shouted Jessica without shifting her attention from constantly powering arrows at the sphinx. "This is your best chance to destroy it! Do it for yourself! Do it for humanity!"

Lucas suddenly let out a barbaric scream with all his might, as if trying to pull every ounce of strength from within. Alan joined him a moment later as the two screamed together. This didn't seem to be from pain or fear, but that they were hyping themselves up.

Waves of AoE were hitting us hard, chunks of HP lost to everyone but me, every second. It was such a weird sensation as well. There was no pain associated with it at all; you just lost ten-percent HP over and over.

Blow after blow continued to smash into the sphinx as sloughs of stone crumbled and burst into dust. Lucas was swinging Wind Slashes faster than I'd seen before and taking off lumps of stone like he wielded a jackhammer. As far as I could tell, none of the bystanders were helping.

Thomas was healing as well as he could, but it was clear that he couldn't keep everyone alive for much longer. "Potions!" I yelled. Bandaging required both hands, and you couldn't attack during that period.

That was the biggest downside between a bandage and a potion. You could pop a potion with a single hand and merely two fingers, but not a bandage. Looking at the constant loss of HP, if we didn't kill the sphinx in less than ten seconds we were all going to die.

Maria was faring worse than everyone, and I realized that she didn't have as many potions as the rest of us. We had only given her two, and her HP was already falling much faster than the others.

Five seconds passed and every skeleton I had died, and then something incredible happened. My abominations grew bright red and swelled a full size. For the first time since I'd acquired them, they had been brought below a HP threshold for a special ability and to my immense joy had revealed that they enraged when close to death. Both of them were pummeling the sphinx twice as fast and twice as hard as previously.

Everyone in the party was around forty-percent HP except for Maria. She was sitting at twenty-five percent HP. The next tick came and she went to fifteen-percent HP, and I could see the frustration and fear in her eyes.

I immediately rushed over to her with a potion in hand. Another tick came and she went to five percent HP. An AoE heal from Thomas came through at that moment and put her back at twenty-percent HP.

I reached her in the same second and basically forced the potion's liquid down her throat. She was at seventeen-percent HP. "Use any stat points you have and put them into VIT now!" I said to her.

"I don't have any!" she cried. The next tick came and she was at seven percent HP.

"I'm out of MP!" Thomas suddenly yelled. In that instant, Maria eyes filled with tears and her face turned grey. The next tick was coming and she scrunched up her face in sour resignation.

Congratulations, you have reached level
21.

The tick of damage didn't come. The second sphinx collapsed into a heap of stone and Maria had survived. She fell to the ground and started to sob uncontrollably, "I thought I was going to die!" Only then did I remember she was merely sixteen years old. Maria was just a child who had to live or die like a warrior in this fucked up world.

I helped her up and we gathered at the corpse of the second sphinx. I had no undead left and casted Summon Skeleton on instinct. There were items there: coins to be exact. I picked them up.

Special Survivor's Medallion: Allows the user to access the Special Shop location for 1 day. The Special Vendor is located inside.

There were ten of these on the floor, and we only needed six. I passed them out immediately, one for each of us.

Besides that, there were thirty Survivor's Medallions, which Jessica had gathered and split evenly: five each. With that, Jessica and I had thirty-five medallions to use inside.

The crowd around us seemed completely stunned. It took a moment for them to regain composure and fathom what just happened. In their excitement they all started to rush forward when something absolutely devastating happened. The two sphinx statues appeared again at the doorway.

"Guys…" Thomas said.

I was prepared to run, but then nothing happened.

Neither sphinx glanced at us, or even acknowledged our existence. The Special Survivor's Medallion seemed to give us immunity and would allow us to enter inside. I couldn't help but look at the crestfallen faces as we entered within. The crowd outside must have been hoping to share the gain, having taken none of the risk. Well, if any of them had helped, I would now be giving them a special medal. Instead, feeling triumphant and that there was a kind of justice to this setup, I walked on through and forgot about the players outside.

Chapter 29: Shopping After the Apocalypse is Fun When the Goods are Magic

Aware that the rest of the group were right behind me, I walked forward while scanning the building ahead of me. It was obvious now that I had passed under the arch that the walls didn't guard a town, or even multiple buildings. Rather, there was one massive, single structure ahead that reminded me of pictures of the Taj Mahal. It was a huge, domed palace made of pale stone. There were no towers or ornamentation though.

A large staircase led up to huge doorway about a third of the way up the building; there the double doors beneath the arch of the frame were already open. Needing no further invitation, I headed up the stairs.

Inside was just one enormous hall that seemed to me to be pointlessly wide and open. And in the center of this white vastness, there was just a single humanoid figure. Jessica and then Thomas called out a greeting, but there was no response. "Is it an NPC?" I asked.

No one knew. We approached carefully and ready for battle, just in case. But after we got to within thirty feet of the figure—a bearded human male in white, Arabic clothes—we were prompted with a menu.

The Special Vendor has been accessed. Nearby monsters will no longer grow stronger. The Special Shop will despawn in 168 hours.

So this was an NPC: the Special Vendor.

"Do you think that message was just for us?" asked Alan.

"No," replied Jessica, "that was a system message for everyone around here."

"A hundred-sixty-eight hours is seven days, so one week. The people outside only have a week to defeat the sphinxes and obtain a Special Survivor's Medallion to enter inside," I was thinking aloud.

"I doubt anyone else will manage it," Jessica shrugged.

By concentrating on the Special Vendor, I found I could open menus with his stock of items for sale. The goods were grouped by sub-menu: Weapons; Shields; Armor; Accessories; Skills; and Items. I started clicking through each in curiosity and quickly realized the lists were huge.

'Weapons' held everything from brass knuckles all the way to assault rifles. There must have been hundreds of selections. The prices weren't that bad either, varying from 5 Survivor's Medallions all the way up to 20.

Each sub-menu was filled with similar amounts, and I was encouraged to see that the other slots were less expensive than weapons. A lot of the combat gear was priced at just two Survivor's Medallions, although the goods under Accessories were mostly 5 Survivor's Medallions. What caught my attention in the Accessories category was that some of the goods granted passive skills as well as their primary benefit, which naturally enough made them expensive, but also very desirable.

I looked at the 'Item' selection and was amazed to see the wide range of all the different miscellaneous goods you could purchase and especially the variety of potions: EXP potions; stat potions; stamina potions; potions that provided resistance to status ailments and elements; generic HP and even MP potions as well. The prices were all reasonable, too.

Five Rations for example, was only 1 Survivor's Medallion. A lot of the deals were bulk like this and seemed tempting. They weren't what I was interested in though. Maybe leftover medallions could be well spent under 'Item' but consumables weren't likely to make a big difference.

Skill books, that was what I was most interested in and I knew Jessica was too. I concentrated on the 'Skill' sub-menu and started to read through carefully. My first surprise was the price: there were a lot of skill books for as little as 1 Survivor's Medallion. Now that was cheap for a permanent gain.

The low-end Skills were abilities like Sharp Shooting, and Energy Bolt, and Fireball. They were barebones basic abilities, and they all started at level 1. As I scrolled higher the price steadily increased, and I was pleased to find my Summon Skeletons on the list at 5 Survivor's Medallions. Heal was there as well, but it was a surprising 10 medallions.

My intuition that supports skills were more rare was pretty much confirmed right then, but I didn't regret allowing Thomas to take Heal. He was superb at his job, and without him I knew matters would have gone much worse, especially in the battle with the sphinxes.

It was when I got to 15 survivor's Medallions that I started seeing skills that were clearly a higher-level than I'd come across before. Most likely, these skills couldn't drop off weaker enemies.

**Book of Life Drain LV. 1: Drains life from
target enemy every 1 second for 5
seconds. Drained life is granted to the
caster.
Cast time: Channeled.
MP Cost: 35
Distance: 3 Meters**

This was an interesting ability that could definitely prove useful. Unfortunately, it wasn't something I wanted. In most encounters I didn't take damage and when I did, Bone Armor made sure to keep me healthy.

**Book of Dominate Mind: Inflicts extreme
fear on the target, making them unable to
perform any action for 5 seconds.
Cast time: 1 Second.
MP Cost: 25
Distance: 5 Meters.
Cooldown: 25 seconds.**

A CC ability that inflicted a 5 second fear; enemies immune to fear would probably not be affected, making it useless against undead-type mobs. The abilities definitely had more depth as they got more expensive, but again this wasn't what I was looking for.

My main source of damage was my minions, and I wanted an active skill that could benefit them the most. Scaling them was my goal. The challenge was that Jessica and I had merely 35 medallions to use. I surveyed every skill above fifteen and slowly turned my attention to those at 20 Survivor's Medallions in cost.

And at 20 Survivor's Medallions, I finally saw a skill that I was interested in.

Book of Summon Skeletal Mages:
Summons a Skeletal Mage with a random
elemental affinity. Caster will repeatedly
shoot bolts of that element.
Cast Time: Instant.
Mp Cost: 45
Distance: 4 Meters.
Requires a corpse to use.

This was the perfect ability for me by far. Skeletal Mastery should scale the mage's damage and HP, and I would also gain the benefit of having additional minions through my Necromancer passive.

"Have you found an ability?" I asked Jessica. Right now, I was holding all of our coins.

"I found one that I want, but…" she hesitated, "its twenty medallions." And my heart dropped. We only had thirty-five and we needed forty.

"What's the ability called?"

"Godless Arrow," she said before reading the description: "Allows the user to fire an arrow that can be material or immaterial. Pierces one hundred percent of defense and always inflicts the Bleeding ailment."

"Material or Immaterial?" I asked, "Is that suggesting you would be able to shoot through walls?"

"I think so, at least somewhat? It doesn't say how it's controlled but maybe with levels I could choose between the two constantly?"

It sounded like an amazing ability, one that warranted the cost.

"Mine was Summon Skeletal Mages," I said and I described it to her. We were both stuck between a rock and a hard place, and I couldn't ask her to sacrifice such a good skill for my sake. But perhaps there was a solution currently sitting in my inventory.

"Hey guys, are you all finding anything worthwhile?" I asked the others. I wasn't sure exactly how many Survivor's Medallions they had accumulated, but I doubted there was even 10 for each of them.

Thomas sighed, "It seems like a shop made for the rich. The really good stuff is only purchasable if all three of us put together our medallions." All four of them started to speak in the same spirit: complaining in unison.

The situation was worse for Thomas, as the support skills I'd say were reasonable at level 20, were even more expensive than both Jessica and my skills.

"We have four more Special Survivor's Medallions," I said. "Why don't we try auctioning them off outside? We won't be staying here for longer than a day." The alternative was to leave, try to farm Survivor's Medals for a week, and for four of us make a second trip before the Special Vendor left. But it seemed to me our time would be better spent by trying to get what we needed today and selling the spare Special Survivor's Medals outside.

"Isn't there a better option?" Lucas suddenly asked. "Why don't we just resell the items the merchant is selling, but at a markup?"

In that moment, I wanted to squeeze him with joy. The goods were tradeable, so we could do this.

"We have a monopoly, essentially," Lucas added.

With nods all around, we quickly agreed on a common approach. None of us bought anything and instead we walked back outside. Our presence caught the crowd's attention as people spoke in whispers at first and then calls, "Look, they're coming out!"

I stepped forward and about forty people hurried forward, bombarding me with questions.

"What was in the shop? Did it have an item that can revive the dead?"

"Was there something that increased life span?"

"How expensive are the items? Is three Survivor's Medallions enough?"

The crowd grew so frantic that I couldn't even hear individual questions and I was forced to retreat below a Sphinx. The eyes of the monster tracked anyone that dared to get too close, and the crowd stopped dead in its tracks.

"The shop is better than you can imagine. It has hundreds upon hundreds of items, equipment, and skill books for purchase. Rations, HP potions, EXP potions—you name it. It's all there." Lucas stepped forward beside me and started projecting his voice. "This is a rare opportunity for you all; as you know, there is only a short time in which you have access to the shop. It will disappear in a week, and even we, victors over these mighty guardians, can only access the vendor for a single day."

There were loud gasps at his comments that further dramatized what he was saying. The crowd grew so quiet a pin drop could be heard, "Furthermore! It is first come first serve! If a skill book is purchased, it disappears from the shop—which means only one person can buy it."

"If you have any survivor's medals, we are willing to take on your orders for a limited time only." When Lucas finished, I got the impression that the listeners would have rushed forward in an attempt to place their orders first if the sphinxes were not threatening to laser beam them.

"How much are the rations?"

"I need Bandages, tell me what bandages cost!" People continuously shouted out for the most basic items, and it was then that I realized I had underestimated how far we had advanced in level compared to the average person. So many of these people were desperately trying to survive, and food was their number one priority. I recalled the prices of Rations 5:1, and Bandages, 4:1. If you were starving and worried about food, it really wasn't a bad deal.

"Five Rations cost two Survivor's Medallions, and four Bandages cost two Survivor's Medallions," Lucas announced. He had marked the price up 100% and yet people nearly pushed over each other trying to put in orders.

The noise and confusion was so bad that I had to send my minions forward to keep people from trampling each other, "Calm down! The consumable items in the shop had no purchase limit. There are enough Rations for everyone. Line UP!" I yelled.

The semblance of a line formed and Lucas walked forward while taking orders. Survivor's Medallions were transferred and then he asked the person to step aside while giving the order to Alan whom rushed inside and purchased their goods.

Our trading was such a success that within ten minutes we had made over 30 Medallions in profit and that figure was still climbing. An hour passed in what felt like minutes, and only then did the desire for items slow down.

Once the rush for basics was over, more experienced players came forward and they were strategic about what they wanted. We heard requests like, "I'm looking for a weapon, preferably a sword…" Others were specific in wanting a particular weapon: a bow, a scimitar, a dagger, most likely requirements of their skill.

With every request, Lucas was like a professional businessman, "The shop does have a range of good swords for ten Survivor's Medallions. There are several options, too. Short-handled, long-handled, double-edged, single edged. Do you have any preference?"

He smooth-talked each new customer for several minutes before shipping Alan off to carry whatever goods needed to come back. Even better was that no one raised a brow, or even complained at all at the prices he quoted.

These items and equipment would be life saving for them, and paying a bit more for them rather than being blocked by the sphinxes and getting nothing didn't seem to be a problem in their eyes.

A man came over to me and asked, "Your skeleton ability, is that in the shop?"

"Summon Skeleton is there, for fifteen Survivor's Medallions," I responded. Inspired by Lucas's trading and the thought that we'd earned this opportunity, I tripled the price. After all, it really was valuable: only one person could buy it and then that skill was gone from the shop. "You need to understand though, that what makes my summoned skeletons so powerful are my passives from the Necromancer class."

The customer thought on it long and hard and while he did, a woman who had been standing on the fringe of the crowd pushed forward. "I'm a Necromancer too. I'll take it for fifteen medallions." She was basically shoving the coins in my hand. I looked at the other gentleman, who could only shrug. *First come first serve* was the rule Lucas had dictated at the beginning.

Other players came forward and asked about skills they hoped existed, and sometimes they did, but the prices we quoted them were too high. This was not because of our markup, but because some of the abilities they wanted cost 20 medallions or above from the Special Vendor.

Besides Summon Skeleton, another group came forward and bought Heal after having witnessed Thomas in action. We charged them 25 medallions, which they happily paid. It was a rare skill, and in an eight-man group it would be incredibly useful to get someone who could AoE heal in the future.

"Last call for the Special Vendor!" Lucas called out and I was glad the trading was coming to an end. Our pockets were fat. Lucas had netted us 120 Survivor's Medallions in profit, which we divided as even split for twenty each.

Before we returned to the Special Vendor, I realized that I had other items that were sellable. I had five Class Changing Stones in my inventory, and after discussing it with Jessica, we decided it was worth selling these while we had the chance of gaining powerful skills. Who knew if this opportunity would ever come again.

"Does anyone need a Class Changing Stone?" I yelled. There was an immediate silence. Dozens of people in the crowd locked their eyes on me, and many of them showed incredible interest. Others were crestfallen as they had spent all of their medallions on Rations.

Eventually there was a small crowd in front of me and I decided to auction a stone. Fifteen medallions was the final call, and the person who won seemed incredibly happy. That was until I pulled a second one from my inventory.

The first went for 15, and the next four sold for 10 medallions each. Jessica and I had gone from 35 Medallions all the way up to 130: our original 35, 40 from our combined split, and then another 55 from selling the stones.

We had each ended up with 65 medallions to do as we pleased, which meant there was no need for us to make an agonized choice between the two abilities we wanted. We could get them both and more. Things were looking up and we were all smiles.

Lucas made one last call, yet before anyone responded, as if it were a divine intervention to rain on our parade, a message was suddenly broadcast to everyone.

Users will now drop their items and equipment on death.

I felt as though a pack of wolves had spawned in front of us. In every direction people were eyeing us hungrily. Not one friendly face remained. Probably, these players were green with envy already at our wealth, but surely no one was foolish enough to think we were acting as a middleman out of the kindness of our hearts.

Those people that had just spent an exuberant amount of medallions on supplies looked like they'd eaten shit. Everyone began to distance themselves from each other. "Let's move...back." Jessica muttered.

It wasn't a slow move either. We all rushed to the base of the nearest sphinx and stood right in front of the paws. "Why the hell is this happening now?" I complained. There was no doubt in my mind that if we tried to leave we would be torn apart.

Those people that had what they wanted and didn't want to push their luck took to their vehicles and hurried away. It was the scavengers and the players that had some levels but no medallions who stuck around eying us.

Even as I watched a crowd that was becoming more and more united in their knowing glances at one another, our SUV was targeted, and the tires suddenly burst. These wolves didn't want us leaving under any circumstance.

"What now...?" Alan asked.

"Let's go inside and use our medallions," said Jessica.

Everyone now had enough to purchase even the highest tier goods in the Ability sub-menu, which seemed to be 25 Medallions. As far as I could tell, those abilities that cost 25 medallions all seemed to be support and lifesaving ones.

Without hesitation, I purchased Summon Skeleton Mage and Jessica purchased her Godless Arrow. I started to scroll through the equipment and item list as well now that I had an extra 45 points to spend.

There was a particularly expensive accessory that I now had my eyes on.

Ring of Undeath: A golden ring headed by a miniature skull. Red diamonds adorn the eyes.
WIS +5, VIT +2, MP +30
Grants the user +1 level for all summoning abilities.
Grants the user: Temporary Grave
Temporary Grave: Creates a graveyard with endless corpses.
Cast Time: Instant
MP Cost: 25
Duration: Five Minutes
Cooldown: 24 Hours

This ring cost 30 Medallions, and I could easily see why. Not only did it have great stats, it also had a +1 to level of my summoning skills. Temporary Grave was an interesting type of effect that I'd not seen before: the ability it granted was not a passive one, but had to be activated.

The effect solved a major issue for all Necromancers. In drawn out fights, I had no way to recover my summoned undead if they were killed. This Temporary Grave basically provided me with the corpses required to repopulate my undead squad.

At a full day, the cool down was long, but I wondered how often I would need to use it? The effect was simply a life-line if things went really south in a bad situation and if something was eating through two whole squads of undead, I was really going to be in trouble.

I only had one accessory at the moment, and the stats on the ring were so good it was essentially a no brainer. I spent the thirty Medallions and equipped it immediately.

Name: Mike Reynolds (27) Class: Necromancer Level: 21 EXP: 0%
HP: 1085/1085 MP: 228/440
STR: 5 Fear Resistance: 5
AGI: 2
DEX: 5
VIT: 29 +14
WIS: 24 +23
Available: 3
Skills: [A]Summon Skeleton LV. 9|[A] Summon Skeleton Mage LV. 2|[A] Decay LV. 2| [A] Reanimate Dead LV. 3| [A] Bone Armor LV. 2 | [A] Vast Shadows | [P]Sixth Sense | [P] Bravery LV. 2 | [P] Mutated LV. 2| [P] Pain Resistance LV. 2 | [P] Skeletal Mastery LV. 4| [P]Intimidate Living |[P] Inner Calm LV. 2 |[P] Necrotic Vision

If there wasn't a feral mob outside the walls waiting to kill us, I would have been extremely happy. I had gained a full level from the sphinxes going down, which put me at 21 and granted me another undead soldier from my Necromancer passive.

On top of that, I received another level from the Ring of Undeath, adding yet another member of my squad. I had +3 base skeletons from Necromancer, which meant Summon Skeleton Mage would summon 5 undead casters at level 2. Summon Skeleton would now summon 12 at level 9.

There was also the potential for a new Skeleton General, as at level 3 and 6 was when I got a new one both times. Maybe there was even something above a Skeleton General, too. Not only that, it seemed Inner Calm had leveled to 2 as well.

For now, there was no way to see if I got another General unless I used Temporary Grave to access corpses, which I decided against. With 15 Medallions left I started to browse the item section. I scrolled and scrolled, and then I recognized something that I was sure hadn't been there when we first visited the Special Vendor.

Random Transfer Scroll: A scroll that allows the user and their party to be teleported to a random nearby location.

The scroll cost 20 Survivor's Medallions, and I only had 15. "Guys, did any of you save some medallions?" Fortunately Jessica and Maria both had a few remaining. Thomas, Alan, and Lucas had gone on a spending spree and were completely out.

"Check the top of the item section." And I could see from their expressions that everyone was doing so.

"Are you suggesting that's our way out?" asked Thomas.

"Well, I don't see a better solution" I said.

"Why don't we check outside and see the situation first?" Jessica suggested. This seemed reasonable, because of course we wanted to save the qt medallions if we could. But boy was it a bad idea. Outside the gate there was mayhem as people were already attacking each other. The fighting petered out when we appeared, and if not for the sphinxes we would have been swarmed.

To make matters worse, our SUV that merely had flat tires before we had entered the hall was now fully ablaze and burning. "Did everyone buy what they wanted?" I asked. I was fully satisfied with my purchases, and the only thing that I would do differently was maybe get some Rations and EXP potions if possible.

It seemed the Random Transfer was our only way out safely. There were people here who were going to sit out all night and wait for us to depart. No doubt there would be a free for all after they had taken us out but first, they were united by greed and a knowledge that we were too tough for any one group to hope to defeat us.

Jessica ended up splitting the cost of the scroll with me: 10 each. I used my remaining 5 medallions to buy three EXP potions and 2 Ration packs, which gave me 10 rations total.

"We should rest before transferring," Lucas said, "in case we land among some tough mobs."

"Agreed," said Jessica and I nodded as well. There was well over 18 hours remaining on our timer, and there didn't seem any prospect that a group could defeat the sphinx: not with all the rivalry outside. If you made a move on a sphinx, there was a real danger someone else would help bring you down for your drops.

"How 'nearby' do you think it will be?" Maria asked while laying her head down. It was only mid-afternoon, but I felt as exhausted as she looked.

"Well, no clue. This location was described as 'nearby' but it was over two hundred miles away from the farm, and we won't have a car anymore," Alan piped in.

With no one else having any better insight, we soon fell quiet; although I wanted to sleep my mind was too busy with the shopping and the implications of the new rule that seemed designed to undermine solidarity between strangers. It took me about an hour before I dozed off.

I woke in the middle of the night, and it seemed most people were still sound asleep. Jessica was awake though, as was Maria, and they were whispering quietly. I stood and walked back to the entranceway, curious if it was possible to sneak away in the night instead of using the Random Transfer scroll.

It was a chilly but beautiful night. The moon was high in the sky with perfect visibility and the air was refreshing. There was a tinge of smoke smell and the sound of cackling fires as I moved closer to the opening.

Plenty of people were still camped outside, maybe even hundreds. Our vehicle was still there, completely torched through. As I looked out, I realized people were actually still awake and watching, like guards.

Jessica suddenly walked up beside me, "This teleport could go very badly."

"Yeah...I know," I said. "But I don't see any other way out of this mess." If we were caught here, there was no doubt we would be enemy number one. We were strong, but not strong enough to hold back this many people.

How would we even escape without a vehicle? We needed to get back to camp two-hundred miles away without a car and probably with people in pursuit. Even if we somehow got past the mob and made a breakout, it was possible we would attract ambushes all the way back to our doorstep.

Jessica touched my shoulder, "I believe we'll cope with whatever we meet on landing."

I turned to her, glad to hear her optimistic words.

"We've come a long way Mike. Remember when we first met? That was a lucky day for me. You have really risen to the challenge of the apocalypse, and you've brought me up with you."

I found my heart beating faster as she kept her beautiful eyes on mine. "It was a lucky day for me too Jessica. I couldn't have done this without you."

"We make a good team. And we'll make an even better one with the help of the others."

End of Book One

Jeremy Chambless was born in Deerfield Beach, Florida and studied Psychology at Florida Atlantic University. Gaming has always been a part of his household: as far back as he can remember, he was holding a NES controller. His own gaming passion has been focused on MMOs and RPGs. Jeremy is an avid LitRPG reader turned writer. A love for RPGs sparked his desire to create *The MMRPG Apocalypse*.

If you have enjoyed this book you'll be glad to know Jeremey has completed apocalypse game-system LitRPG series: *The RPG Apocalypse*. You can find the first book in the series on Amazon and Audible.